THE CAPITAL OF
LATECOMERS

THE CAPITAL OF
LATECOMERS
NINA NENOVA

Translated by Vladimir Poleganov

amazoncrossing ⟲

Text copyright © 2013 Nina Nenova

Translation copyright © 2015 Vladimir Poleganov

Previously published as Столицата на закъснелите in Bulgaria in 2013. Translated from Bulgarian by Vladimir Poleganov. First published in English by AmazonCrossing in 2015.

Published by AmazonCrossing, Seattle

www.apub.com

ISBN-13: 9781503947078
ISBN-10: 1503947076

Cover design by David Drummond

Printed in the United States of America

"Physical theory in its present stage strongly suggests the indestructibility of Mind by Time."

—Erwin Schrödinger, Nobel Prize recipient in physics

"The very study of the external world led to the conclusion that the content of the consciousness is an ultimate reality."

—Eugene Wigner, Nobel Prize recipient in physics

"Elucidating the mysterious flux [of time] would, more than anything else, help unravel the deepest of all scientific enigmas—the nature of the human self. Until we have a firm understanding of the flow of time, or incontrovertible evidence that it is indeed an illusion, then we will not know who we are, or what part we are playing in the great cosmic drama."

—Paul Davies, professor of theoretical physics and cosmology

* * *

The shimmering river spread its wide flat surface before abruptly plummeting down to the rocks, breaking into sprays of white, killing everything in the water, even the fish. It then continued its flow— a darkened mass of slow liquid that entered a narrowing tunnel. It descended along the tunnel, farther and farther down, so deep into the rock that those who walked above could neither feel it nor imagine it was there beneath their footsteps. People passed over the hidden river, each on his or her way, while down there, the river roared and raged in the darkness. For the river remembered that before the hollow rock and the concrete tunnel restrained its passage, it was as wide and bright under the sky as ever. It knew it was not an underground river.

1.

Rhein, Rhein . . . Remember, Rhein. This river is your godmother. You were conceived in it, and if you could go back thirty years in time you would see the small boat, oars tucked in. You would see the sun in the sky and the tiny white clouds—like boats, too, carrying lovers down another blue river. They, too, drift with the current, but only this boat will plummet down the waterfall.

It will, unless you keep it from falling. Otherwise, you will be nonexistent, conceived but dead nonetheless. The thirty years of your life would have been merely possible, yet unlived.

"Wonderful," I whispered to myself. "I don't want my life."

"Come on, hold the boat, Rhein!"

I don't want my life. Besides, how could I hold the boat? I was not born yet. Still, if I'm here now, my mother must have survived.

My thoughts seemed logical and I resented it. The river darkened, disappearing into the past, and I stayed here, without even the illusion that I could change anything.

Now, I couldn't help it. I had to say it, my voice loud and clear:

"How stupid. Stupid!"

Lately, this had become my trigger word. As soon as I heard myself saying it, I knew I was finally out of the trance. I opened my eyes, and as always, first looked at my hands. I wasn't holding a brush or a palette, yet both my hands were covered in paint of different colors. I had been painting, then.

I turned slowly to face the painting: dragons, lotuses, tiny Japanese women with enormous fans. I face the screen, that is. The painting is behind it. It has to be there, but what does it look like? I don't know. For a long time I have been only the executioner. While *the other* paints with my hands I am blind and deaf and I have no memory. With my eyes he studies the result, judges it, approvingly or not. *He* decides what the paintings will be like, and when he's done he simply locks them away in the storeroom. He has somehow made me believe that if I see the paintings, I would destroy them. This is his revenge, his relentless punishment for my attempt to kill myself and so kill him, whose self has not been one with mine ever since. The Artist.

Today, however, I have decided to finally uncover the truth about these paintings. All I have to do is wait for Kort's arrival. "Get them from the warehouse and see for yourself," I would tell him, before heading off somewhere. When I come back he would say . . . What would he say? What *could* he say?

I left the studio, dropped off my overalls in the laundry room, and headed for the bathroom. I stopped in front of the mirror there. For almost a year, I had seen no one besides myself, and now it seemed that I hadn't seen myself, either. Who was this man in front of me? With hair down to his shoulders and a chest-length beard? He had an athlete's frame, but his body was pale and gaunt. And these eyes? Supposedly blue, but so desolate their blue had almost disappeared, as if someone had meant to refill them with color, and then had forgotten about them.

I took a shower, put on clean clothes, drank a cup of coffee, and went outside. As I had chosen full isolation, no one was taking care of the property, which now looked ragged and wild, just like its tenant. I went into the meadow. The grass had grown overly tall since I first stepped on it full of hope that here, in the heart of this oasis, my spirit would heal and soar again. Here I was a year later, my spirit obviously still ailing. Was I able to soar again? The answer was to be provided by Kort, because I couldn't tell. I didn't know.

I sighed, resigning myself to yet another absurdity, and raised my head to the sky, waiting.

The helicopter appeared from the south, entering my sector without passing over any of the other nine, and landed on the meadow just as the two hands of my watch merged, marking the twelfth hour. Good! I smiled vaguely. The agency, Guaranteed Peace, was fulfilling its commitments to a tee.

A moment later, though, I blinked in disbelief. Instead of the pudgy and bald Kort, a female stranger came out of the helicopter. She was young and slender and had very long hair. She walked toward me, stumbling in the grass.

"Oh, Rhein, you're crazy!" were her first words.

A stab with a knife would have bothered me less. What a swift and precise diagnosis.

"I think I would have gone crazy, too," she continued as she stepped closer and clutched at my arm. "Alone for hours over the desert. What if that contraption got mixed up and dropped me off somewhere out there?"

"Contraption? In what sense?"

"In the sense that it doesn't have a pilot. No one's flying the thing. There's no pilot!" She laughed exuberantly.

I laughed, too, probably as hysterically as she did. The helicopter was remote-controlled, no mystery there. But who, in God's name, was she?

"I see," I mumbled, "but I . . ."

"You're a total freak, you know that? How could you live here? And for how long now? A year, right?"

I looked at her. Kort's daughter, most probably. I rummaged through my mind, trying to remember her name, but it was nowhere to be found.

"Hurry up," she yelled, wrinkling her forehead. "My luggage, go get it before it takes off again."

I rushed for the helicopter and dragged out two voluminous bags and a smaller one with a shoulder strap. I was horrified. There could be no question about her intention to have a long visit. I was lugging the bags with me, and she was already mincing toward the villa in her high heels.

I followed her into the foyer, put the luggage on the floor, and smoothed my beard a little. The damned thing had gotten curlier after the shower and it seemed to be getting curlier under this uninvited young lady's critical gaze.

"If we were in the outside world," she said, "I would've never recognized you."

"Same with you," I could have replied, but she probably wouldn't have believed me. Girls like her could stand before a blind man and still think they were unforgettable, irresistible, and so on.

"How's your father?" I asked dryly. "I was expecting him, actually."

"Obviously he forgot to tell you," she said with a casual wave of her hand. "He's been so busy recently with Hosepha's exhibition and all."

"Who the hell is she?"

"She? I'm talking about Marcian Hosepha himself, man. Don't tell me you haven't heard of him."

"I'm sorry, I haven't."

"There. See what this isolation has done to you? You're losing tempo, Rhein, losing tempo! How could you not be? If you don't even know who you're up against."

"I am not a horse," I sighed, "or a hound."

"Oh, yes, you are a horse." She patted me on the shoulder. "You are my first racehorse. That's why I'm here. I will take you out of the stable

6

and spur you on so hard that Hosepha will be staring at your tail as he eats your dust. While I make faces at my father from the grandstand."

She half-closed her eyes, drifting off into some reverie, while the helicopter outside began humming quietly. I turned and saw it gaining altitude. It floated up into the sky and flew away.

"Now listen, young lady . . ."

"Vanda." She took off her shoes and started walking about the foyer in her socks. "Just keep calling me Vanda. Despite my new position I insist that we remain friends."

Vanda, Vanda, I began repeating to myself, with the unpleasant premonition that her name might slip from my chaos-ridden memory again.

"What's this new position of yours?" I asked, closing the front door.

"You don't know about that, either? My father and I, we're business partners now, Rhein. On equal footing, but the truth is he's seriously underestimating me. He's become so bumptious recently because of Hosepha, his discovery. Well, never mind. I will *rediscover* you. You've been at the top and you'll get back there again. Because you are my favorite."

I smiled at her. Only youth could have such insolent yet charming spirit. Especially when it lacks self-confidence. Or when it's afraid of something.

There was something, or rather, someone, to be afraid of now, here in the desert, in this unfamiliar complex in a small oasis, hundreds of miles away from the nearest city. Vanda was alone with me in this computer-operated villa.

She stood there, silent, as if reading my mind, watching me with feline cunning through half-closed eyelids. Her eyes were bright green, elongated, and slightly slanted, emphasized by her jet-black eyebrows. Her beautiful, though unusual, face was almost triangular because of the wide forehead, the sharp cheekbones and chin. Her skin was smooth and amazingly white against her shiny black hair, which fell, perfectly straight, down to her shoulders. Her nose was narrow, with miniature nostrils, and her mouth was small and aggressive at the same time.

"Well?" she said.

I shrugged. If this most succinct of all questions was meant to evoke a response to her babble about the stable, the spurring, and the dust, I had no idea how to respond. With a joke? Irony? Or should I have just told her how I really felt? *Back to civilization, little lady. Find yourself another favorite horse.*

I picked up her bags and carried them up the stairs. I climbed the stairway in silence, straining my ears, expecting her to follow me. I couldn't hear anything, but this meant nothing. She was probably walking behind me in her socks and that outfit. What was she wearing? I couldn't remember. I started to panic. What kind of artist could I be? I used to pride myself on my keen observations.

I reached the second floor and walked along the hallway, struggling to recall her image and her clothes in particular. Instead, I "saw" her completely naked, sporting curves much more voluptuous than she had in reality.

Well, that's the way it is. Imagination is always better than reality or mere sight. These are only the canvas and the frame, whereas imagination is . . .

". . . the father of art," I blurted out loud.

I stopped and turned around, embarrassed. Vanda had been following me so close that she almost bumped into me.

"I meant your father," I said to her. "Sometimes he thinks he is . . ."

"The father of art? You're right," she said, laughing. "I'll tell him that as soon as I get the chance."

She was wearing a cream-colored sleeveless dress that fell just beneath her knees. It was nothing worth noticing. She had her shoes back on. Yes, she had been clacking along the marble floor with her high heels and I hadn't heard a thing. As if I had been somewhere else all this time.

"Oh, it's fantastic here," she announced, looking around excitedly.

I looked around, too. We were in the guest room, and I had somehow missed the moment of our arrival. I dropped her bags on the carpet and spread my arms.

"Make yourself at home. Rest up while I prepare lunch."

"No lunch for me. I'm still recovering from that horrible journey. I'll just take a shower and then a nap."

"Perfect! I mean, I'll see you this evening." I quickly withdrew into the hallway, closing the door behind me.

What am I to do? What will happen now? I asked myself in vain, hopping down the stairs. I was discovering that I had become even more idiotic than I had thought. It was going to be really hard, if not impossible, to cover up this fact.

2.

That afternoon, I managed to refrain from doing quite a few things. I didn't call Kort, I didn't shave my beard, I didn't talk to myself, I didn't lock the studio door. I didn't write a single word in my diary—as if nothing interesting had happened. I didn't search for information on Marcian Hosepha online, although the urge was almost irresistible. Right now, however, I had no other option. It was the only way to preserve my dignity.

"You've been at the top . . ." What if I'm still there, Kort? You'll be sorry for writing me off, leaving me to your ignorant little daughter so she could learn from me. "Rediscover" me! She, a girl who obviously could tell neither a painting from a photograph, nor an artist, an ARTIST, from a horse. Nor a horse from a stallion.

I kept fuming until I realized that my fuming itself was becoming increasingly pleasurable. Apparently, after spending such a long time in isolation, one stopped being picky when it came to entertainment. Whatever happened to be at hand was interesting, as long as it was new. So in that sense, Ms. Vanda Cortez was a welcome addition here.

I didn't have to wait for her until sundown. She made her appearance considerably earlier. She was wearing sandals, a pair of shorts, and a short T-shirt revealing her perfect waist. Her legs, however, were skinny, and she had tied her hair back, so the possibility of another erotic reverie was unlikely. I had never been one for childlike girls and right now that's how she looked.

I was sitting in my favorite chaise longue on the terrace and it took her a while to notice me. As she did, her face showed such rapture that my heart skipped. She had gone to the studio. *She had seen them.*

"Oh, Rhein," she said, rushing to me as if to embrace me. "This is . . . I'm speechless. This is truly fantastic, all around. It's as if I'm in the residence of some maharaja!"

I said nothing.

"Or of a prince?" She smiled slyly and sat across from me. "This entire villa is a piece of art. The splendor of the Middle Ages and the digital technology of the future combined in such a superbly balanced way. It must have cost you at least a million!"

"I took a two-year lease on it and it cost me everything I had. But I didn't do it because of the medieval splendor and the digital sophistication. I'm paying for the isolation."

I thought my hint was obvious enough, but maybe I had to ask her directly if she wanted me to get her a helicopter for tomorrow, or whether she would prefer to leave the day after, which was *already* kind of late.

"When are the servants coming?" she asked.

"They're not. I have no servants."

"Every corner is so clean, everything's tidy. Don't tell me you're doing it all by yourself."

"I only use the kitchen, the bedroom, and the studio. Did you take a look at the studio?"

"I peeked in there, too. It's spacious and bright, but to be honest, I was a bit disappointed. It's the only thing that doesn't really fit the overall design of this place. It's much too plain. What's with that screen? It's downright kitschy."

"You're right. I'll get rid of it first thing tomorrow," I said. "Would you like some coffee?"

"I already had some. I couldn't resist. I've never seen a fully automated kitchen. I found champagne, black caviar, strawberries, whipped cream. I wonder if there are any candles around."

"If you're worried about a power cut . . ."

"Come on, Rhein. Candlelight is more romantic. We'll also light the fireplace. It's going to be an evening to remember."

She stood up and took me by the hand. She pulled me up and led me along the terrace. We entered the living room, but we didn't stop. We were headed for the second floor and, ultimately, for my bathroom.

I stopped at the door.

"Come on," Vanda said, pulling me after her.

She had been rummaging in here as well. On the table by the mirror she had lined up all the shaving and haircutting accessories that I had stuffed into one of the drawers, discarding them along with my intention of ever using them again.

This girl was definitely going too far. But what was I to do? If I started arguing with her or if I became rude I would end up in an even more awkward situation. Smiling dumbly, I sat before the mirror, and she immediately spread a large white towel over my chest. She tied it behind my neck.

"To rent such a luxurious villa," she murmured reproachfully, "and not make good use of it."

"I had no other choice. There are only ten villas in the complex and this one is the simplest and the smallest."

"You don't say."

"The Agency counts on quality, and not quantity, and on its special services of *utter seclusion*."

"I see. So all the other clients are like you."

"You mean crazy?"

"Well, no, but . . ."

"I have no idea what they're like, Vanda. I'm not even sure if there are any."

"I bet there are. At least nine. All of them eccentric, all of them millionaires," she said, grabbing the scissors. "I can't wait to meet them."

"No, no, that's impossible. That's out of the question," I said, cowering in the chair.

"We'll see."

"We'll see nothing and no one! You should follow the rules or . . ."

You can go to hell! I tried to stand up but she pushed me back down with surprising strength. The scissors in her hand stopped a mere inch from my temple. I took a quick glance at her reflection in the mirror. I was surprised. She looked helpless and frightened.

"Please, Rhein," she said softly, "don't, don't get mad like that."

Like *what*, for God's sake? Yes, I had raised my voice, but that was hardly a reason to become so frightened. She was shaking. I took my eyes off her reflection and fixed them upon mine. There was nothing scary there. Not anymore, but there might have been. Who knew, maybe I had glared at her?

"I'm sorry," I mumbled.

She nodded, then leaned over me and began trimming my beard. Her hand moved with the precision of a surgeon. No more shaking, no more fear. Damn! Had she tricked me?

"You're doing well."

"My grandma used to run a beauty shop," she said as the scissors clipped away. "She was a wonderful woman."

The view in the mirror was constantly changing, growing increasingly unsettling. Her reflection would come closer to and merge with mine, or it would cut through it, taking away the ear, the cheek, the eyebrow, the eye. Then it would retreat, leaving my face changed, somehow more exposed. The tiny hand with the swift little fingers held the two glinting blades that looked ready to stab.

Enough! I said to myself. I leaned back in the chair, as if to make myself more comfortable, and got the mirror out of my view.

After a little while, however, I sensed that something strange was happening. I had fixed my gaze on the medicine cabinet, and the fact that it stood above the table now struck me as something of enormous importance. It seemed to hold a fateful secret that I was supposed to have uncovered a long time ago. Because it was connected to *that morning*, and because the table was white.

Vanda put down the scissors and started using the hair clippers. I drifted away under their quiet buzzing. White, white, yes, this table was white.

But what of it? I asked myself. But Vanda's eyes showed me that I'd spoken out loud. "I meant the situation in the complex. Or rather the fact that there's no situation to speak of. Otherwise, it wouldn't be so peaceful, and that's the whole point. One shouldn't expect anything extraordinary, shouldn't be anxious wondering what might happen tomorrow, or in an hour."

"Utter boredom," Vanda decided. "You don't look that calm. Just sit still and keep out of my way."

I locked my fingers together, and only then did I remember the scar. Good thing my shirt had long sleeves. I decided I would wear only long-sleeved shirts while she was around. But then it occurred to me that it would be more convincing if I put a bandage around my wrist. *Tendovaginitis, you see . . .*

"I've been working a lot lately," I said.

"I am happy to hear that."

Vanda smiled, turned off the clippers, put them down on the table, and released me from the towel's grip.

"But perhaps we're meant to live under pressure," I said. "When everything around you is calm and quiet, your mind starts producing pressure of its own, and it often goes too far. So we arrive at this paradoxical situation: the calmer your surroundings, the more frantic and

turbulent you become on the inside. As if under a lid and with no valve
to let out the steam."

Standing next to me, with another white towel in her hand, Vanda
was still smiling. I had to smile back.

"Poor thing," she whispered.

She leaned and kissed me lightly on the forehead. It felt so nice I
almost passed out.

"Vanda, I . . ."

"Hush." Her fingers barely touched my lips. "Come on, Rhein,
you've been avoiding looking at yourself for a while now. What do you
expect to see? I haven't turned you into a vampire."

She was right, I realized bitterly. I reluctantly turned my eyes to
the mirror. It was as if I was looking into the past, once again finding
my own reflection from that haunting morning. My face was the same
now as then: beardless, pale, bloodless. Yes, but back then, my blood
had been drained from me, while now . . . The Artist! He had sucked it
all from me. *He, he* is a vampire.

"I can tell you haven't been out much," Vanda said with some concern. "Look at you, your complexion's practically colorless. If one can
even call it a complexion."

"I agree. That's why I look like I've been sucked dry."

"You seem perfectly healthy to me. A bit of sun is all you need, and
I'll take care of that tomorrow. I'll take care of everything."

She wrapped the towel around my shoulders and began to comb
my hair in a leisurely manner, her movements tender like kisses, gentle
and relaxing. Now, neither my face, nor anything else, looked like it
did before. Because back then, it had been death that stood beside me,
and now, life itself, embodied in this beautiful, vivid girl with ruby lips
and sparkling emerald eyes. A true jewel. She was going to take care
of me—she had said that loud and clear. She was going to take care of
everything.

3.

I was standing in front of the bedroom wardrobe in my bathrobe, wondering what to put on. "Dress formally," she had said. Okay, but the only suit I had was too formal and, truth be told, I had brought it here for purely sentimental reasons: to remind me of the triumphant night after my final exhibition. All my other clothes, however, were casual or working clothes—even less appropriate.

I took out the suit, the shoes, and the white silk shirt. *So what? What if it's white?* I asked myself again. Not about the shirt, of course, but about the table in the bathroom. I was still unable to get it out of my mind, although I hadn't even noticed it before today. I hadn't given much thought to my pathetic suicide attempt, either. It had never crossed my mind that it could be connected to some secret, which in turn could be connected to . . . the color of the table.

I burst out laughing. I quickly put on the shirt and the suit, but then I spent a long time rummaging through the wardrobe for suitable socks. I was ready much earlier than the hour she had specified. I was excited, to be honest. I circled the room a few times, my nearly mint, shiny shoes squeaking. So what if they squeaked? Was I to put on sneakers instead? The pants, though, were a bit loose, as well as the jacket. I had lost weight. But not so much as to feel feeble or anything like that.

Was I going to make a fool out of myself? I stepped toward the large mirror with determination, saw my full reflection, and immediately replied to my question with a "No." I rather liked the sight. The paleness had gone from my face, and without my beard, I looked considerably younger. Vanda had not demonstrated great hairdressing skills, which was a point in her favor. She had continuously tried to make it even, and she trimmed my hair down until she called it a buzz cut. I grinned. Buzz or not, it looked good on me and also made me look younger. Besides, thirty was far from old age.

I laughed again. I met my eyes in the mirror and whispered to myself, "I'm alive." Here I was, saved, and about to have a romantic candlelit dinner. I could have been a nine-month-old corpse if . . . If what?

"Oh, come on!"

I turned my back to the mirror and headed for the bathroom. As always, I had left everything perfectly clean and in order. Everything was put away, the floor was shining—not a single hair on it, and the table was cleared: as it had been *back then*. Although maybe it wasn't supposed to be.

I had put myself in the role of a suspicious cop coming in here to carry out forensic experiments on himself. How fitting for a man who became his double every day.

I squinted, concentrated, and without getting overly emotional, I tried to remember.

A tragedy. The feeling of bottomless creative impotence. Nothing helps, least of all this overpriced place of solitude. It's early morning and I'm in the shower, although I don't need waking up since it was yet another sleepless night, which will likely be followed by another, and yet another. My insomnia is merciless. It is killing me.

"I will kill myself," I say to myself.

Although I have no intention of doing it, the very possibility somehow makes me feel more alive. I get carried away imagining it. Pills? No, that's the way cowards do it. With a rope? No, it's ugly afterward, lacks aesthetic sensibility. A gun? If only I had one. A knife? That's it! I shall depart from this world like a Roman patrician.

I go to the bathtub's control panel and press the water button. Death needs no shampoo, fragrances, or extras whatsoever.

"Hey, am I really about to do this?" I ask myself, shaking my head, doubtful.

I put on my work clothes, still thinking I'll drag myself off to the studio again. But the bathtub is already filled and the water inside is so tempting. I get in, with my clothes on. Of course, it would be inappropriate to die naked. What about the knife? I have one. I take the pocketknife out of my pocket. I press a button and the blade springs out, ready to be used. I do exactly that: I use it, crudely slashing the veins on my right hand. This is my way of punishing it for not being able to paint anymore.

I don't know what happened after that. When I woke up, I was still in the bathtub, soaking in my own blood, but my wrist was tightly bandaged, resting on a dry spot on the side. I remember thinking—if the haze in my head could be called thinking—that my instinct for self-preservation must have kicked in at some point. Half alive, I had gotten out of the bathtub and somehow managed to wriggle out of my soaked clothes. I had washed myself in the shower and had gone to get more bandages and disinfectant from the medicine cabinet.

I could remember now! On the table, right beneath this cabinet, there was not a single drop of blood. If I had taken the bandage from the cabinet the first time around, with bloody water dripping from my clothes, there should have been some stains at least. There should have been a puddle on the floor, as well.

That was it. I couldn't recall how I had done anything to save myself, because I hadn't. Someone else had. But who?

4.

She was dressed in a long black dress with an open back and a plunging neckline. A ruby necklace sparkled on her neck, and on her ears, drop-shaped ruby earrings. Her black hair was tucked back with a couple of hairpins that were also encrusted with rubies: tiny droplets, like blood.

I approached the marble table by the fireplace, which, to my chagrin, was *white*. I slumped into one of the armchairs and stared at the soothing, lively flames. Vanda turned off the light, and all around us, like doomed souls forever trapped in pale flesh, the tiny flames of dozens of wax-white candles flickered.

"It's too bad I couldn't pick up some flowers," Vanda sighed.

I was silent. What could I say?

"Well?" she asked. Her favorite question.

"Be more specific," I suggested.

"How can you be so insensitive?"

I racked my brain, wondering how I was supposed to take this. I was at a loss.

"But you're handsome," she added. "So I forgive you."

"No, no! I mean, yes, forgive me, but also tell me what for?"

"You silly thing. Can't you see how much effort I've put into this?"

"Your dress is lovely."

"I didn't make the dress! I'm talking hard work here. Do you think this whole thing got arranged by itself? Did the fireplace light itself?"

"I'm sorry, Vanda. You should have waited, I would have helped."

"I wanted to surprise you!"

"I *am* surprised. How could I not be? That's why I'm acting like this. I'm just not used to such things. I can barely remember what a woman's attention, human attention even, means."

"But you like it, right?" she asked, pointing at the table.

The table threw me into yet another nightmare. It was covered with all kinds of delicacies, but until this very moment I had only seen it as white, in other words, empty. I broke into a sweat even though the window across the room was wide open. *How am I going to endure this evening, if this is just the beginning?* Suddenly I heard the pounding sound of baroque music. Jesus! I tried to summon Him in desperation. In the end it was not Him but Vanda who showed mercy and lowered the volume.

"It will be a night of drinking and fire. A fiery night that will melt all the ice between us."

"Be careful, I might take you seriously," I said, trying to sound playful.

"Please do," she said, waving her hand in the direction of a bottle of champagne in an ice bucket.

I did not need another prompt. I opened the bottle with the skillfulness of a sommelier. I filled the glasses right to the brim and Vanda applauded.

"To this night," I said, making a toast.

"To us, this night's children."

We looked at each other in a way that was not entirely childlike and clinked glasses, their crystal ring mingling with the polyphonic chords. We drank to the bottom. I filled the glasses again and drank again, this time by myself. I would rather have had something stronger, but after an entire year of abstinence this was good enough.

"I only drink with company," I thought it necessary to note.

"That's another reason you should be glad I'm around."

We struck up a light, breezy conversation and started flirting. Indiscriminately we snacked on oysters, lobster salad, sandwiches with black caviar, salmon, and all kinds of paté. My anxiety was gradually disappearing and my mood was brightening. We finished the bottle and I opened another one. Everything was going from good to better, with the promise of becoming perfect.

I was already imagining lifting Vanda in my arms and gallantly carrying her upstairs to the bedroom when she abruptly changed the subject.

"What's that on your hand?"

"Tendovaginitis, an occupational trauma."

"I don't mean the bandage. What's that gadget on your left hand?"

"A medical wristband. It measures my pulse, temperature, blood pressure, and some other life signs."

I went to throw more wood on the fire, recalling how I'd taken off the wristband back then, but only after it had started vibrating under the water.

"So you're under constant surveillance?" Vanda asked as I returned to my seat.

"Not exactly. It only alerts the medical facility if a dangerous deviation from the norm is registered. In that case, I would be instantly informed by a special signal on the wristband."

"What happens if you take it off?"

"That would be registered by their computer and, according to the contract, would be an explicit indication that I don't want any help, even in extreme circumstances. It would also mean that I relieve the Agency of any responsibility for my health and life."

"For how long?"

"How long what?"

"What I want to know, Rhein, is for how long the Agency personnel would leave you undisturbed and without medical attention. A day, a month, a year? Until the contract expires?"

"I have no idea. The relevant clauses are quite vague and that's the reason I would rather not experiment."

I needed silence. I stood up and walked over to the opened window, gazing at the night outside. For a whole nine months I had been living with the notion that after I'd bandaged my arm, I soaked myself back into my own blood. Only a psychopath would do that, I would tell myself. Everything was so simple. The people from the Center had come. But since they weren't allowed to come—because I had taken off my wristband—they had probably decided to keep their visit secret. That's why they had given me only the most basic treatment and had then hurried away, while I was still unconscious.

Hundreds of moths, flies, and beetles were trying to get inside, attracted by the glow of the candles and the open fire. They were bumping against something my senses could not perceive, and hovered closer again, and bumped again, subject to their innate impulse toward the light that would singe them, hurt them, kill them. Wasn't I the same? What was I still pressing toward, like some mindless bug? Instead of staying in the darkness of the night.

I turned.

"Well?" Vanda asked, seated seductively in her chair, holding a glass of champagne.

"It's nice that you can open the windows whenever you feel like it. They're protected by an infrasound screen, or a microwave one, I don't know. But no bug ever comes in."

"Yes, I noticed," she said. "Come here and sit down."

I did as I was told.

"Let's finish our conversation," she said. "Where is the medical facility located?"

"Imagine two circles, and one of them, the smaller one, is inscribed within the larger one."

"I can imagine that."

"Okay, but they are not really circles. They are decahedrons, which means they have ten angles."

"You don't say," she laughed. "Thanks for elucidating."

"I'm sorry, just trying to be clear," I said. "So the larger decahedron is divided into ten trapezoid sectors, whose top sides are actually the sides of the smaller decahedron. The lateral sides are the same for two neighboring sectors, and the exterior sides border the free territory of the oasis. You see?"

"Absolutely, but what have I done to deserve this? Why are you punishing me in this geometrical fashion?"

"Because the sectors, Vanda, are parks with the villas in them, and the inner decahedron is the Center, where the medical facility is. That's the answer to the question you asked."

"I'm sorry I asked."

"Besides the medical facility there is also a communications unit in the Center, as well as an underground part of the complex with a power station, water supply equipment, and other such facilities. I suppose that's where the employees live. Well, not underground, of course."

"Of course not," Vanda said, shrewdly staring into my eyes.

"Actually, I haven't been over there yet," I said, trying not to blink more often than usual. "I simply never had to, but, according to the Agency's prospectus, they should have pretty much everything there. Whatever is not available could be delivered from the city within a few hours."

"The other clients are probably making use of these options."

"God knows what they're making use of. Personally, I don't need anything. Absolutely nothing."

"Except, maybe this."

Before I could even react, she lifted herself from her chair and sat on my knees, and, not wasting any time, kissed me passionately. I carefully pushed her off my knees.

"Let's not rush this, Vanda."

"Why not?" she said standing there and taking my hand. "We both know it's going to happen at some point. Why not do it now?"

"No, we don't know that. I don't want to know. I'd rather it remained a mystery."

"What?"

How I was saved, I thought.

"The girl," I said. "I mean, you."

"I'm not here to play a mystery game, Rhein," she said, tightening her grip on my hand. "I came to you with an open heart, and with the dream to become your sole inspiration. Your muse."

I raised my head and, sincerely touched, stared at her face, which seemed illuminated by her bright, sparkling eyes.

"But, my dear child," I said, "I hardly think I deserve . . ."

I thought I could feel her fingers slowly moving over to my wrist. And the bandage. I didn't look down to see if I was right.

I stood up.

"Go on, get some sleep."

Then, using the remote, I stopped the music that had become almost unbearable. I turned the lights back on and extinguished the candles, one by one.

5.

I was woken up by the unpleasant glare of the sun, which pierced the eastern window and my eyes. That had never happened before. The sun was always at its zenith when I came out of the trance. I couldn't have done much work today, I said to myself, but as soon as I went through the usual checks I realized that I hadn't worked at all. My clothes and hands were clean, the brushes and the palettes untouched.

I looked at the clock. It was barely past ten. Could it be that I had just sat here, like a stuffed animal, from six thirty until now? I summoned my courage and faced the screen.

It was folded. There was no painting there.

I had put it away. *He* had put it away without finishing it. But why? Was it unsuccessful, too wretched? Or on the contrary, had he sensed that it needed nothing more? Was it already a masterpiece?

I wandered aimlessly about the studio, glancing at the storeroom door every now and then. I knew today wasn't going to be the day to go in, but maybe I could have a peek. I stopped by the coffee machine and got myself a double espresso without sugar. I drank it, leaning against the wall. I was feeling an unfamiliar soreness in my shoulders and in my lower back, as if I had spent the past hours not just standing, but making a series of bows.

I threw my cup in the disintegrator, took the penknife out of my pocket, and made another cut on the special lath. Now they were exactly thirty. The number of his paintings. The number of mine? Zero. Well, he certainly deserved a good rest. Although, judging by my physical condition, his idea of rest was quite different from mine. God knows what he had been up to.

"What have you been up to, eh? Come on, show yourself and answer me! I have to know how you're *using* me."

The door behind me opened. My hair stood on end. It's him, the Artist. He exists outside of me. He is moving closer and closer.

I turned sharply—Vanda. I had completely forgotten about her.

"Ha! First you call me, then you get startled when I come."

"I didn't call you."

"Who were you talking to, then? Yourself?" She stared at me and changed the tone of her voice. "I'm sorry, Rhein, I didn't mean to eavesdrop. But I was going to come in anyway. I want to see your paintings."

"No! I mean, you can't see them. They are in the storeroom."

"Big deal. We'll take them out."

"No."

I grabbed her by the elbow and took her out to the hallway.

"Rhein, what's the matter with you?"

"I don't know."

I shut myself back in the studio and heard her walking away. Where was she going? I dashed back out.

"Vanda, wait. Vanda!"

But she turned toward the stairs and was soon out of my sight. I could hear that she walked past her room, which meant she wasn't going to collect her stuff and leave. I wondered if I should be disappointed or glad, and ended up feeling both. I was starting to turn into two people in my relationship with her, and I wasn't even in a state of trance.

I headed for the bathroom, but went back after a few steps and locked the studio door using the fingerprint sensor.

Half an hour later, freshly shaved and changed into decent clothes, I went down to the first floor. I walked around the rooms, but Vanda was nowhere to be found. I was impressed by the fact that she had tidied up the living room, even putting away the candles. I continued looking for her, determined to apologize for the way I had behaved earlier, and maybe also for the previous night.

I found her in the indoor swimming pool. Her breaststroke was relaxed and not particularly regular. She saw me, but neither came out nor accelerated her rhythm. Her movements had the languid quality of someone absorbed in a pleasurable activity. She had taken care of her surroundings, too. The vents were breathing out the aroma of fresh lilacs. I sat down in one of the chaise longues and waited. Her bright yellow cap stood out against the blue water, and her presence, just like her cap, stood out against the monotony of my life.

She finally climbed out of the pool. Her suit was black and relatively unassuming. She took off the cap and picked up her bathrobe. She didn't put it on but only wiped herself with it.

"How about something refreshing?"

"Yes, of course," I said, standing up. "What should I get you?"

"No, no, I'll go. I want to choose for myself. The choice here is always so varied. What would you like?"

"Water, sparkling water with ice."

"Just that?"

"For now, yes."

Vanda put on her slippers; their high heels left no doubt that she was unhappy about her height. The realization gave a boost to my self-esteem. A woman like any other, why should I fret over her tricks?

She took some time at the bar. When she finally returned, she brought sparkling water for both of us. She placed the tray on the table, the expression on her face somewhat solemn and dignified.

"Hey, come here, come," I said, pulling her toward me.

The touch of her skin shot through my body, silky and cool, and I caught a glimpse of her lips, parted as if she were frightened. I let her go and she threw her head back. She was in fact smiling.

"Rhein, come with me."

She turned her back to me and started walking along the pool. Her hair was so black it glimmered. I hurried after her, following her upstairs.

Next thing, I threw her on my bed. I was feeling hot, trembling all over. She reached over and pushed the blinds button. She lowered them halfway and we were immersed in enigmatic twilight. Her eyes, now staring at the ceiling, flashed white, glittering like mica.

"Oh, Rhein," she whispered.

I leaned over her while she unbuttoned my shirt. I wanted her passionately, but at the same time I didn't want her at all. I am crazy, I really am! One of "us two" wanted her, and the other didn't. My body was beginning to feel divided. We were tearing it apart.

I stepped back.

"What? Now what?"

"Quiet."

"Why?"

"Someone was ringing the doorbell."

Shaking her head, she laughed with contempt.

"I might have been mistaken," I mumbled.

But then, from out of nowhere, there came a clear, distinct ring from the front door downstairs. My heart stopped. Was such a coincidence even possible?

The ringing came again.

"Who is it?" Vanda asked dumbly.

"I have no idea. But this is absurd."

"Maybe it has to do with me."

"With you? Why would it have anything to do with you?"

"If no one has visited this villa since you came here . . . God, I hope nothing has happened to my father."

After a short pause, the bell rang again. I stood up, buttoning my shirt.

"How do you know that no one else has been here?"

"I checked," she told me. "I simply checked."

"When and where?"

"Last evening, with the so-called Butler. At least I had no trouble communicating with the computer," she said. "Go on, answer the door."

6.

The kid standing outside looked weird, to put it mildly. His head barely reached my waist but it was as large as an adult's, and it sat atop such a thin neck that I felt the urge to reach out and support it somehow. Help it stay in place before it fell down like an overripe melon. His legs were also shockingly thin, unlike his arms, which bulged under the short sleeves of his T-shirt, almost tearing it at the stitches.

"Hey, you're being impolite," he said, nudging me.

I nodded but I kept staring at him like an idiot. I was stupefied by the very fact of his presence here, and I was unable to muster the strength to act with the sensitivity that his looks seemed to require.

"Is everything all right, Rhein?" Vanda called on the videophone. "Should I come down?"

"No, don't! I'll only talk with him," he snapped, turning to me and offering his brawny hand. "Chavdar Gromov, but I'd rather you called me Chari."

"Okay," I said.

"Can I come in?" he said as he entered the villa. "We don't have much time. My father's probably looking for me by now."

I relaxed. The kid had simply run away from home. We remained in the foyer, sitting on the ottomans by the window. We could see the little terrace outside the front door.

"How old are you, Chavd . . . Chari?" I asked.

"Twelve. Now, Ray, here's some advice. Get yourself a glass of whiskey, it'll help you overcome the shock."

I finally looked at his face instead of his head. I was surprised to find it had regular, even mild, features. I smiled at him.

"Listen, Chari, I guess there are no other children in the complex to play with, so you're bored, aren't you?"

"Yeah, right. As if I care about playing."

"Well, I am not a child, so how about finding somebody else to shock?"

"Sorry, Ray, I have to do this. So, brace yourself and hear me out. We're dead. The trap snapped closed! Now no one will ever leave this oasis. With the exception of her maybe," he said, his eyes rolling up knowingly. "Although I'm not sure about that, either."

"Trapped here with her? Now that's truly worrisome."

"I knew you wouldn't believe me. I have neither hard evidence, nor any logical explanation. But what was I to do? My only choice was to come here and try to warn you."

I was hoping his father would find him here soon. But until he did, why not brighten his life a little?

"If you're warning me then we must still have a chance."

"I guess so. I'm sure that if our rescue is at all possible it entirely depends on you."

"What should I do?"

"Nothing heroic, Ray. Simply make her leave today."

"You think that this would resolve the issue?"

"Probably. Especially if you send her away before twelve. Here, see, it's not too late," he said, tapping his wristwatch with his finger. "It is barely ten past eleven. Call a helicopter from the Center right now. Help her pack her bags and *Adios, Señorita Cortez.*"

"How do you know her name?"

"You should've noticed by now that I know a lot of things, Ray. I have various ways of finding out about things and in most cases, I can see the connections between them."

"So you've found a link between Vanda's appearance and the snapping of the trap?"

"The oasis began changing yesterday at noon. I can feel it. I also witnessed some very unnatural events that I'd rather not talk about. I can assure you, though, that this is still only the beginning, Ray. It's going to get much worse."

"You think Vanda is to blame?"

"No. It's more likely that she doesn't realize what she's causing. Although, tell me, has she been asking you about stuff since she arrived? Is she prying? Actually, were you expecting her yesterday or someone else?"

I remained silent, but nervous shivers ran down my spine. Moving his ottoman closer to me, Chari peered into my eyes.

"I'm right. The lady is such a pest. She somehow managed to throw this entire place out of balance. That's how she turned the engines on!"

"What engines?"

"The engines of the oasis, Ray."

I patted him on the shoulder, laughing, and stood up. "You want some ice cream?"

"Yes. Chocolate cornetto."

I went to the kitchen and got a beer, and for him I got some chocolate as well as the ice cream. I looked at myself in the mirror. I was still grinning, although the paleness had crept back into my face. I returned to the foyer and walked by the window just in time to see a huge, lop-eared dog sitting on the terrace outside.

"That's it. He's found me," Chari sighed.

He tucked the chocolate bar into his pocket and began briskly eating the ice cream. The dog started barking. It looked and sounded like something out of a horror movie.

"What breed is it?" I asked.

"He's a cross between a mastiff and a pit bull. Hector, shut up!"

The dog heard him. He stopped barking and dashed away.

"He's off to get my father," Chari said bitterly, eating his ice cream even faster. "Listen to me, Ray. We might never see each other again. So, please, remember my words. The engines just sit revving for now, but very soon this oasis will really start off. It will take off! We will know neither where we're going, nor how to stop it. It will carry us through mirages and this timeless void until we all become dust and bones."

His eyes were large and dark, filled with curiosity and fear. This child seemed to have gone too far into his fantasy world. Who knew what nightmares tormented him at night?

"How long have you been living in the complex, Chari?"

"Over a year. My mother was with us in the beginning but she couldn't stand it. The moment my father also decides that he's had enough . . ." His head, an unbearable burden for his thin neck, drooped. "I know that he won't wait for me for too long, Ray. After that, there will be no one to take care of my dog."

"Hey, Chari, it's a good thing you've warned me, but I think that it would be more fun for you if we took off. Am I right? Come on, admit it!"

"I admit it. But you decide."

His hand clutching the dog's collar, the boy's father was already coming up the front steps. I went to open the door for him. He was a well-built man, about forty with surprisingly imposing looks. He was visibly uncomfortable and annoyed.

"I'm sorry for troubling you." He spoke hastily as he gave a small kick to the dog, who was whimpering and trying to get inside with

Chari. "I'm also sorry that I entered your park without ringing, but the gate was open and the animal rushed in, following the scent. I couldn't stop him, and I didn't want the kid to get away again. Yes, I am sorry."

"Don't be."

"Come on!" he called to Chari, who was standing behind me as if hiding from the wind. "Yes, sir, please accept my apologies. I promise this won't happen again."

"I hope your son will visit me again. I assure you, it was very pleasant. Chari is wonderful company. He's so intelligent. You've done a good job."

"Thank you! My name is Gromov, by the way."

As I introduced myself, Gromov grabbed Chari's shoulder and the three of them left, heading down the stairs in a compact formation.

"You know you're ill," Gromov was murmuring loud enough for me to hear, perhaps on purpose. "You shouldn't have gone out, especially not without your wristband."

7.

"Who was that brazen little fellow?" Vanda asked when I returned to the bedroom.

She had traded her swimsuit for a flimsy robe and was comfortably lounging on my bed. Next to her I saw my diary.

"You read it?"

"Yes, Rhein, I did."

"Leave! Get out. Out!"

"Don't you see, dear? Everything is falling into place. It's all to our advantage. Especially how you have two different handwriting styles."

The anger made me shake, and I didn't know if I'd be able to control myself.

"You're raving again," she said as she looked me up and down. "I'll let you calm down and then we'll talk."

She rose from the bed, put on her fancy slippers, and left on clacking heels. What arrogance! Lying here, paging through my diary, rummaging through my most intimate experiences, peeking into my very soul.

Peeking into my madness. And yawning!

Grinding my teeth in rage, I threw the diary into the drawer of the bedside table. I went into the study, sat behind the desk, and called the Butler. Until now, I had completely forgotten its existence. From the very beginning, I had accepted the Butler with absolute trust, almost like a child does his mother. Or maybe like a sucker who accepts a well-marketed product. Why not? As a rule, all goods and services supplied by the Agency were of the highest quality. The computer butlers who ran these electronically equipped villas were of even higher quality. They could probably run a space station.

Of course, the computer in the villa I was renting was doing a perfect job, too. Everything, from the toasters and coffee machines to the air conditioners, freezers, disintegrators, and the security system, was under its constant and diligent care. It monitored, regulated, charged, fixed, cleaned, and turned everything on and off. Most importantly, it never forgot anything.

I raised my head, startled by the noise of a revving engine. For a moment, the crazy thought that the oasis was taking off flashed through my mind. But it was only Vanda taking the jeep out of the garage. I ran to the window and watched her drive toward the Center. What was she going to do there? Well, what she was used to doing: whatever she wanted.

I sat behind the desk again. I leaned over the keyboard and brought up the register. Not a single visitor was recorded until yesterday.

I tried to approach the matter in more detail, but ended up wandering through the computer's files. It turned out that, unlike Vanda, I had difficulties communicating even with the Butler. I only wanted it to show me the data from the day of that terrible morning. But despite my asking in several different ways, the Butler only kept displaying the complete list of actions it had performed in the last nine months, arranged not chronologically but in categories.

Naturally, I was in many of these categories, little more than a link between the Butler and the appliances it was managing. For example, it had documented the types of coffee I had made; the number of times I had opened the freezers, the fridges, the windows, and then the times I had closed them; the times I had turned on the cleaners; when and what programs of the washing machine I had used, and the same for the dishwasher and the stove. I could even track down the exact time I had been in the shower, the bath, or the pool and the temperature of the water during every single minute, as well as many other bits of dumb data.

In the end, I got fed up and left the study.

Vanda returned after more than two hours. I heard her steering the jeep back into the garage, and I went out onto the terrace right away. I sat in the chaise longue there and waited. After all, she said that we would talk again after I had calmed down.

I made an effort to look perfectly rational, wondering at the same time if I would be able to look her in the eye after everything she had found out about me by reading my diary.

"Hello," she said cheerfully, relaxing in the chair across from mine. "I went to the Center. Rhein, it's amazing. You have to come with me first thing tomorrow and see for yourself."

"Why should I? I believe you."

"Could you, please, get me a lemonade? Or some iced tea?"

I brought her both.

"Well?" she asked, after drinking the lemonade.

Damn it! I discarded my thoughtful look, opting for distanced and slightly arrogant. After all, I had been at the top. I used to be a great artist. Artistic people are always more or less crazy. This would be my defense.

"So," she said, briskly tossing back her hair, "I will introduce you to our plan, step by step, outlining all of its advantages for you. But first, stop thinking so much. The Artist saved you and that's it. Don't you get it? That's it! Because it was exactly then that your personality split for the first time."

"Vanda, can't you see that it's a very delicate issue?"

"Enough with all these feelings already. It's your feelings that made you schizophrenic, which isn't a bad thing, by the way. Quite the contrary, it was for your own good, and it will continue to be. I will take care of that. All I want from you is to start perceiving it rationally from now on. Or, as my grandmother used to say, 'Don't cry—use your eyes to look for the advantages.'"

I had no response. The words *split* and *schizophrenia* just bounced around my thoughts.

"So, twenty-nine paintings?"

"Thirty since this morning."

"Bravo! Excellent!" Vanda cheered. "More than enough for a big exhibition."

"No," I said firmly. "I wasn't saved by the Artist. It was the medical station guys. Afterward they cleared out all the data related to their visit. The Butler has no record of anything."

"Could be, yes, it could have happened like that, but that's of no use to us. That's why we'll stick to the Artist. It's all so sensational. But we'll have to develop it, embellish it. 'As I lay unconscious, he rose from the bloody water, put a bandage over our hand, crawled back, swaying.'"

"Vanda!"

"Hold on, hold on," she said, putting her hand on her forehead. "You take turns writing in your diary. Get it? You write, then he does. This is how you two communicate; there's no other way. So here's an example of what he would write about that fateful morning: 'I snatched this body back from death and it is now mine, much more than it is yours. Take good care of it or I will seal you off completely. Only I will remain in this world.' To which you would answer: 'Do not threaten me, my dear.' And it would go on like that. We'll figure it out, have no worry."

"Worry? What on earth are you talking about?"

"I'm talking business, Rhein. A very profitable business. We'll launch the exhibition with a bang."

"What if the paintings aren't good?"

"Who's going to even look at the paintings? We'll sell them even if they're just doodles. We'll attach a copy of your diary to each one, which you will personally sign for every buyer. By that time, your diary will already have become a bestseller. We'll release it first."

"Uh-huh."

"It's a good thing you started writing in your diary before you went crazy. This way it will be obvious how much your handwriting changed. There are two of you, no doubt. Rhein-RHEIN, the Artist. Compared to him the one-eared Van Gogh looks like a mischievous kid who got hold of a pair of scissors. Yes! This will be our motto." Vanda stopped, having thought of something else, and said, "I shouldn't have shaved your beard. Let it grow back again."

"So you want me to cash in on my own tragedy?"

"What else should we do with it? Put it in a frame, next to your unsold paintings?"

She sprang from the chaise longue, grabbed my hands, and looked into my eyes with excitement.

"Come on, darling! Show them to me right now. I can't wait anymore. They might not be very good but we can still make it work. But they might be brilliant. Or monstrous. Why not monstrously brilliant? Or brilliantly monstrous?"

"Leave me alone, Vanda," I said, shaking my head listlessly. "I need some rest."

"Oh, yes, I'll leave you," she said, stamping her foot. "I'll leave you forever. If you don't show them to me right away, I'm leaving."

I closed my eyes, feeling dizzy, but she dug her fingers into my shoulders and shook me, forcing me to look at her again.

"I am determined to succeed, understand? At any price! If I can't make it with you, I'll find another. I will even steal Hosepha from my father."

"All right, all right!"

"All right what?"

"Leave me. I want to rest."

8.

My sleep was disturbed by the buzz of an approaching helicopter. By the time it landed on my lawn, I was fully awake. I pretended to be asleep, though. This would drive her mad, I told myself. She's not one to leave silently and peacefully, while someone napped on a chaise longue in the sun. She would come to stir me and we would argue again, and then maybe make up again.

Before even a minute had passed, I heard the front door open. That was a bad sign. She hadn't procrastinated, nor even hesitated. I relaxed even further, almost ready to start snoring. Very soon, however, my ears were assailed by the sound of a peculiar shuffle, which soon started to fade. I raised my eyelids warily and saw Vanda dragging her bags to the helicopter. She had on a comfortable but very ugly pair of pants and flat shoes. She didn't give a damn about her looks anymore. I was definitely no longer on her agenda. She was walking away without looking back at me.

"Listen," I could say to her, "we didn't come to any agreement, but why all the hurry? Stay a few more days." That would surely tempt her; she liked it here. How low I had sunk. I, who only a year ago enjoyed more attention from women than I could handle. Now I was trying to figure out how to keep this pain in the ass here. Trying to charm her with a kitschy villa, instead of my personality. I was crazy.

"Stupid!" I quietly repeated the trigger word I used in order to get out of the trance.

Vanda reached the helicopter. She climbed the tiny stepladder, lugging one of her voluminous bags; the small one was hanging from her shoulder. She left them inside and climbed down to get the last one. She went back inside with it. I saw her stowing it in the back and taking her seat.

"Vanda!" I jumped to my feet and rushed to the helicopter.

She remained seated inside but didn't press the takeoff button. She watched me and waited—neither frowning nor smiling. She was not disdainful. Or anything. It was as if she was no longer here. She'd already moved on to Marcian Hosepha, the painter she was going to steal from her father. He'd already written me off so it only made sense that his daughter would do the same.

I was at the very bottom. I raised my head.

"Come down here. I'll show you the paintings."

"When?"

"Right now."

She climbed out of the helicopter and said, "I won't release the helicopter. My luggage will remain here."

"Why?"

"To give you some incentive. Otherwise, you'll go back on your word again."

"I won't do that."

"Deal."

Instead of shaking on it, Vanda put up her hand for a high five and then we were on our way. Her head was no higher than my shoulder, but that didn't matter. I still felt small.

"You're doing the right thing. Besides, you have no other choice. One must constantly fight for survival. You can't just break down and head straight into the bathtub," she said. "I know this is hard for you, but I don't think I'll be of any help just whining with you."

"I'm not whining."

"I disagree. Your entire diary is a chronicle of whining. But that's okay. We'll gather all the art snobs and grab their cash. The sums your paintings will fetch at auction will be astronomical, believe me."

We reached the villa and went in. I slowed down.

"Shall we have a drink first?"

"No."

We crossed the foyer, then started climbing up the stairs.

"It's not just about the money, Vanda. I feel sick to even think of my paintings hanging on a wall somewhere where no one understands them, loves them, or even likes them."

"Did you pile them in the storeroom because of the enormous love and understanding you have for them?"

Once again, she was right. She wasn't stupid. I looked at her in a new way—with more respect, but less sympathy.

"Tell me this," I said, stopping. "How come I have no other choice?"

She stopped, too. "Don't you realize how deep in trouble you are? You've given up everything you had just to rent this villa. You're beyond poor now. When your time here basking in luxury is up, you'll return to civilization, where you'll most likely end up homeless."

We continued up the stairs, reached the second floor, and walked down the corridor.

"There's something else to keep in mind, too, Rhein. What if your condition gets worse? Where will you go with an empty wallet? They will lock you up in some filthy psychiatric ward where you'll remain forever, forgotten by everyone."

"See," I said, smiling bitterly. "I do have a choice, after all."

We stopped in front of the studio door. Vanda, her arms akimbo, squinted at me venomously. Apparently, she had tried to open it while

I was sleeping and already knew that it was locked. I quickly touched the sensor, not wanting to hear another word from her, least of all that dumb "Well?" I stepped back. She nodded at me and went in, closing the door behind her.

I leaned against the wall and took a couple of deep breaths. Then I headed for . . . I didn't know where. I ended up in the library. I selected an encyclopedia of art and made myself comfortable in the armchair by the window. I tried to read, but in vain. The letters were shifting before my eyes, forming words one would never find in a book like this. *Rhein-RHEIN, doodles, cash.*

I turned to the window. It was half past four, early afternoon in the long days around here. Burning in the cloudless sky, the sun poured its heat over the grass, the trees, and the wild bushes, yet they all looked so good. Unnaturally fresh, bright green, constantly watered by the Butler.

I stood up abruptly and pressed my head against the glass.

Vanda was outside. She crossed the driveway and looked back. She saw me and ran across the meadow, straight for the helicopter. She climbed in and a few seconds later the rotor started turning. The impeccably maintained aircraft took off and flew away, off over the desert.

9.

No, she was not just gone. She had fled! Which could only mean that she had been horrified upon seeing the paintings.

I left the library, feeling devastated. Now I had to go inside that damned storeroom. But first I stopped in the living room, opened the liquor cabinet, and poured myself a generous dose of whiskey. I sat and took my time drinking it. I wished this could go on forever. It occurred to me that I could pour myself another glass. I had no reason whatsoever to stay sober.

Soon, though, I was interrupted by someone ringing the buzzer. This villa, which until yesterday had been the epitome of solitude, was now starting to feel like a highway motel.

I went to see who it was, but there was no one at the front door. Still, the ringing came again. It took me some time to realize it was coming from the gate that led to the Center. I turned on the monitor and a woman appeared on the screen. I sighed so loudly that she seemed to hear me, so I had no choice but to open the gate.

I went out onto the terrace, leaned on the railing, and waited. In a minute or two, a small sports car stopped in front of the villa. The woman climbed out and walked in my direction. She was about thirty, medium height, with a cute face and fit body.

"Hello," she said with a smile.

"Hello to you, too."

"I'm a bit early but considering the amount of work we have to do, maybe I should have come even earlier. Where's Vanda?"

"She left."

"Did she? I hope nothing unpleasant has happened."

"Her father called her about some exhibition. It was an urgent matter and she was in a hurry. That's probably why she forgot to let you know."

"It doesn't matter. I'd agreed to help her with the preparations for the party. Do you know about that?"

"I know nothing, obviously."

"Vanda was at the Center this afternoon," the woman explained. "We met at the café and she invited us, me and a few other people. But don't worry, I'll tell them not to come."

"Okay. Please, do . . . Actually, don't!" Overwhelmed by the thought of what awaited me in the storeroom, I quickly added, "Let them come. I hope you don't mind helping me."

"Of course," she said. "My name is Magdalene. Maggie for short."

"Rhein."

"I actually can't believe I'm meeting you. You are my favorite artist."

"Shall we get to work, then, Maggie?"

"Sure, but I have to warn you that I'm not awfully handy."

"Me, neither," I laughed. "That's why we'll resort to prepackaged food. We'll leave it to defrost and get to know one another. How does that sound?"

"Perfect. The menu Vanda had in mind seemed impossible. Although she could probably pull it off."

"Yes, probably."

Soon, we were fussing about in the kitchen. It turned out that we were expecting five people at seven, which was in two hours, and a few more who would arrive later.

"There's enough time," I murmured to myself.

"Don't worry. They're all so curious to meet you they probably won't even notice the food and drinks." Maggie stopped and put her hands on her hips. "Now, however, I'll have to ask you to sit somewhere. There's plenty of space here, but I keep feeling like we're about to bump into each other."

I dutifully sat on a stool, tilted my head, and looked at her. Her skin had a healthy golden color, and there were sun-faded streaks in her auburn hair.

"You have a nice tan," I remarked. "Unlike me, you seem to be spending a lot of time in the sun."

"I used to. Although I've been mostly underground lately," she said, opening one of the freezers.

Underground . . . Another nutcase, then.

For the next several minutes, she kept busy choosing frozen meals and arranging them in the microwave ovens. Then she rubbed her hands like someone who had just finished with some onerous task and sat across from me.

"We'll turn them on in an hour," she said. "Then we'll choose the wine. Now what?"

"Tell me about yourself," I said. "Why are you in the oasis? You don't look like someone who needs seclusion."

"I'm not here because of the seclusion, Rhein. I think that if the Remorites really existed, their capital must have been situated right here, since the underground part of the complex is connected to the caves."

"Are you an archaeologist?"

"No. I have a degree in psychology, but maybe this will prove to be more useful, although the Remorites were not at all like us."

"I know nothing about them, either, Maggie."

"I keep forgetting that you are in fact a hermit," she said. "It's just what we call you."

"Very appropriate."

"But we say that with all due respect, I assure you."

Uncomfortable silence set in. It was obvious that there had been ridicule—whoever "we" were. My soon-to-arrive, uninvited-by-me guests, I presumed.

"Listen, Rhein," she said, her face lighting up as if an amazing idea had dawned on her. "Come with us to the caves tomorrow. I will tell you both the legend and my theory about the Remorites. You'll find it interesting."

"All right," I heard myself saying. "I'll come."

After that, the conversation became easier. We agreed to meet at the café around ten and then we exchanged numbers.

"Everything's settled, then. Now we can gossip openly," Maggie said. "Don't look so surprised. You're about to spend an evening with people who are . . . quite peculiar. If you're not prepared, you'd be sure to make a blunder. For example, does the name Natalia Shidlovskaya mean anything to you?"

"I've seen her dance in several performances. She's fantastic, especially in *Swan Lake*. But why are you asking?"

"Because a woman will come here who will seem vaguely familiar. You'll start staring at her, trying to remember where you've seen her."

"Impossible," I objected. "If it is Shidlovskaya I'd recognize her right away."

"I doubt that," Maggie sighed. "I live with her. Four months ago, I moved into the villa she's been renting for a year. She couldn't stand the solitude, that's why she took me in. After many recommendations and guarantees from important people, of course. I had a hard time dealing with them. They had to write her about me without knowing where she was. She insists on keeping this a secret from absolutely everybody."

"That won't last long if all the other people here know who she is."

"They do, but they also want to keep their whereabouts secret, so it is a collective secret."

"It's not a secret anymore if Vanda knows."

"Don't worry. She wouldn't recognize Natalia, and the others are not as famous as she is. Plus, they're all using aliases here. Now, Rhein, tell me, have you read *Pride and Prejudice*?"

"I have."

"It doesn't matter. Make sure you deny everything about the book. You haven't read it and you know nothing about it. Otherwise, you'll be dragged into a discussion of its plot and we won't be able to drag you out of it for the whole evening. When it comes to *Pride and Prejudice*, Lord Darcy is completely obsessed."

"I see. We're getting to the second guest. Is Lord Darcy his alias?"

"Yes, but he doesn't consider it an alias. He believes he is the actual Lord Darcy. Or maybe he just pretends to believe it. Honestly, I don't know. I don't understand him, and I'm supposed to be a psychologist."

"Well, never mind, let him believe what he likes. Are all the other guests as eccentric?"

"No, no, they are rather harmless. One of them, he goes by Ludovic, is a very pious person. Something like a repentant sinner. He used to be in the mafia, this I am sure of."

"Why not a serial killer or a terrorist?"

"Because he's here, Rhein. You can tell he's very rich. He's made a killing dealing drugs, weapons, or devil knows what else. Now he's hiding both from his accomplices and from Interpol, the KGB, and the FBI. He's waiting for the storm to blow over before going back to a normal life as a decent businessman who's devoted to charity. Yes, that's my version of his story. Here's my advice: don't mention the mafia or the cops and he'll be your friend."

"Sounds encouraging. Who else can I expect?"

"Hans and Wilma are newlyweds. They've sought refuge here, hiding from her vengeful first fiancé. Supposedly, the man is pathologically jealous and he's got nothing to lose since he's about to die of cancer or AIDS. I can't remember."

"You mean they'll wait until he's dead and then go back home."

"Exactly."

"Good. So with Hans and Wilma I should steer clear of soap operas."

"Look now, Rhein," Maggie said, frowning, "I understand that everything I say sounds nuts, but I don't know how to put it otherwise. Because *it is nuts*. This complex was made for such people—people with plenty of money and an even greater abundance of problems."

She leaned toward me, exuding a great deal of patience, as if she was ready to listen to my problems for as long as it took. *Come on, my dear Hermit, I know you have plenty of problems, too.*

"How many are there in all?" I asked. "People, I mean."

"There's thirteen of you. Not counting me and the staff."

"Why shouldn't we count you?"

"Lack of problems, naturally." This time she seemed to be joking. "And also lack of money. I can't even afford to rent a tree here to build a tree house in. I was lucky Natalia needed company."

"She was lucky, too, Maggie."

10.

The Lord appeared first—not at seven, but well before six, and not from the direction of the Center, but from the free territory. We opened that gate for him and he soon slammed the brakes of his dusty jeep next to Maggie's car. Over six feet tall and lanky, he leaped out of the jeep dressed in a hunting suit, a feather trilby on his head.

"Greetings, greetings," he called at us, waving his long arms, looking like a windmill.

He bent down, pulled out a bag from inside the car, and hurried toward us. His boots were as dusty as the jeep, and as soon as he came closer, I saw that his clothes and even his face were in the same condition.

"You are Rhein," he said, offering me his dry and wiry hand. "I am Lord Darcy, Fitzwilliam Darcy!"

He waited for my reaction, and after receiving none, he turned to Maggie.

"Guess who I met."

"The Wanderer," she said.

"Indeed. Only this time I didn't try to talk him up. I shot him down and I've brought you his head. Here, it's for you."

With a slight bow, he handed her the bag, which was dripping blood. Maggie jumped back and her face turned pale. I was probably as pale as her.

"Look at him." Darcy grinned, looking down. "He chewed through it."

"No," Maggie moaned.

"No? Isn't this what you wanted?"

"It was a joke."

My eyes darted back and forth between the two, occasionally landing on the red stain growing larger on the terrace.

"This is a joke, too," Darcy said, bursting into laughter. "It's just game that I've brought you."

Now I had an idea of his particular sense of humor. But I couldn't understand why Maggie took it so seriously, as if there was no doubt in her mind that he really could have brought her someone's head.

"Who's the Wanderer?" I asked.

"A man who pretends to be deaf and dumb," Darcy replied, dropping the bag at my feet. "He wanders around the oasis, instead of sitting in his villa. Since our Maggie likes to wander, too, he scares her. He's in love with her. But hey, where's your girl?"

"She left."

"Too bad. Why didn't you make her stay? She was a hottie."

"Darcy," Maggie started, "what should we do with this meat?"

"It's a young and tender antelope," he said as he pulled out his phone and dialed a number. "Four people in villa number 5. You have a barbecue?"

"I don't know."

"Everything for a barbecue, including a few of those insect-repellant gadgets. We'll be dining outside." Darcy hung up and smiled kindly at Maggie. "Are you happy now, lazy girl?"

"Very much so," she replied. "With Vanda gone, I was worried about having to spend the entire evening serving everyone."

"I would never let that happen," Darcy assured her. "Come on, let's go. We'll change clothes and be back at about seven."

They got into their cars before I could say anything. Soon they were gone, having placed me in a very awkward situation.

I went back to the kitchen and threw all the Chinese food back into the freezer. Why hadn't I thought of ordering cooks and servants? Despite my lean wallet, I could have afforded as much. I was angry both at Maggie and at the false Darcy. Unless of course he really was a lord. When I thought of Vanda, I felt so helpless that my anger just evaporated.

I returned to the living room, finished my whiskey, and stepped back outside. I shot a glance at the bag. I should have noticed right away that it was much larger than it would have been if it contained only a head. Poor creature. An hour or two ago it had been running free in the lush greenery of the oasis, and now it was here at my feet.

A gray minivan came up the driveway. As soon as it stopped, four creatures dressed in gray uniforms got out of it. At first, I thought they were aliens, then strangely small people, and finally, children. Of course, they weren't children, either.

They started taking cardboard boxes out of the minivan, probably filled with stuff for the barbecue, and stacked them by the vehicle. I was standing on the landing, only thirty feet away, but they didn't seem to notice me. Each of them grabbed a box and plodded in the direction of the trees nearby. They left the boxes there, on the grass, and dashed back, their heads lowered. A ridiculous notion—that they actually avoided looking at me on purpose—crossed my mind, confusing me even more.

I lifted the bag, descended the stairs, and joined them, just as they were about to grab the next batch of boxes. They were all of equal height, not exceeding five feet. I felt like a giant and stooped somewhat.

"Hello," I said to them.

They froze, as if I had pointed a gun at them. What in God's name was going on? What kind of behavior was this?

"Here's the meat," I said, trying to hand over the bag. But since no one took it I just left it on the ground. "If you need anything from the kitchen, feel free to come in."

I went back inside and looked at my watch. All the unpleasant impressions I had collected from both the personnel and the clients of the Agency immediately lost their significance. It was ten past six, which meant I had a whole fifty minutes and not a single reason to put off the inevitable. I headed for the second floor.

The studio's door had been left ajar. I pushed it and the first thing I saw was the wide-open window across the room. Why did she open it? I lingered in the corridor for a bit longer and after summoning my courage I stepped forward. But I didn't go in. I clutched the doorframe, feeling that something was pushing me back, as if hitting me in the chest. My breathing quickened, and the air seemed to set my lungs on fire. The heat was unbearable. The air conditioners must be set for heat, I thought, but I immediately realized that the temperature in the studio was normal, even cool compared to that of my body.

My knees bent and I was about to collapse. I sat on the floor, where to my great surprise I instantly felt better. I stared at the window and slowly rose to get back in its range. I prepared myself for a new thermal shock, or stroke, or whatever it was, but none came. The moment I tried to stand up, however, everything was repeated and I was forced to sit down again.

I turned my head to the storeroom door, also left ajar, darkness seeping out through the opening. *She turned off the lights before running away*, I thought to myself, and, soaked in sweat, I started shaking. At least I knew what was happening to me. I was possessed by an overwhelming, all-consuming fear. How could I not be, after losing myself for hours every day for nine months? Who was I during that time? What was I turning into? I hadn't even asked myself these

questions until today. I'd been painting in a trance, simple as that.
Now, however . . .

What if the paintings really were monstrous? Expressing some side
of my being that I was unaware of, that had terrified Vanda and would
most likely terrify me? That's what scared me.

I dragged myself sideways, leaned on the wall, and slowly rose
again. Teetering like a drunk, I made for the dark storeroom. I reached
through the crack and gropingly hit the light switch. I peeked inside.

I heard my own laughter, as if from afar. The paintings were all
wrapped. That's what I had been doing this morning. I walked beside
them, counting—all thirty of them. Not a single one was unwrapped,
which meant that Vanda hadn't seen any of them, either. So why did
she run away?

"I honestly don't give a damn why," I replied out loud.

11.

The antelope was already eaten, the barbecue set put away, and the table, set up under the palm trees, cleared off. We were sitting around it in comfortable chairs brought by the servants, sipping our drinks, enjoying the sunset, and chatting in a leisurely way. Or rather, the others were chatting while I sat silently, feeling wonderfully well.

The newlyweds, Hans and Wilma, were sitting across from me, an astonishingly bland couple who held hands and looked very much in love. It struck me as quite natural, considering how unlikely it seemed that anyone else would fall in love with either one. As soon as I laid eyes on them, I knew that the whole story about the vengeful, jealous, terminally ill first fiancé was entirely made-up. Unless the guy was hoping to acquire the funds he needed for his treatment through marriage. Anyway, these two were the ideal guests. I could treat them as if they weren't there at all.

Unlike Hans and Wilma, however, Darcy could not be ignored. He was as loud as an entire hunting company. His stories of safaris and defeated predators had no end, or beginnings. They cut suddenly into the conversation, then died out unfinished. He would light his pipe and smoke for a while, absorbed in his memories, before suddenly embarking on another story, even more confusing and implausible. Baron Munchausen would have been a more appropriate alias.

"At least nine hundred pounds live weight," he was saying at the moment, "hurtling toward me, despite the fact that I'd already put three bullets in him. He knocked me down. The gun was no longer of any use so I took out my knife."

And so on.

Maggie was sitting to my left, and to my right was Ludovic, the Russian mafioso, whom everyone endearingly called Ludo. He was a wide-shouldered hunk of about thirty-five, with nearly white blond hair, a round face, and childishly innocent sky-blue eyes. He drank a lot, talked little, and frequently sighed—either out of sadness or piety, I couldn't tell. We had exchanged only a few words so far. First at dinner, regarding our lack of desire to become vegetarian, and later, while we were choosing drinks, on not being able to abstain from alcohol, which was also a pity. All in all, thus far he hadn't surprised me on any level. If not a thug, he was definitely Russian.

"I couldn't believe my eyes," Darcy said, raising his voice passionately. "The wicked thing was baring his teeth at me, even after I had his heart in my hands. By the way, the heart alone weighed as much as my dog."

Maggie reached and took his lighter, which, unsurprisingly, was the shape of a gun. She clicked it and raised the flame to his cigar. He heartily started puffing, while she continued with her own conversation, which was directed at me, I think.

"I sometimes feel that the Remorites themselves summoned me here. I dreamt about them at night. I was haunted by them during the day. 'Search for us, find us,' they whispered to me, not with words but telepathically. I don't know. Even if they are, in fact, a figment of the imagination of some ancient beings, they are still so alive to me."

"Excuse me, Maggie," Darcy said through layers of smoke, "but it's high time to pull yourself together. You are obsessed with a fairy tale and it's becoming a fixation."

"Don't listen to him, dear," a mellifluous voice said from nearby.

"Oh," Maggie exclaimed, "I was starting to think you weren't coming."

I stood up. A woman had arrived—plump, withered, her face caked with makeup. Was it really her? The world-famous ballerina whose dancing entranced everyone, whose pictures, only a few years ago, had graced the covers of the most prestigious magazines?

"Well, I came, and mind you, I walked. It's obvious that I need a more active lifestyle, isn't it?"

Her question was aimed at me.

Dressed in a long silk robe, she was standing on the lawn. She was not smiling. I approached, as she looked at me tensely from beneath her artificial lashes. I took her hand, leaned forward, and gently touched it with my lips.

"It's an honor, madam," I said softly. "I love ballet because of you."

"I admire your art, sir," she replied with dignity. "I own two of your paintings and I am very proud."

We exchanged polite bows and I led her to the seat at the head of the table, which was kept for her from the very start of the evening. While she was taking her seat, the men stood up.

"We were waiting for you, Natalia," Ludo rumbled. "Without you, the most important is always missing."

"It's missing when I'm here, too," Natalia softly objected, while a servant, who had appeared out of nowhere, carefully placed a glass of some green liquid in front of her. "Thank you."

"Good Lord," Wilma chortled as the servant scurried off.

"She's right, Willie," Hans said. "I also suspect them of being vengeful. So we have to be polite to them."

"But, Hans"—Natalia raised her eyebrows in bewilderment—"I don't suspect them of anything. I just like people who do their job well, that's all."

"Pe-eople," Darcy mockingly drawled. "They're just a bunch of dumb, well-trained animals. A pack of monkeys brought here from the wastelands."

"That's enough," Natalia said. "Do I have to remind you that you need to mind your language in my presence?"

Darcy's bony face, with his crooked nose and round, yellowish eyes, proved surprisingly expressive: several different emotions passed over it in quick succession, all of them negative.

"Why did you tell Maggie not to listen to me?" he blurted out.

"Indeed, Natalia, why?" Maggie said. "After all, you don't believe that the Remorites exist, either."

"Indeed, I did not believe, my dear, but this afternoon . . ." Natalia paused, shaking her head. "I'll just spit it out—I saw them."

"Who? The Remorites?"

"Well, yes."

"Oh, God," Wilma chortled again.

"Shut up." Maggie cut her off and turned to Natalia. "Is that a joke?"

"Not at all. I don't feel like joking after what I went through."

"Then keep it a secret," Darcy suggested.

"I was in the living room," Natalia continued, without paying any attention to him. "I was just about to leave to come here, when I suddenly felt sick. I barely reached the couch. Just then I saw them. They appeared as if out of thin air, passed by me, and gradually faded away, vanished."

"What did they look like?" Maggie asked excitedly.

"Hard to tell. I could see their outlines clearly, but their postures made them hard to distinguish. They were stooping. Or maybe they were shriveled, twisted in shape? I don't know. And I don't have an answer to the question of why I saw them."

"You were hallucinating," Darcy said. "There's the answer."

"It is possible." Natalia shrugged. "But whatever it was, I now think that if the Remorites really exist, they have remained here, just as the legend says."

For the first time that evening I felt that we were all in agreement that this was most bewildering.

"They stopped here only to rest for a while." Natalia lowered her voice to a whisper. "For a long time they lived with the illusion that this was not their journey's destination. This oasis, however, was far too comfortable. It inclines one to overstay, and ultimately leads to the fatal delay."

"When a supposed transit station proves to be the final one," Ludo said and finished his drink in a single gulp.

"Yes, precisely," Natalia said. "We must not forget that *Remorites* means 'latecomers.' Just what we are now."

"Oh, God," Wilma chortled again.

"No, no, she's right, Willie," Hans said. "I, too, think that you and I have stayed here dangerously long."

"Hans"—Natalia looked at him reproachfully—"this was not what I meant."

"What did you mean, then?"

"I have no opinion on the matter. But I think that we should not be focusing on how long anyone has been here, but on the fact that none of us wants to continue the journey."

"Wow," Darcy declared. "You felt unwell, then your brain manufactured a few outlines, and what a yarn you've spun! Analogies, allegories, a whole philosophy. I wonder what would happen if you had a nightmare? Or if you decided to impress not one but a collective of famous artists?"

Well, this man knew how to make others uncomfortable. I wondered if I should say something, but Ludo beat me to it.

"She doesn't need to try to impress anyone," he said through clenched teeth.

"Why, of course," Darcy said, grinning at him. "She is brilliant by nature."

Ludo placed his huge palms on the table, preparing to lunge forward. Reaching over, Natalia gently put her hand on his shoulder, while one of the servants quickly put a new glass of vodka in front of him. The servant took the empty glass and stepped back, a melting shade among the palm trunks.

The whole situation had a certain comical quality to it, but the most comical of all was that no one found it funny. On the contrary, we remained serious and tense, until Darcy finally pressed his lips together and took to clipping his cigar. Ludo sighed and looked up. Only then did we all relax.

"Let me tell you what I did," Maggie babbled. "Today I achieved a real breakthrough with the two A's!"

"Really?" Wilma and Hans said at the same time.

"Yes," she said, turning to me to explain. "I'm talking about Alvaro and Adela. They rent villa number 10."

"Louts," Darcy grunted.

"Absolutely," Maggie agreed. "But they were born like that. As for their second nature, they're like moles. No wonder they wouldn't let anyone in their park. They have dug it up for acres. Strawberries, tomatoes, cucumbers, potatoes."

"Potatoes," Wilma repeated in amazement.

"And onions," Maggie said, laughing away, "and pumpkins. I have never met such obsessive people. They say that they create new varieties of fruit and vegetables. They had me walk through seedbeds and melon fields for over an hour, and it was about three in the afternoon. It was stifling hot. But not only did I make it through, I managed to show constant admiration: 'Oh, what enormous melons! These leeks are amazing.'"

"If you ask me, Alvaro and Adela do deserve admiration," Natalia said. "They might be somewhat simple, but at least they don't waste their time here. They are doing something useful."

"The defender of self-taught agricultural innovators," Darcy said.

Ludo bristled again. Apparently, both the remarks and the reactions of these six people revolved in cycles of predictability.

"Anyway," Maggie said, "what's important is that I managed to set them at ease and they told me their secret!"

Everyone expectantly stared at her.

"Oh, come on, Maggie," Wilma said. "Tell us their secret!"

"It's quite simple, really," she said. "They won the lottery. Which is why, of course, they very soon received the Agency's prospectus. They have four adult children who did not give a damn about them while they were poor but suddenly changed their minds after the windfall. Well, the two A's decided not to give them a cent. They rented the villa here and set out to accomplish their dream of creating new varieties of leeks and such."

"I don't want them in our company anymore," Darcy said with disgust. "Let them dig in their melon fields."

"Hey, Fitzwilliam," I said, "or was it Fitzpatrick? Do I sense in you the hunter's primitive hostility toward the gatherer?"

"Why, yes." He cheered up unexpectedly. "You must be right. My ancestors' blood rises against all these vegetables and . . . and bumpkins. They are the ones who have always driven the game away from their fields. They cut down the woods. So, not long ago, I was after a grizzly bear that had eaten two young children . . ."

I took a deep breath, preparing to stop him, but behind his back, Maggie gave me a sign not to say anything.

". . . They were Native Americans, but still children. I had not yet added a grizzly to my collection. So I made for its lair, alone, as always, with only my rifle . . ."

And so on.

There in the twilight, my guests seemed somewhat two-dimensional, only barely outlined. But in all likelihood I looked the exact same way.

12.

Just as I expected, their stay extended late. When it started to get cold, we moved into the living room, the flow of gossip and slander undiminished. Thus, while silently waiting for them to leave, I learned quite a few things, all of them, unsurprisingly, concerning absent people. For example, I learned that the Wanderer, who had been the first to rent a place here, was neither deaf, nor mute, in everyone's opinion, but only pretended to be so. Felix was a student, exiled here by his parents, who wanted to put an end to his drug addiction and force him to study for his medical school exams. Strauss was a physicist, wading chin-deep in the realms of mysticism or the paranormal, maybe even both. The topic of the two A's surfaced again at some point: they were apparently both appalling and somewhat sympathetic. And then again, Felix and Strauss "knew no limits," although I didn't understand in what respect.

For a while, it was interesting to listen to their chatter, but I started to feel sleepy. I did soldier through, however, and in the end saw them off as a polite host should. I sent the servants away. Finally, I was alone again.

I hastened to bed, reaching for my diary by force of habit. But no, I would not write in it anymore, I told myself. I felt bad and decided not to destroy it yet. I placed it under my pillow and switched off the lamp, and the darkness spread over me, penetrating my thoughts, filling my soul. It dragged me down into dreams in which, I hoped, I would return to my river, which only temporarily had run underground.

But it took me nowhere. I sank into some kind of intermediate state, neither wakefulness nor sleep, which took me back to the day that had just ended, rife with images and voices: the smell of cigars, the taste of freshly killed meat. The touch of the ballerina's puffy hand and the brawny arm of the boy—*"We're dead, Ray. The trap has snapped!"* I could also feel Vanda's silky-smooth skin, and our kisses here, on this very bed where I was lying now, pressed between darkness and the revolving day.

I was in bed with all of this flowing through my mind when I sensed someone or something crawling, slowly, in the hallway. I could really hear it, yes. Although barely audible, this strange, intermittent sound reverberated in my head as if amplified. I tried to move but I couldn't. When I finally struggled out of my petrified, sleepy haze, everything had gone quiet.

I felt for the switch on the lamp, hesitated, and decided not to turn it on. I groped my way to the door, where I listened again: silence. I went out into the hallway. It wasn't as dark here, but this frightened me even more. I turned in the direction of the light. It was coming from the studio. The door had been left ajar.

I walked toward it, silently tiptoeing. Coolness rose from the marble floor, up through my bare feet, and spread through my body until reaching my heart, where it transformed into ice.

The light was actually coming from the storeroom. I clenched my fists, ran through the studio, and stopped to peek in. I looked about. The paintings were still wrapped, but one of them—the largest—was displaced. Someone had pushed it a little to the side.

"The Artist . . . it's *him* again," I whispered to myself, and for some reason the words calmed me down.

I turned off the lights and shut the door. When I left the studio, I shut the second door, too. The hallway, however, didn't grow as dark as it was supposed to. Light was coming from the stairway. I was startled, but then I realized that on the landing, there was a window with open blinds, letting in the bright, moonlit, starry night.

I went past the bedroom and down the stairs. I reached the first floor, where I suddenly decided this whole sneaking-around business was silly. I waved my hands about, looking for the switch, staggered, and cursed.

Then came the familiar sound of crawling, but now somehow hurried. The noise came from the corner room next to the kitchen. But who was it? I heard a bang, then whimpering. I rushed, pushed the door, and the bright light blinded me. I was rattled by a piercing scream.

Slumped by one of the freezers, Vanda was shrieking, her mouth gaping like a wound. A moment later, she stopped and began sobbing silently, while scratching her fingernails over the floor.

"You scared me, Rhein, oh, how you scared me."

"Well . . . I'm sorry, but what are you doing here?" I mumbled, shocked.

"I looked for you in the studio, but you weren't there, and I felt even sicker in there. I dragged myself down the stairs, crawling in here. Oh, Rhein, Rhein, Rhein."

"Yes?"

"What do you want from me?"

"Me? I want nothing, nothing. Get a grip on yourself!"

She began sobbing again. I stepped closer. Her hair was tousled and matted, her clothes stretched and sand-stained. There were bruises on her hands.

"Vanda." I leaned in, patting her lightly on the back. "Everything's fine, you're safe now."

"Safe?" she said, tossing her head back to look at me.

She laughed with unspeakable bitterness. I had the feeling it was the first time she'd been honest with me.

"Come on, get up," I said.

"I'm hungry. I'm starving."

"Well then, come, I'll take you to the kitchen."

"This is the kitchen, this!"

"No, it isn't, and this freezer is empty."

"Why?" she suddenly shrieked. "Why is it empty?"

She was either acting up or completely disoriented.

"Because it is for special orders, and I have never made one," I explained to her in a gentle, conciliatory voice. "Come."

I helped her to her feet, then slowly led her to the kitchen. I made her sit on one of the chairs and promptly began taking sandwiches and sausages out of the fridge.

"No, that will only make me sicker. Just pour me some juice. Considering I haven't eaten in three days, my stomach—"

I turned sharply.

"Three days?"

"Maybe even more. Just give me something to drink."

I poured her a glass of orange juice, handed it to her, and sat down. I watched her as she painfully swallowed. Her lips were sore to the point of bleeding. What had happened to her?

"Vanda," I began carefully, "why did you go to the studio?"

"I told you, I was looking for you."

"You thought that I would be there in the middle of the night?"

"Night, night," she repeated. "Why, yes! It's night, otherwise it would have been light outside."

"Naturally," I said.

"What's so natural, Rhein? It was day when they brought me back here!"

"Who's 'they,' Vanda? Who brought you back?"

"I don't know. They were only shadows, faceless shadows. They kept me in the helicopter for three days, or longer, and outside, there was . . . there was nothing. Not a thing!"

I stood up and carefully lifted her in my arms. I took her upstairs.

"In the bathroom," she moaned. "Leave me there."

"Are you sure you won't feel worse?"

"On the contrary, it will make me feel better." She began to toss feverishly in my arms. "I feel terribly dirty. Oh, Rhein."

So I left her there. I remained at the door for a while, listening. The shower turned on and I could hear the rattle of a hairbrush. I gathered that her movements were not those of someone who was about to faint.

I returned to the kitchen, where I was again plagued by vague doubts. I walked back to the corner room, went to the freezer, and tried to open it, but it wouldn't yield. I clutched the handle harder and pulled. I even considered kicking it. Then it dawned on me. That's why she had collapsed next to it. When she had come here, she had already felt weak, and the dumb thing, refusing to budge, had brought her to the edge.

I checked the other three freezers in the room. Unlike the first one, they opened effortlessly. Poor Vanda, she had tried to open perhaps the only faulty object in the entire villa. Maybe the Butler decided not to mend it simply because it was empty.

All in all, faulty *is the key word for everything,* I thought.

About fifteen minutes later, I carried a tray up the stairs, heavy with fruit, toast, juice, and several kinds of cheese. No sound was coming from the bathroom. Vanda was apparently not there anymore, so I stopped in front of the guest room door.

"Shall I come in?"

"No," she shouted, but opened the door almost immediately.

She had put on a nightgown and wrapped a towel around her head. She smiled at me faintly and slipped back into bed, tugging the covers up to her chin. I placed the tray on the movable table, pushed it closer to her, and sat on one of the ottomans.

"Listen to me, Vanda," I said in a low voice. "It's not good to fall asleep with so many confusing things on your mind. You have to figure out exactly what happened to you so that you can overcome it now."

"And you know exactly?"

"More or less, yes. The helicopter simply had to land in the desert due to a malfunction. Instead of waiting for the people in the Center to fix it, you succumbed to panic. You went out in the unbearable heat, lost your way, fell down, and hurt yourself. By the way, do you have any other bruises besides those on your hands?"

"No, but my head hurts."

"See, you probably hit your head, too, and that's why you can't remember anything. What's clear is that you went back into the helicopter, otherwise the rescue crew would have come."

"Yeah, right! They left me stranded for three days."

"You're wrong, Vanda. No more than two hours have passed since you left here."

"Hah!"

"It's true. I guess they brought you back here simply because the failure occurred closer to the oasis than the city."

"Simply, simply. You keep saying that."

"It is simple. The helicopter took you from here at about four thirty and most likely brought you back at about six thirty, while I was shaving in the bathroom. That's why I didn't hear it. Then you entered the villa and went looking for me in the studio, and there, as you said, you felt even worse. You lost consciousness."

"God!"

"Yes. You were unconscious for hours there. You only came to after nightfall and your memories got muddled, your perception of time got distorted."

"What about those faceless shadows? Were they just my imagination? Did I dream those up because of that legend they told me in the café?"

"Forget it," I said, standing up and kissing her on her forehead. "Relax, eat something, and go to sleep. No nightmares this time, promise?"

"I promise."

But as soon as I left the room, I heard her rushing to the door and locking it.

13.

For the past nine months, I'd been getting up at six every morning without exception. But today I allowed myself to linger in bed until eight. I thought about all kinds of things, mostly about how much my life had changed in two days. *What else is in store for me?* I asked myself, charmed by the question. *What else?*

Yes, I lay quietly, staring at the ceiling, feeling unusually alive. I was no longer a mere receptacle used by some mysterious Artist. I had significance, desires of my own, predilections.

"That's right," I said, jumping out of bed.

No trance and painting today. I took a quick shower and put on warm clothes that were reasonably suitable for visiting a cave. I also chose a pair of comfortable, sturdy shoes. On a page in the diary I wrote: "I'll be back probably late in the evening." I tore out the page and left it in the kitchen. I went down to the garage, and for the first time since I had come here, I got into my jeep. I drove off and, again, for the first time, left my sector.

Straight ahead, a beautiful white lane led toward the heart of the Center, and another one, also beautiful and white, curved around the sectors. I had a lot of time until my meeting with Maggie, so I turned right. I drove slowly, gazing at the fences. Nothing could be seen through them, as they were all decorated with picturesque metal knotwork and garlands of evergreen plants.

I drove by three gates, above which, in huge bright digits, hung the corresponding numbers, *6, 7,* and *8,* as if designed for visually impaired people. I had no doubt that they were lit during the night, shining in red: bloody signs carved into the body of darkness.

I reached the final gate and turned down a lane identical to all the previous ones, leading to the Center. The view was magnificent. Exotic trees, bushes, and dozens of different flowers were arranged in multicolored compositions, interspersed with fountains and artificial waterfalls. I found myself in a proper botanical garden and was amazed by the fact that an entire complex had been constructed here and that now, on this splendid day, people were working. It was simply unbelievable to me.

The trees and the bushes thinned out and I saw the outlines of a stylish two-story building, perfectly designed to fit the scenery. I stopped by it, got out of the jeep, and circled around the house, as the main entrance was on the other side. As it turned out, there was a small lake on that side. There, on the shore, stood a thin, short man carrying a basket, his gray-white hair puffed like a cloud around his head. He was standing with his back to me, feeding a flock of about a dozen swans. One could tell from a distance that the man was completely absorbed in what he was doing.

I approached, coughing on purpose, so as not to startle him.

"Good morning," he said, turning to face me.

He stuck out his tongue. My bewilderment didn't last long, however, once I saw his face. He looked so much like Einstein I couldn't blame him for replicating the famous picture.

"Uncanny resemblance, huh?"

"If you are the physicist, then the coincidence is even more unbelievable."

"Hah, *coincidence!*" he said, taking a piece of bread from the basket and throwing it to the swans. "My face was like minced meat. A car crash. So I had to undergo several plastic surgeries, and that's when I chose to look like him."

"Yes, but not everyone can so easily assume such an iconic face."

"True. The structure of my skull was quite favorable. Once I lost some weight my figure became about the same as his."

"And the mustache and the hair. Especially the hair."

"True! Can you imagine what it would've looked like if I were bald?"

We exchanged glances of feigned horror, then both laughed out loud.

"Of course, around here I could've even used his name, but I decided not to. I kept mine: Gunther Strauss. Remember it, young man. One fine day, it may be as famous as that of the great Einstein!"

"I hope so," I said.

"Me, too," he replied with longing in his voice. "You are . . . the river. What was it?"

"Rhein."

"That's right! I am glad that you'll be joining us down in the caves. But I have to warn you, Maggie and I have opposing opinions on the Remorites. We will never agree. Not until she stops looking for material traces down there, which I don't believe exist."

"So you think that the Remorites never existed."

"On the contrary. I think that they couldn't leave any material traces exactly because they existed and they do exist. Do you understand?"

"Of course," I lied.

He seemed to believe me because a wide, approving smile brightened his intelligent, Einsteinian face. I was beginning to have fun, and found this weird fellow increasingly likable. I had been a fool to spend a whole year living as a recluse. It was interesting here, and everyone was crazy in their own way. I had finally found kindred spirits.

Nodding at me, as if to confirm my thoughts, Strauss returned to feeding the fat swans.

"I doubt these critters would be able to fly," I said.

"That's my goal. I like them and want them to stay. But is this good for them, though . . . ?"

"Obviously not."

"Or maybe it is," he objected. "After all, migratory birds frequently die on their way."

He frowned, threw the empty basket to the side, and walked toward the building. I followed him. Considering that he looked to be around seventy, he was a fast walker. An agile, energetic old man. Whereas Darcy displayed a more or less deliberate eccentricity, Strauss's seemed genuine. His madness suited him well.

"I might stop feeding them," he murmured, somewhat menacingly.

I looked back. The swans had left the lake and were eating the crumbs around the basket, while a servant in a gray uniform was trying to chase them away, probably to get the basket.

We entered the building. The café was on the right, and a restaurant was on the left. I followed Strauss into the café, which, unsurprisingly, was spacious, luxurious, and richly decorated with greenery, with a perfectly supplied bar and glass cases full of delicacies.

We sat in the armchairs around one of the few tables. Next to the table stood a pair of gripper shoes, two thermoses, and a backpack with a thick jacket thrown over it.

"You're not well equipped," Strauss said disapprovingly. "You don't have a flashlight. Good thing I've got a spare one you can use. Have you had breakfast?"

"Not yet."

"Wonderful," he said, clapping his hands loudly.

A servant appeared, dressed in gray like all the others, but with a white table napkin over his arm. He took our orders and withdrew, without uttering a sound.

"How many are there?" I wondered.

"At least forty, but they're still too few for the work they do, especially in the parks."

We were soon served our breakfast and started eating.

In about half an hour Maggie arrived with Chari, and Chari was accompanied by his dog, which instantly bared its teeth at me.

"That's his way of greeting you," the kid explained.

"What are you doing here, pal?"

"I'm coming with you. Here, take this," Chari said, pushing a jacket into my hands. "I brought it for you. I knew you'd forget how cold it is in the caves."

"Thanks. But if you have run away again—"

"I spoke to his father," Maggie chimed in. "He's not worried when Chari is with me."

"Not worried," Strauss grunted.

He bent down and started taking off his shoes, apparently to change them for the other, sturdier pair. The dog buried its nose in his hair.

"Rhein," he said, pausing in an uncomfortable position. "Get them away from here. Both the dog and the kid. Maggie and I will . . . Get away! . . . We'll choose some food and drinks."

"All right, but put them on my tab," I said.

"Okay, okay. Get away, you beast!"

"Hector," Chari corrected him. "His name is Hector. Don't tell me you're not smart enough to remember."

"Oh, no," Maggie said, putting her hands over her ears. "I won't have you quarrel today. Rhein, please."

I grabbed Chari by the shoulder and the dog by the collar, and led them out of the café.

"You're brave," Chari said, "considering you're an artist and you need the use of your hands."

I didn't say anything, but I remembered that I had forgotten to put a bandage over my wrist. I would have to rely on my long sleeves again.

Over the next ten minutes, Chari showed me around the building, saying that besides having a place to eat and drink, "the parasites" also had billiards, bowling, and table tennis, as well as roulette and other kinds of gambling. He also informed me that "the parasites" almost never played, because they preferred to weave intrigues.

I finally realized that, as a grown-up, I was supposed to rebuke him.

"It's not nice of you to call them names like that," I said.

"Maybe not, but it's the truth," he said obstinately. "They are parasites. But soon you, too, will be one of them. Because you, too, find it comfortable to live in lies."

"What lies?"

"The ones about your life and the oasis."

"Which could take off any moment now?" I said, remembering his words from yesterday.

"No, Ray, it's neither *could* nor *will*. It has already! You'd better get your head around the fact quick. You had your evidence last night, didn't you? You got your Miss Cortez back."

"You're quite a smart aleck, little friend."

"I am, but in this particular case, I just saw the helicopter. We live in villa number 4, right next to yours. Now let me tell you, it's not nice of you to call me 'little friend.' One is either a friend or not. No place for belittling here."

"You're right. I'm sorry."

"I'm sorry, too. I went too far . . . a little. I shouldn't have compared you to the other parasites. After all, for the time being, you're not entirely like them."

I accepted his somewhat offensive apology. When Maggie and Strauss joined us, things between us were settled. I gallantly unburdened Maggie of her backpack and we took off.

14.

It turned out that one of the emergency exits of the underground complex was quite close to the building. We entered a small antechamber and from there started down a very steep staircase, which didn't lead us as deep down as I thought it would. There was a metal door at the end, which obviously could be opened only from the inside, and a few yards to the side of it, a rectangular hole gaped in the wall.

We switched on our flashlights and crawled through it, one at a time. Hector disappeared in the darkness ahead. Behind our backs, the lights switched off automatically. That was it. Our world was gone. We had left it just like that, in the space of a few seconds, simply by passing through a hole.

We were not under the ground, but inside it—beneath everything mutable and transient that lived up there, above us. We were under the inexorable flow of time, which engendered and destroyed all, which gave life and took life with equal haste, like some impatient mad inventor whose experiments never quite lived up to his expectations.

Here, however, the world was different. This was eternity's dominion, the realm of eternal darkness, which engulfed our tiny lights without being affected by them. Our flashlights only made the darkness visible for a moment, so we could see that, from here on, we could only descend deeper, following the meandering labyrinth halls fretted into the rock by eons of subterranean water flowing with incomprehensible patience. We could only wander, entering deeper into the rocky bosom of this planet, though we could not even be sure that it was our native planet.

"It's ours only on the surface," I said suddenly, my voice ricocheting, clashing with the cave's silence. "We humans are superficial creatures and that's why in most cases our sight is horizontal. That's why our way of thinking is as it is: wide, but flat. Rarely soaring and never diving into the deep."

"What are you blabbering on about, Ray?" Chari nudged me, looking up at me before saying, "Well, hello there! How have you been, Artist?"

Chills went down my spine. I took Maggie's backpack off my back and put on the jacket Chari had brought for me.

"I would be freezing without it," I said. "You're a true friend, Chari."

"You say that, yet you have no idea how right you are," he remarked.

We were standing face-to-face, cross-lit by the flashlights hanging on our chests, and images of him were piling up in my mind in quick succession, as if I was taking pictures of him. Here he was, with his strange, mangled proportions. He looked as if he were assembled from two different figures, one with a wide chest and strong arms, the other, from the waist down, short and shockingly skinny. Here he was again, with the head of a man, a large man, and a tiny neck. Yes, but here was his face, with its adorable features and a smart, lively look in his deep, dark eyes. Eyes through which I could see his soul, wounded by the stupid play of chance that had assembled him like this. Longing for attention and love. Just like any other child's soul.

"Hey, what's wrong with you two?" Maggie said.

"They are communicating with each other, that's what's wrong with them," Strauss snapped at her. "We are among the Remorites now."

I looked around. Except bats and mice, I doubted there were any other creatures here. I put the backpack over my shoulder and started after Chari, who was walking away from us with quick steps.

At this point the cave appeared to be nothing special, just a tiny slanted cavity with limestone walls, punctured here and there by low passages. The floor was nearly smooth, which meant that no rock had collapsed here for ages, and the bedrock was strong, monolithic. But was it going to be like that farther in? I still found the lack of any precautions on our part bewildering. We hadn't even bothered to put on helmets. As soon as we started walking through one of the passages, though, I began to see why everyone was so confident. Bright phosphorescent arrows marked our way from here on. So there was going to be no wandering at all. We were headed for a particular place and they knew how to get there.

After we took the first turn, our bracelets, one after the other, signaled that we were no longer connected to the medical center. Chari stopped, secretly signaling for me to stop, too. We waited for Strauss and Maggie to pass us by.

When they disappeared around the next bend, he whispered, "Finally. We can speak freely now. There is no way they can overhear us by these rocks, not even with state-of-the-art equipment. Come on, Ray!"

"What?"

"Start talking. How did she act? Was she stressed out, or did it happen without her noticing? Was she drugged or unconscious? Or awake, but under the impression that she was experiencing hallucinations? It is important for me to know."

"All right. She acted completely normal. She told me that the helicopter made an emergency landing in the desert. The breakdown was resolved, and the guys from the control center returned her after she asked them to."

"You're lying!"

Indignant, the kid turned his back to me and started forward. I went after him, plagued by the unpleasant suspicion that from now on I wouldn't be able to attribute everything to his imagination. He really knew a great deal. I also remembered his visit yesterday, suspiciously well timed. I lied to Vanda that someone was at the door, and there he was, ringing the doorbell less than a minute later. Quite a friend, huh? And how did he enter the sector? How did he unlock the door?

I called after him sternly. My intention was to press him with some questions, but when he stopped and faced me, I suddenly became worried about him.

"Chari," I began, avoiding his eyes, "yesterday I accidentally overheard your dad saying that you . . . that you are not quite well."

"Please, don't play it delicate," he said. "You heard him nagging me, repeating that I was sick. Now you're wondering how on earth he could let me roam the caves. Am I right?"

I nodded, quite confused.

"I'll give you the answer, Ray. My father simply hopes that something terrible will happen to me in here. He can't wait to get rid of me. Despite the fact that I have no more than two or three months to live."

"I don't believe you, kiddo."

"Your call," he said, pushing away the hand I had placed on his shoulder. "Ask Maggie and Strauss. They know that I will die soon."

We continued on our way, walking quickly in silence. The silhouettes of Maggie and Strauss appeared before us. For about a hundred yards, we walked in a group, but then the passage became so narrow that we had to walk single file. I was last, or at least I thought I was, until a rustling sound made me turn back. The dog, which had rushed ahead the moment we entered the cave, was now behind me. He was lurking, then, stalking me.

I faced him and he bared his teeth at me and stooped. Illuminated by my flashlight, his eyes looked like burning embers. The fur on his neck was standing on end; a snarl came from his throat. It was clear that he was preparing to attack me. We remained like that for a moment, staring at each other. Then he suddenly wagged his tail, as if he had just recognized me.

"Well, hello there! How have you been, Artist?"

"No, it's impossible," I whispered to myself.

But the dog wagged his tail again, jumping around me playfully. I leaned down mechanically and patted him on the back.

"Come on, Hector," I urged him, and he immediately rushed forward.

His claws rattled on the stone floor, sending off sparks, while he disappeared, merging with the darkness. I shook my head and hurried after him. I took the next turn and caught up with the others.

"I don't understand why you are so convinced that the main city, no matter whose city it was, could be somewhere around here," I said, panting.

"These caves are very convenient," Maggie replied over her shoulder. "That's why the irresponsible Agency has placed subterranean machinery for the complex in one of them. They used it, ready-made, and destroyed everything in there."

"Nonsense," Strauss said from the front of our little pack. "There has never been and there still isn't anything to destroy. For the thousandth time, I'm telling you, the Remorites could not leave material traces."

"But why?" I asked him. "Why can't they?"

"What?" he shouted, suddenly stopping and blocking our way. "So you haven't even mentioned my hypothesis to him? You wanted him to come here unprepared so that he won't be on my side?"

She wanted to object, but in the end she just waved her hand.

"Wait, wait," I said. "I meant that, generally, it's not logical that the Remorites would build their capital in the caves."

"On the contrary," Maggie objected, "otherwise they would have to dig."

"There you go again!" Strauss pointed at her with a denouncing finger. "You're deliberately confusing him. But no, Rhein, they have neither built anything, nor dug anything."

"Because it wasn't necessary, right? Why would they stay underground, when it's so nice aboveground?"

"Precisely because it is so nice," Maggie said. "That's why their capital was here and not there. They came from the future and they didn't want to destroy the lovely harmony of nature in the oasis with their construction."

"Nonsense, lies, profanities," Strauss griped.

"If you think that insults are arguments," Maggie responded.

"Wait, wait," I said.

"Silence," Chari whispered, barely audible, perking his ears.

We stopped talking and listened, too.

"Good, good," he commended us, grinning, happy that he had tricked us. "Now listen to me. How could you be so dumb? The fact that Ray knows nothing about your hypotheses or the legend is only an advantage. Let him try to find out the truth from the Remorites! If he succeeds, could there be better proof that they still exist? That's right, Ray! From now on, you will only rely on your perceptions and sensations, and in the end, when we reach the bottom, you will describe them to us in detail. What do you say?"

I smiled, throwing a "child's-nonsense" look at Maggie and Strauss. But, to my surprise, they didn't return the smile. They seemed to have taken his words seriously and were now awaiting my answer.

"Well, okay, sure," I mumbled. "But don't count on it too much. It's more likely that I won't sense anything."

"Oh, you will, you will," Strauss assured me sympathetically. "I've seen a couple of your paintings in Natalia's villa. I can tell you're far from thick-skinned. But be careful down here, you might end up with no skin at all."

After giving me this piece of advice, we started walking again so that we could reach, as I now knew, "the bottom." Whatever that meant.

15.

The passage was getting narrower and the ceiling was becoming lower. Only Chari could walk without bending down. But while Maggie and Strauss only had to stoop, I was forced to drag along so bent over that my hands sometimes touched the floor. Every time I tried to straighten up a bit, the backpack scraped against the ceiling, and my shoulders rubbed against the rough walls. It was awful. My back hurt, my heart was beating erratically, I was sweating even though it was cold, and I felt like I was suffocating.

On top of all that, Hector had somehow ended up behind me again. Only the devil knew how this animal was maneuvering in these tight quarters. All of his grunting and smacking and sniffing at my clothes was really getting to me. It was as if he were trying to communicate with me again.

A small widening of the passage allowed me to glue myself to the wall and let him squeeze past me. He didn't want to, though. He only kept sniffing at me. The jacket belonged to Gromov, so maybe he was mistaking me for him.

"Easy, boy," I said. "It's me."

"Really?" Chari said, poking me in the ribs. "Are you sure it's actually you?"

"Listen, kid, I'm tired of you and . . . Call off your mutt! I don't want him breathing down my neck."

"He's just doing his duty, Ray. Maggie only brought me along because of him. He's her protection."

"From whom? The Remorites?"

"No, the Wanderer. Otherwise, he constantly follows her. But with Hector here he wouldn't dare. Even if he did, Hector would sniff him out right away."

After hearing his name, the dog began to creep by me slowly. He reached Chari and buried his ugly muzzle in the boy's armpit. Chari embraced him somewhat soothingly and led him ahead. I trudged after them in my torturous position as all kinds of suspicions tormented me. *My father simply hopes that something terrible will happen to me down here. Maggie and Strauss, too, know that I will die soon. I have no more than two or three months to live . . .*

"I don't believe you, kid."

"On the contrary, you just did," Chari objected.

Once again, I'd verbalized my thoughts without realizing it.

I grinned jokingly but he was gone. I stared ahead in horror. His light was gone. The passage before me was completely dark. I listened for his footsteps, for the dog's breathing. Then I realized that I was only hearing noises from the past. Noises I hadn't heard before, but that were familiar to the Artist: the creaking of the screen's unfolding, the rustling of the wrapping foil used in the storeroom . . .

"But you're wrong again," Chari told me.

I relaxed and even the scraping backpack became a comfort. I had been staring ahead, while he was right beside me. I sat down and felt his warm breath on my face. Our eyes were so close that I saw my reflections in his pupils.

"What?" I asked. "How am I wrong?"

"In pitying me, Ray."

I began nodding and didn't stop nodding, even after he moved away, even after he and Hector walked off. Yes, I pitied him but I also admired him. Whatever illness he carried in him, this kid took it like a hero. He had even found a way to play with it.

I stood up and followed him, and only then did I think of Maggie and Strauss, who had disappeared somewhere quite a while ago. I got angry at them, especially at Maggie. She needed a guardian, and now she also got a porter. I was dragging around her backpack but she didn't even bother to wait for me. She also didn't care about the kid; she was just using him for his dog.

"Chari!" I called. "Wait!"

"No use," he called back. "You wait for yourself."

I clenched my teeth to avoid cursing. I tried to walk faster but something was wrong with me again. This time, however, it was not my hearing but my sense of motion. I was walking, pebbles scraping under my feet, but at the same time I had the persistent feeling that I had not moved from my previous spot. It was driving me mad so I stopped and slowly turned back. But I instantly regretted this decision because *I saw myself.* I really saw myself *there*—about twenty feet away. I stood out starkly in the space between the passage's walls. Standing up straight, no pack on my back, no flashlight in my hand, and no jacket on. I was in my usual working clothes. My hair was shoulder length and my beard reached my chest. I closed my eyes.

This is a hallucination, I thought. *Otherwise I couldn't be standing up straight.*

"It's too low!" I said aloud.

"Low?" someone asked me. "How do you feel?"

It was Strauss. He was walking beside me, watching me curiously with his head raised. I looked around. We were in a large cavern. The ceiling was at least ten meters high.

"Why don't you answer, Rhein?" Maggie said.

She was right next to me.

"Why should he answer you?" Chari called from behind. "Isn't it clear? If it's too low for him in here, then he must feel like a giant. Right, Ray?"

"Yes, yes, like a giant here, and back there like a dwarf."

I laughed at my joke. But the acoustics of the hall distorted my laughter and transformed it into a series of screams. I hastened to shut up. Maggie and Strauss—the psychologist and the physicist with a penchant for anything paranormal—exchanged bewildered looks.

I imagined myself carelessly waving a hand and explaining, "Oh, nothing to worry about. It has just become a habit for me to split in two. Because during this time of day the Artist is usually painting, and in order for him to do this, we both have to be in a trance."

Maggie and Strauss would think me a total weirdo, immune to the power of the Remorites. For now, though, I was the only one making faces, and Maggie and Strauss had moved away again, probably to discuss my behavior out of earshot. I glanced at my watch and felt utter exasperation. There was more than an hour left until the end of my normal working time.

"Don't worry," Chari said, pulling on my jacket. "If the Remorites don't borrow our eyes, we won't be late."

"Oh, come on, enough with this nonsense," I mumbled.

But when he hurried ahead, I noticed that the dog was now following Chari so closely that it looked as if his nose was hooked onto his clothes. All he had to guide him was his sense of smell, it seemed. His behavior had changed since we'd entered the cave. He was going blind, slowly. I whistled sharply. The dog stopped. He turned his head and looked right past me.

"He's going to be all right, Ray," Chari shouted. "It's only temporary."

"Who?" Strauss said from somewhere up ahead. "Who is going to be all right?"

"You," Chari said, "and everyone else who thinks that I talk nonsense."

"Stop it, both of you," Maggie shouted. "Leave the man alone. He's not some junkie."

"Felix isn't, either," Strauss said. "Not anymore."

"I doubt that," Maggie said. "How else do you explain the influence of your innuendoes on him?"

The three of them gathered together and continued to argue in low voices. What were they trying to do to me? Suggest all kinds of outlandish things so that in my dazed disorientation I would fall for them? Like believing that the dog had gone blind because the Remorites were borrowing his eyes.

Suddenly, ignoring me completely, they turned into one of the hall's side exits, marked with a huge phosphorescent cross. They filed out, taking three-fourths of the light with them. I was left wondering whether I should follow them or let them go to hell.

I decided I would take a good look around the hall and if none of them came back for me by the time I was through I would leave. I went to the marked exit, took off the backpack, and left it there. I continued along the wall, using my weak flashlight, following its many bends and bumps.

I had never been in a cave before, and this one was nothing like the ones I'd read about or seen in photos and movies. There were no stalactites and stalagmites or anything of that sort. It was all the same: rocky floors, angular walls, and a ceiling that could successfully pass for a mirror image of the floor. Along with the ubiquitous grayness, it could best be described with the word *boredom*.

I reached the end of the hall where there was another exit. I stepped through it and found myself in a dark, rock-studded corridor sloping up, defying my expectations. I followed it despite the unnerving, deep cracks along the walls and especially in the ceiling. It was clear that here the rock had collapsed in places, littering the passageway with rubble.

I forked off in a direction that looked less dangerous and continued climbing. At least for the time being, there was no risk of getting lost—there was only one way to go.

The steeper the slope became, the greater my hope I would finally get aboveground. I was climbing energetically, scrambling up on talus rocks, slipping on the clay beds of long-gone streams. I negotiated my way over something that resembled a natural staircase, with steps fit for giant feet. Climbing up these felt like overcoming one Alpine peak after another. I didn't stop to rest, but pushed myself even when I had no need to. This way, I figured, I could probably avoid falling into a trance. I was puffing and panting, often stumbling on stones jutting out of the surface. It felt good to hear only the sounds of my breathing and my scrambling feet, and nothing from my past.

I regained my composure and slowed down just in time to stop a step away from a wide crack in the floor that stretched between the two walls. There was no way I could go around it. I kicked a large stone into it. It fell and made a noise. It's shallow, I gathered, and stepped back with the intention to dash and jump. But just then, from somewhere down there, came the sound of water splashing. The stone had only now reached the bottom.

I couldn't go on; the risk would be completely unjustified. On the other hand, however, even the thought that I would have to pass through that narrow passage again was enough to make me claustrophobic. So I stepped farther back, dashed, and jumped. I landed far beyond the crack but slipped on the stones, lost my balance, and fell down flat on my stomach. Something under me cracked. When I raised my head, I was as blind as a mole.

My eyes! They had taken them. I was shaking with fear. I slid my hands across the ground before me and, cutting myself on some edge, felt for the flashlight. With great relief, I realized that it was out of order, not me. My relief, however, lasted only a few seconds. I looked around, in vain, of course. The darkness here was of the kind that could only be found underground. It was as dark as death.

I crawled forward to increase the distance between me and the crack, and then stood up and slowly crept sideways. My shoulder touched the wall. My knees were bent, I was breathing heavily, rivulets of ice-cold sweat ran down my back. I had two choices: I could sit here and wait for someone to find me or I could start walking blindly along the wall, and if the branch turned out to be a dead end or I reached another crack, I would sit there, and wait for someone to find me.

I chose the second option precisely because my better judgment leaned toward the first one. I had too many reasons to believe that the expression "use your better judgment" was not one for me.

16.

Alternating between walking and crawling, I thought I saw many lights, including some that looked like ghosts. I didn't pay much attention to them. I had real problems, and I was tired. My body now seemed to avenge itself for my sedentary life, for all the months of complete neglect. If I made it out of here alive I would train every day, I kept promising myself.

My mental state was as bad as my physical condition. I managed to advance upward, clutching at every bump on the wall, feeling that I was just about to suddenly change direction by falling into some wide, deep crack. Instead, though, the floor was getting smoother and flatter, until I was no longer climbing, but only walking. But this was nothing to cheer about. I had heard of long horizontal galleries going on for tens or even hundreds of kilometers. Was I even in a gallery? Or had I reached another hall with many exits, and therefore, no exit for me?

I shouted in an attempt to get a feel for the size of the place. My yell echoed once, twice. It thrashed about like an animal, then suddenly stopped, as if someone had cut its throat. The one thing I learned from my experiment was that I had better keep my mouth shut.

When my other shoulder touched a wall the question of "Where am I?" became irrelevant. I raised a hand and touched the ceiling. It was only a couple of inches above my head. So I was back in a narrow, low space. The darkness around me seemed to be getting thicker and somehow solid.

"Calm down," I whispered to myself.

After all, what is darkness? It's nothing, really. The absence of light, and nothing more. Yes. But there was no other absence in the world that looked so thick, so black, so material. I swiped at it and thought I felt its resistance. The ghosts around me had multiplied. My panic now seemed to produce them in throngs. I wondered how many could fit in this narrow space.

I smiled bitterly, bent over, and continued creeping at the speed of a lame turtle. I had taken so many risks just to avoid walking through one narrow passage on my way back yet here I was, in a place infinitely worse than the previous one.

Time passed, but I couldn't say how much exactly. My watch, a sentimental gift from my grandfather, did not glow in the dark. From the moment I had broken my flashlight, I'd had no proof that my sight was functioning properly. So, couldn't I suppose that in here, just like the dog, I had gone blind?

I closed my eyes, which at least got rid of the ghosts. My other senses gradually became more active. They informed me that the situation was changing. Barely perceptible vibrations now permeated the silence, and the air had turned from cold to cool. I could feel a slight draft, completely different from the deep breath exhaled from that ghastly crack. The rush of air seemed to be coming from somewhere above and carried pleasant, refreshing humidity.

I kneeled and, running my fingers over the floor, found that it was more clay than rock. I could feel thin concave furrows here and there, like traces of tiny dried-up streams. I was extremely thirsty. I leaned on the wall with the intention of standing up, but I had reached another turn. To be on the safe side, I decided to take it crawling.

I reached out my hand and bent it sideways to feel if there was another hole after the turn. A short melodic chime rang out. My bracelet! It was signaling that the connection with the medical center was restored. It was good news, to be sure, but I was still squeezing my eyes shut. I didn't open them yet.

I drew my hand back and the bracelet signaled again, announcing a disconnection. I crawled around the bend and another signal followed, the same melody as before. Pressing my back against the wall, I sat down and only then summoned the courage to open my eyes. I blinked a few times, but no, I couldn't see anything, not even the ghosts.

I'm finished, I'm blind, I told myself. But as I did, the darkness turned to dusk, and the dusk began to disperse. That devilish child had an exceptional flair for stories, it seemed. He had made up the tale of borrowed eyes, which fit perfectly into the fears of an artist going mad. Soon my sight adjusted completely and the phrase "light at the end of the tunnel" acquired a literal meaning for me.

"Thank you, God," I said.

I jumped to my feet and the flashlight swung over my chest. It had been a hindrance the entire time, but I never made the decision to throw it away. Now, though, I pulled it over my head by the strap and hurled it to the side. I hurried toward a blurry rectangle of light.

"No, God!"

Bars. The end of the tunnel was closed up with a metal grate.

This was too much for my nerves. I dashed up the slope, glimpsing bits of blue sky and the green branches of a bush. The bars were now clearly visible. As soon as I reached them, I clutched one with both hands and pulled and pushed, enraged. I bruised my shoulder, and only then calmed down.

I peeked outside as best I could. I saw carefully trimmed grass, the trunk of a tree, and the pruned branches of a topiary bush. I wasn't in the free oasis, but in a park surrounding one of the villas. I felt joy, but only for a brief moment. If this exit, or rather, this barred prison, was far from the villa then nobody would hear me.

I turned my attention to the metal grille, and just then realized that not all of the bars were fixed into the concrete. Some were welded to a metal frame, attached by a padlock to the adjoining frame fixed into the concrete. *Who would need such a door?*

"Help, help!" I yelled, sounding hysterical. I tried again, making my voice deeper. "Hey! Is there anyone out there? Hello! Hey there."

I became exhausted, my voice grew hoarse, and I stopped. Now what? I seemed to have no other choice but to sit here and wait until my bracelet registered the dehydration. The guys from the medical center or security would find me. It would only take a day or two.

I grabbed a rock and started pounding against the metal. It was easier than shouting.

17.

I was soon surprised by the agreeable rhythms I was producing by simply banging a rock against a few steel bars. Funny, that. No wonder some people play all kinds of ordinary objects. Bottles, for example—empty, half-filled, or filled. Filled with clear, cold water.

Dehydration in a day, or even two? I had overestimated myself quite a bit. But now I had the feeling that in no more than an hour the thirst was going to dry me out completely, mummify me here as I sat in a concrete tunnel with a stone in my hand. Moreover, it was getting darker before my eyes, as if I were already under the shadow of my own demise.

Wait. It really was someone's shadow. I looked up. Yes, there on the other side of the bars, a man! Joy and relief washed over me but just as quickly disappeared. Because, hand on his heart and horror on his face, this man was staring at something behind me.

I jumped as if stung and, clutching the rock, looked back. I didn't see anything. Why, then, was he staring like that?

"Ghosts?" I said, turning back to face him. "Is it the ghosts?"

His face was still twisting and writhing, but not from horror. It was a tic or a series of tics, and he appeared cross-eyed. I dropped the stone and spread my arms in a friendly gesture. I waited for him to pull himself together. He needed time, the poor guy. I probably looked like a scarecrow.

"Hey, don't be scared," I began amiably, although each word scraped my throat like sandpaper. "I'm not coming out of a beauty salon. I'm coming out of a cave. That's why I look like this."

Instead of replying, however, he began shaking his head and pointing to his ears. The Wanderer, of course. The one who pretended to be deaf. He was far from my idea of a wanderer or a tramp. He was a large, well-fed middle-aged man, clean-shaven, carefully combed, and neatly dressed; he was wearing beige trousers, with perfectly ironed creases, a light-blue shirt, under whose open collar shone a thin silken scarf. Actually, if you didn't count the tics, which had almost died away by now, there was nothing strange about him. I thought that his decision not to communicate with anyone in this complex was more common sense than delusional thinking.

But maybe he thought that *I* was crazy. Who knew how long he had stood there, watching me drum on the bars.

"Listen, buddy," I said, smiling conspiratorially, "no need to pretend with me. I don't know if you're mute, but you are definitely not deaf. Otherwise you wouldn't be here. You heard me and came over. If you have the key with you, unlock the door, and I promise you we'll separate as if we've never met."

He pointed at his ears again, making a sign to say that they were of no use to him and that I was talking in vain.

Good, then, let him pretend to be whatever he liked. I started using signs, too. I pointed at the lock, made a rotating motion with my hand, and mouthed "Unlock it." I also showed him that I was thirsty and that I was asking him to help me. The whole pantomime was sincere and, I am sure, comprehensible. But even if incomprehensible, did my situation really need any explanation? It would have been obvious to anyone that I had to be freed immediately.

I dropped my hands and waited for his reaction. He fell into such a tense hesitation that his eyes crossed even further. He was facing me while his eyes began twisting sideways, one sinking into his nose and the other into his temple, until only the sparkling whites remained. Then, with obvious effort, he returned them to their normal positions. He pointed at me and then pointed into the tunnel. Seeing that I couldn't understand him, he suddenly made the jerky gesture one would make to swat away an insect. "Go away. Go back where you came from." That was what he was telling me.

I'm not a bad person. I would even call myself kindhearted. I have always tried to accept all my troubles with at least some sense of humor. In this case, however, I was way beyond my tipping point, and this guy wasn't helping in the least. So I just nodded in agreement with him. I raised a hand, waving good-bye. But then I reached out through the bars and grabbed his belt. I pulled him toward me. Now we were only an inch away from each other.

"Hey, you, 'deaf' guy," I said through clenched teeth. "Listen carefully because I won't repeat myself. Make one movement, and I'll break your neck. Is that clear?"

I lowered my body quickly and grabbed him by the ankle with my free hand. With another strong pull, I knocked him off balance. He swayed backward and before he fell, I managed to pull his leg in between the bars. Once he was on the ground, I grabbed his other leg and pulled it inside, too, which resulted in his crotch being pressed against the middle bar. He definitely was not going to move now.

I locked his legs by sitting on them. Then I reached out and went through his pockets. There was no key. In fact, all of his pockets were empty.

I released him, stood up, and started down the slope, once again entering the tunnel I had believed, with such vain hope, I had left. I looked at my watch. Only forty minutes had passed. Time really seemed to move more slowly in the caves.

As soon as I reached the bottom of the slope, I found the flashlight, picked it up, and started back to the bars. I was hoping to be able to fix it in the light, despite knowing better. But what else could I do? I had to do something, after all.

Nearing the closed exit, I began imagining that while I was gone, something might have changed with the bars. I was right. Some of the bars were missing. In other words, the door was open. But my senses were now too dull for me to feel anything stronger than slight surprise. I wondered where the key had been. Hidden somewhere nearby or simply hanging by the door?

I stepped out and blinked my eyes. The last thing I expected was to encounter the smell of chloroform. But it was in the plastic bag that was being pulled over my head.

18.

I woke up with a severe headache, rushing heartbeat, dry mouth, and heavy eyelids that felt glued together. I had to use my fingers to lift them up so that I could see. It took me a while to shake off the haze from my vision. I could hear the thundering beat of my heart, mixed with something reminiscent of chirping birds. Then the ceiling spread above me: endless, bottomless, and blue.

"I am not in my bedroom," I said.

I strained and, little by little, rose to a sitting position on the smooth, white surface. Yes, it was a lane, and by the shade I gathered that there was a wall or a high fence behind me. My neck was stiff, and I couldn't turn my head to check. I started to stand up, and only turned my whole body when I set myself on my feet. The number 3, enormous and bright red, spread its glow through my tormented mind. It appeared that I had been lying right in front of someone's gate. But I hadn't been drunk and I hadn't woken up because I hadn't fallen asleep—that was my next conclusion, after which I remembered everything. Everything up until the moment with the chloroform, of course. I realized that the guy did not just put me under, but also threw me out here like a rag.

"Bastard," I croaked feebly under the gate's surveillance camera. "You will pay for . . ."

The spasms in my throat did not let me finish. I walked down the lane, reached the fork, and stopped. I had to decide whether to go right, which led to my sector, or continue straight, toward the Center, where I had left the jeep. The distances, as far as I could tell, were almost the same, but after the image of cascades, small waterfalls, tiny rivers, and streams flashed through my mind, I headed for the Center. I tried to hurry and noticed that I was limping. Because of the unbearable headache, however, I couldn't tell whether my leg also hurt or had just fallen asleep. I rubbed my knee, which seemed to be the source of the problem.

Clenching my teeth, I hurried on, despite the limp. The sun was mercilessly glaring over me. I looked at my watch—it was ten to three. I had been out for ninety minutes. He had gone too far with the chloroform and almost poisoned me, the bastard.

But why? If he was afraid of me, he could've simply left the door locked. Instead, he drugged me and threw me out. And how did he get the chloroform and bag so quickly? None of it made sense.

I kept asking myself questions until, in one brief moment, they all vaporized. Now the only thing that interested me was the fountain in front of me. As soon as I saw it, it became the meaning of my life. But I managed to pull myself together. I waded into the grass and walked toward it slowly, reverently, just the way I would one day walk toward the Savior.

19.

A car was parked in front of my villa when I returned in the jeep. Before I even reached the landing Vanda opened the front door.

"Rhein, good thing you're back!"

"Have you invited guests again?"

"No. But where did—"

"Whose car is this?"

"Einstein's. I forget his name. They came just now, looking for you."

"We were worried about you, Rhein," Maggie said, peeking out from behind Vanda.

I stepped in past them and walked to the living room. Strauss was sitting there, still in his spelunking outfit. He held a cocktail glass and, staring at me, said nothing. I slumped into the armchair across from him.

"Anything to drink?" Vanda asked me.

"Orange juice."

"Just?"

"No. Two orange juices."

She went over to the fridge and carried out my order while Maggie looked at her with slight condescension, sitting on the sofa next to Strauss. She hadn't changed, either. Only the jackets and the flashlights were missing from the last time I saw them.

"When we saw the backpack there by the exit," Maggie said, "we thought you'd left us because we somehow offended you."

"Nonsense," Strauss said. "That was your suggestion. I knew the reason right away. What do you say, Rhein?"

I took the first glass of juice from Vanda and drank it in one gulp.

"I was disappointed," I said. "The caves turned out ugly and boring."

"Nonsense," Strauss said. "You knew very well that we weren't going in to admire the scenery. You realized that we purposefully left you alone in that cavern. You had to remain alone with your thoughts so that they could contact you."

"If we're going to discuss the Remorites again," I said, "let me just say this. They neither telepathically conveyed a message nor—"

"Stop," Strauss broke in, spreading his arms dramatically. "Don't deny it, fella! You sensed them, you were acting strange, I was watching you. I know!"

"He behaves strangely on a daily basis," Vanda said, her voice unusually timid.

"I have always been quite odd."

"When you sensed them," Strauss persisted, "you got scared. That's why you decided to leave."

"Hold on," I said. "You think I got scared, she thinks I was offended. All in all, very mundane reactions. So why were you worried?"

"If everything was fine," Maggie said, "you would have exited the caves no later than twelve. We came out at about three, and saw that your jeep was still there by the café."

She fell silent, after which she and Strauss looked at me quizzically again. I smiled at them and casually reached for the second glass of juice. I had no intention of sharing my adventures with them. They were as dumb as they were disgraceful.

"Nothing happened," I said, shrugging. "I just walked about the Center. It's quite nice there, like a botanical garden."

Vanda buried her face in her palms and heaved a tormented sigh. When she dropped her hands, her eyes were teary.

"But, darling," Maggie said, "why so sad? You see him, alive and well. See, he was even lucky. He was walking about, while we . . . we can never erase from our memories the terrible tragedy we witnessed."

"Tragedy," I whispered. "But he . . . he's alive, isn't he?"

"No, he isn't," Vanda screamed through her tears. "No, he's not alive, not *at all*. Not after his brain splashed all over the rocks."

Swaying, she crossed the hall and stormed out, closing the door with a bang.

"I really don't get her," Maggie said, looking puzzled again.

The glass slipped from my hand and thudded on the carpet. I clutched my head and felt like it was about to explode. A child. Such a lonely child he was. But also bold, and brave, and smart, and with such incredible, unbelievable imagination.

"How did it happen?" I asked quietly.

"I'm sorry," Maggie said. "I didn't think you would be so upset."

"Death is always upsetting," Strauss said.

"Enough," I said. "Don't give me small talk. Just tell me everything, clearly and to the point."

Embarrassed, he lowered his eyes and mumbled something unintelligible. But Maggie didn't seem to need much encouragement.

"Even though you slowed us down, we reached the bottom in time . . ."

"What bottom? In time for what?"

"The bottom of the chasm. The sun illuminates it only for an hour, and then . . ."

"Then everything becomes different," Strauss said. "You have to go there, Rhein. You have to! I am positive that *they* will reveal themselves to you precisely in the light of—"

I threw him a warning look and he shut his mouth, which formed a thin, dreamy smile. Wretched man. He was so obsessed by those fictional things that he had lost all connection with his soul.

"Your callousness is outrageous!" I yelled.

"Yes, it is," Maggie snapped at me. "None of us is going to sit here and mourn for that low creature! What do you want? That we pretend to be sad just for you? Do you want us in mourning from now on? What a hypocrite."

"Maggie, Maggie," Strauss said, waving his hands. "Don't—"

"How dare you?" I said, suffocating on my outrage. "How dare you speak like that of a child!"

"What child, for God's sake? We're talking about that nasty, intrusive fatso," Maggie said.

I was standing up now, laughing with relief. I went over to them and patted them on the shoulders.

"I'm sorry. I thought that Chari . . . that his brain . . . Oh, whatever! I am sorry."

They were silent for a second or two, then laughed, too. We went to the fridge together and poured ourselves new drinks. I mixed myself a "heavy" cocktail this time.

"But who's the fatso you're talking about?" I asked.

"The Wanderer, of course," Maggie replied.

"Well, the guy wasn't . . ." I almost gave away too much information. "Didn't he lose some weight from all his wandering? Last night, when you were talking about him, I imagined him as some scrawny street bum."

"Nothing like that! Fat, greasy, and always dressed sharp, that's how he was."

"Listen," Strauss said, stirring awkwardly, "let's not go too far. If you ask me, 'don't speak ill of the dead' is good advice and we should follow it."

"I don't understand," I said, thinking to myself that someone else must have abducted me. "How did he manage to find you? It was really bad luck that the accident happened right in front of you."

"Luck has nothing to do with it," Maggie sighed. "He did it that way on purpose."

"*Did?* You mean he killed himself?"

"Alas, yes," Strauss confirmed.

Everything changed in my mind. The accident became the ending of someone's heartbreak, and the image of the unpleasant, rude man disappeared, replaced by the horrified face writhing in nervous tics.

"The chasm is in his park, so we had gotten used to his presence," Maggie told me. "Every time we carried out research, he would stand up there and watch us. When we went without the dog, he would come down. He really was always after us. Actually, after me, even in the free oasis. He was stalking me, Rhein, that is the truth!"

"True," Strauss murmured, "yet, his death was . . ."

"Completely unexpected," Maggie said. "Because in the beginning, everything went in the usual fashion. We reached the bottom of the chasm, sat down to rest, had lunch, and then started for our destination. When the Wanderer appeared up there, we pretended not to see him. We're with the dog, we were telling ourselves, he wouldn't come close, just watch us from there. As it turned out, however, his intention was different this time. He began banging, gesturing, throwing stones."

"At you?"

"No, no," Strauss said, shaking his head, "he was throwing them to the side."

"After making sure he had our attention, he suddenly waved his hands . . ."

Maggie flinched. She gestured at Strauss to continue for her, and, burying her fingers in her hair, started rocking back and forth with half-closed eyes.

"He waved his hands, lunged forward, and jumped! He jumped right into the chasm, more than a hundred feet deep. Without making a single sound. He really was mute, I am sure now."

"He forced himself upon us when he lived, and he forced his death upon us," Maggie said, rising from the sofa. "I will go tell Vanda. She must have misunderstood, too."

As soon as she was out of the room, Strauss leaned forward and whispered, "The poor woman is deluded. She thinks that he killed himself because of her, out of unrequited love. But the guy had no intention of committing suicide, Rhein. He believed that he would fly. I am sure of it!"

"What time was it?"

"When?"

"When the guy tried to fly."

"Twenty past one."

"Or maybe later, hm?"

"No, it was *exactly* twenty past one."

When I went back down the slope to collect the flashlight, I looked at my watch and it had been five to one. This meant that I returned to the bars and the already unlocked door no later than ten past one. How fast was this suicidal man? Did he drug me, drag me to the gate, dash toward the chasm, bang, gesture, throw some stones, and jump? All in just ten minutes?

"What happened next? I mean after you left the caves."

"We saw your jeep, called Gromov to get the kid and the dog, and came here."

"Without meeting anyone from security?"

"We called them first, but they said the wretch's bracelet had signaled them and they had started doing their job."

"So, you didn't have to give them a statement?"

"No, Rhein, *no*. What do you think? That they would start interrogating us and pull some police tricks? In what was obviously a case of suicide? They aren't out of their minds. The Agency would lose us as clients if they did that. They are going to get the body, write their reports, and continue trying not to disturb us."

They would definitely disturb me, though, if they found the broken flashlight and my bracelet. I only now realized that it was not on my wrist. The Wanderer had taken it off, of course. Otherwise, it would have sensed my unconsciousness and signaled for me to be rescued.

"Hey, fella, you've gone pale," Strauss said. "What's wrong with you?"

"I'm not feeling well," I said. "I'm hungry, I need sleep, my head hurts."

"Your leg, too, I suppose," he said. "As soon as you came in, I saw that you were limping. How did you hurt it?"

"Back there in the passage."

"Bad, very bad," Strauss said, smiling slyly as he leaned in close to me. "You should've come back here right away and bandaged it. It wasn't necessary to torture yourself for three hours by walking about the Center."

I fell silent. What could I say? I made to stand up, but he stopped me, touching my shoulder with a delicate gesture. He bent down over me, and his face, a perfect copy of the face of a great man, loomed over mine.

"Listen to me, Rhein," he whispered. "My hypothesis about the Remorites might not be completely correct. Yet, today, in the caves, you really did meet one of them. You have to understand this, because otherwise you won't be able to help him. *This* Remorite."

He slid his hand over my shoulder, stepped back, and nodded to me almost imperceptibly.

20.

From the living room window, I watched Maggie and Strauss leave. Vanda saw them out. Strauss threw Chari's jacket on the backseat and sat behind the wheel. The two women continued talking for a few minutes, then hugged each other. So, they had either become perfect friends, or just the opposite. Whatever. Finally, Maggie sat next to Strauss, he started the car with a jerk, and Vanda remained in the driveway, waving them good-bye.

I went to the kitchen. It smelled of something delicious and freshly cooked, but that was a temptation I easily resisted. I grabbed a couple of packs of junk food and headed for the second floor. My leg started hurting even worse on the stairs. I reached the landing between the floors and heard the front door shut. I stopped and listened, which proved to be unnecessary.

"Rhein," Vanda shouted.

"Yes?"

"When are we having dinner?"

Never, I felt like answering.

"Seven," I answered.

"All right, take a rest. But don't be late."

I left the packs in my bedroom and locked myself in the bathroom. As the bathtub filled I took off my dirty clothes. My knee was swollen and bruised but all in all it didn't look so bad. My face, when I saw it in the mirror, did not scare me, either. I was so overwhelmed with all kinds of emotion that the physical exhaustion actually helped me; it somehow helped me keep my balance.

Soon I was in the bathtub, thinking, of course, of the man who had killed himself. He and I had something in common. We had both treated our lives like rubbish to be thrown away. Unlike me, however, he didn't get a second chance. *Because he never split into two,* I thought, and after that seemingly absurd conclusion, I decided that the man had neither dragged me to the gate nor left me outside.

Here is what must have happened: By some whim of fate, he had decided to jump in the chasm just today. On his way there, he had heard me banging for attention. So, he had gone back to his villa for the bag and the chloroform. He had wanted to help me, but not to waste time with me. This was why, while I went back for the flashlight, he had unlocked the door and hidden, waiting for my return. He had drugged me and taken the bracelet, and then he continued on to the chasm.

Time had passed, how long exactly was insignificant, and I had come to. Actually, the Artist had come to, and had then dragged me out. There, in front of the gate, *I* had come to.

That was it, even though it didn't make sense. On the contrary: both his and my actions were absolutely devoid of any sense. But on the other hand, what else could be expected from delusional minds like ours?

I stepped out of the bath and went to the medicine cabinet. I put a piece of adhesive tape over the deep cut on my thumb, which reminded me of the broken flashlight and the bracelet again. Were the security people going to find them? Most probably, yes. But so what? They would return the bracelet, and if they decided to interrogate me, I'd tell them the truth. If they didn't, however, it would be even better.

I bandaged my knee, put on my bathrobe, and went into the bedroom. It was already five; no point opening the prepackaged food. I set the alarm for ten to seven and sprawled on the bed.

I was woken up by a melody that was nothing like the ringing of my alarm clock. It was coming from inside my bedside table. Finally I remembered: my mobile phone. I hadn't heard it ring for over a year. It had to be Kort, I told myself, although we had agreed that only I would call him.

I answered.

"Rhein?"

It wasn't Kort.

"Who's asking?" I said.

"Felix. We don't know each other, but I really need to talk to him."

"All right," I grunted. "Speaking."

"Rhein, right?"

"For the time being, yes."

"For the time being, yes," he repeated like an echo. "Because you don't know whether the next moment it would be you or someone else. Right?"

"Of course."

"The same is happening to me, Rhein."

"What is?"

"Yes, you're right," Felix said, lowering his voice. "It is not something to discuss over the phone. That is why I must insist that you come here right away."

"Why don't you come here?"

"No, no. I understand you already have a guest. We can't discuss these things while she's around."

"We won't discuss anything, Felix."

"I see, I see. My villa is number 8."

"I have a lot of work to do, and you must be busy, too. After all, you're here studying for your exams. Was it medicine, or law?"

"Yes, yes. I will wait for you, Artist. It is extremely important!"

He hung up. I was outraged, not by him but by Maggie. I gave her my phone number only yesterday, and she had already started giving it to whomever she felt like.

The alarm rang a little later. I dressed quickly. I was so hungry that even the idea of having dinner with Vanda seemed attractive. I slid my hand over my chin, and, deciding to shave, went into the bathroom. The dirty clothes were gone and the bathtub was empty. The girl was really trying. She kept the villa in order, just as diligently as she kept my mind in a mess.

She had done her best in the dining room, too. The table was set for a feast. I sat down and waited for Vanda to appear. She would probably wear another chic dress tonight, and jewelry and high heels. My imagination conjured images that were increasingly pleasing until she emerged and proved all of them wrong.

Pushing the serving cart, Vanda appeared from the kitchen wearing a T-shirt of mine that reached down to her knees. There was no trace of her previous desire to seduce me. I would somehow survive without it, I noted to myself, albeit with some bitterness, and reached for the wine bottle.

21.

I was in the bed, tipsy from the wine, but I didn't dare to fall asleep. I had the feeling that sleeping would wipe some important sign from my memory. Something I had heard or seen during the day without paying attention to it, something I had missed amid the chaos of events.

I sat up and switched on the bedside lamp. *It's the chaos that's bothering me.* But if I wrote everything down the way it happened, I would easily separate the wheat from the chaff. I reached for my diary. It had disappeared; it wasn't on the bedside table. I lifted the pillow but didn't find it there, either. It wasn't in any of the drawers, or under the bed.

Vanda again. Putting on my bathrobe, I started for the door, but my phone rang at the same moment. I went back and grabbed it angrily.

"Rhein, Rhein," Felix said. "Now. Now you will *have* to come! I need help. Your help!"

"Call a friend."

"I can't. They won't believe me."

"Believe what?"

"That the Wanderer is here. With me!"

"What makes you think I would believe you?"

"Because he told me."

"The guy used to be mute, Felix. And now he's dead."

"I know, I know! He told me about that, too, he wrote it down. But he doesn't look like a dead man."

"Listen to me, Felix—"

"No! Get away . . . Rhein, come here!"

What followed was a thud, accompanied by screams, and then silence. The not-so-studious student had ended his little charade by hanging up.

I took off the robe and threw it on the bed. I tightened up the bandage around my knee, got dressed, and, tucking the phone in my jacket pocket, limped across the bedroom and then down the hallway. I stopped in front of Vanda's door. It was ten o'clock, but she was probably sleeping.

"Are you sleeping?" I shouted.

"What?"

"Give me back my diary. Right now!"

"What?"

"Damn it!" I tried to get in. It was locked. "Unlock the door."

"Why?"

"Give me back the diary."

"I have no idea where it is. It's not here. You probably misplaced it somewhere."

She was now on the other side of the door. I could hear her quickened breathing. Her voice sounded shrill and shaky. She was playing frightened again. Everyone here seemed to be playing with me. But in Felix's case, he was a junkie—an ex-junkie or not, who knew. So I couldn't just go back to bed and fall asleep. It was quite possible that he really needed help.

I lumbered down the corridor.

"Where are you going?"

I turned. She was peeking from her room, the position of her body showing that she was ready to lock herself in again, should I decide to try to enter.

"Don't go, Rhein. Don't go anywhere."

It was a reasonable piece of advice that filled me with the premonition that I would be very sorry if I did not follow it. On the other hand, I would be sorry if I did follow it.

"I'm only taking a walk. Good night, Vanda!"

When I reached the stairway, I sat on the railing and slid down.

Five minutes later, I had left my sector and was stopping my jeep in front of the gate of number 8. I got out of the car, rang the bell, and waited, my heart sinking. I waited a long time, or at least it felt that way. I rang the bell again.

"Rhein, is that you?" Felix answered at last.

"Yes, it's me," I said, staring at the eye of the camera. "You can see."

"But I haven't seen you before. Say something else so that I can be sure it's your voice."

"Who else could it be? Could there be another idiot who would fall for your tricks?"

"Yes, yes, it is you. He recognized you."

"Who? The dead Wanderer?"

"No, maybe he's not dead but only thinks that he is."

"Send him my best regards."

I got back into the jeep with the intention of driving back home, but at that moment the gate opened, and an inarticulate scream came from the loudspeaker.

"No! Don't come in, Rhein! He wants to take his vengeance on you!"

I popped my head out of the car window.

"What for?"

"Let me go . . . You're alive! Come to your senses!"

I put my foot down and shot through the gate. He had recognized me, he was alive, he wanted revenge. What the hell was happening?

I stopped in front of the villa and jumped out. My knee snapped painfully. I looked up at the wide-open window on the second floor—it was the only one lit. I stood there nonchalantly, hands in my pockets, and whistled a few times.

"Hey, Felix!"

No reply came, but I noticed that the front door was slightly ajar. I headed that way, when the lights upstairs went out.

"So, is that good night, then?" I shouted, feeling humiliated.

He wouldn't get away with it, I decided. He would get the slapping I had come to deliver. I moved to the door, pushed it with a bang, and stepped in. I turned on the lights and kept moving until I sensed some motion and looked around. I stiffened with horror.

I was surrounded by monstrous semblances of human beings. Twisted, broken, bloated, squished. Indescribable. They had been lurking here, waiting for me! I slowly began to step back, and so did they.

"That's me," I whispered to myself.

I burst into uncontrollable laughter. I saw the creatures around me opening their mouths—pink-and-white slits, holes in the softened, waxlike faces—laughing soundlessly alongside me. I stopped. I wiped my sweaty brow with my sleeve, and, relieved, gave in to my amazement.

I was in a narrow and long anteroom. On the walls, crooked mirrors were installed in such a way that they reflected and multiplied their own images. But why? What kind of man would want to see himself this way every time he left and returned home?

Looking ahead at another warped mirror, I could see words spelled out in huge letters: "YOU WERE NOT CREATED LIKE THIS!"

I went to the end of the anteroom and found a concealed button. As soon as I pressed it, the mirror slowly slid open.

I continued through a spacious foyer with a stairway in the middle and a lift to the right. Naturally, I chose the lift, where I was again greeted by my twisted reflections, accompanied by another sentence: "YOU'RE LOOKING AT THE FUTURE OF YOUR SOUL— UNLESS YOU STOP!" I felt uncomfortable, as if I had encroached on the private world of someone suffering from a shameful disease. But he really was sick, I reminded myself. Here he was making efforts to cure himself, although this hardly looked like the best type of therapy.

There were no crooked mirrors or messages in the hallway on the second floor, and the place appeared normal. Except for the signs of the zodiac forged from iron and suspended from the ceiling by thin chains.

I stopped by the room where the lights had been turned off in some ostentatious gesture. On the door: "KNOWLEDGE IS POWER! LEARN AND THE VICTORY WILL BE YOURS!" I knocked— Rhein, the polite idiot. I had taken the bait and was now waiting for permission to jump into the frying pan. Only silence came from the other side.

I went back with loud, shuffling steps, and as soon as I was under the Capricorn sign, I raised my hand. I made a painful jump, grabbed it, and snatched it from its chain. Carrying it so that its horns, long and sharp as knives, pointed out, I made for the room again. It wasn't silent anymore.

I rushed in and my eyes were flooded with light. A motion detector, of course. Which meant that a while ago, the lamps had switched off simply because Felix had left the room.

There was no one in the room. I was sure of that almost immediately, as there were only a few pieces of furniture, arranged in a way that made it impossible to hide anywhere behind them. Not counting Batman, Neo, Spiderman, Lara Croft, the Terminator, and several other such heroes that were on the walls, I was all by myself here.

So where was Felix?

I turned around quickly. He wasn't behind me and he hadn't appeared in the hallway. Now what? Should I embark on a limping tour of the villa? Go looking for him when it was more than clear that he didn't want me to find him?

Nothing was clear about any of this. I thought about it briefly and ultimately decided that I had to take a closer look around the room with all the posters. Maybe I would stumble upon a sign. Or traces of a struggle. With the dead man?

In order not to be surprised from behind while rummaging, I closed the door. On the back of the door, a scantily clad, long-haired, voluptuous blonde with lusting eyes and a wicked smile beckoned me from a poster. I smiled back. So, the student seemed to have rather ordinary tastes, which meant that he could turn out to be an ordinary person with no serious mental deviations.

I could see that this poster had been put over another crooked mirror so I rolled up the poster. There was another message: "GET RID OF DRUGS OR THEY WILL GET RID OF YOU!" I looked at my reflection—it was deformed in such a way that it showed what I would look like a week after I was buried. I returned the model to her rightful place and spent a few moments staring at her, just to neutralize what I had seen in the mirror.

As I headed for the desk in the room, the sound of a starting car engine caught my attention. I dashed to the open window and leaned out, just in time to see my jeep disappearing down the driveway.

Many thoughts ran through my mind, none of them pleasant. The fact that I would have to go back home on foot simply drove me mad. I stepped away from the window and tore down a poster of the Renegade on his motorcycle. Underneath it, however, instead of my own distorted image I saw the pimply face of a teenage boy. I had no doubt it was Felix. Skinny and unattractive, dressed in a formal suit with a bow tie and a white handkerchief tucked into the jacket pocket.

His squinting, probably myopic, eyes had a tormented look, and his smile was so artificial that it resembled a grimace.

"HERE IS WHAT YOU USED TO BE LIKE—A HAPPY CHILD!" The insolent accusation was written on a piece of white tape, stuck right above his head. At the bottom of the picture it said: "BE LIKE A FENIX, SO THAT YOU CAN BE FELIX AGAIN!" followed by: "WE SHALL ALWAYS BE WITH YOU! MUMMY AND DADDY."

"Look at these nasty idiots!" I said.

Quickly my anger was tempered by the thought that with parents like these, Felix really needed help. But I was not the one to provide it. I decided to leave. I limped past the desk and only then noticed the computer was in standby mode. I stepped closer and moved the mouse.

"I'LL BE BACK!" appeared on the screen.

I sat in the desk chair. So that was it. The kid just felt like making a few laps around the complex and decided to dial my number. Some nerve.

I looked at my watch—it was almost half past ten. Hopefully, he would get sleepy soon. I was exhausted, but with good reason, considering what a long and terrible day it had been.

22.

I remembered leaving, was sure that I'd left, but now I found myself back in Felix's study. That's right, I found myself, just like a lost item. I was sitting in his chair, my elbows on the desk, and all I saw were thin yellow zigzags against a black background. The computer had returned to standby mode.

I had fallen asleep here, like some homeless bum. I had fallen asleep while waiting for my host to return and give me back my car.

Again, I decided to leave. I leaned on the desk to ease my knee while standing up, but remained seated because the screen brightened just then. I stared at it in bewilderment. Now, along with the promise of *"I'LL BE BACK!"* it said, *"IF YOU TELL HIM ANYTHING ELSE, I'LL KILL YOU!"*

After a few minutes of sleepy thought I decided these messages hadn't been left for me. According to the story Felix told me over the phone, this was probably a conversation between him and the Wanderer. I looked at the screen again. The chat went on so I scrolled to the beginning:

"How did you get in here?"

"I am dead. I can enter wherever I want to."

"Why come to me?"

"I want you to call the Artist again."

"How do you know that I have called him before?"

"I was with him when you did."

"Did he see you?"

"No. At first he was asleep, and then his double took some of my energy. When the energy dwindles, I become invisible."

I was startled. The sleeping part was easy. Felix had guessed that I was sleepy by the sound of my voice. But the double? No one knew about him. Except Vanda, who'd spilled it all at the café yesterday. The gossip had spread quickly. Under normal circumstances, this would have angered me, but now it calmed me down. I continued reading Felix's piece of pulp fiction. After all, he had written it for me.

"Invisible? Enough with the nonsense! Don't you see that you're alive?"

"No, I'm not. That's why I want to have my revenge on the Artist. He pushed me."

"You're lying. I have no idea how you've survived, but Maggie told me that you jumped."

"She's wrong. The Artist was there, he attacked me, I had a chloroform spray can, but that didn't help me."

I closed my eyes and rubbed them, but to no avail. So they were trying to provoke me! The security people, of course. They had found my bracelet. I had become a suspect, and now they were testing me, watching me from somewhere, observing my reactions.

"Okay, even if it happened like that, why would you take your revenge on him here? You could've done that while you were at his place and he was sleeping."

"No. I cannot encounter his double. It's dangerous for me. That's why you will kill him."

"Dude, you're crazy!"

"Probably, after all I've been through. Come on, call him! Now!"

Well, Felix did call me, and I came. But when I arrived he suddenly decided to warn me. Upon hearing that, the Wanderer threatened to kill Felix if he said anything else. So Felix managed to escape. He jumped into my jeep and drove off.

Yes, that was the story they were trying to sell to me. But who were "they"? It couldn't be the security people. Perhaps it was Strauss. Being fond of all things paranormal, he concocted this whole mystery with Felix's help. "Those two know no limits." That's what Maggie had said about them.

There was another possibility, of course. Felix, shocked by the Wanderer's suicide, had gone on a bender and from his altered perspective the whole story was real. And now he was driving around in such a condition.

I stood up. I had to report this so they could start looking for him. I took the phone out of my pocket, an automatic gesture that was actually useless. I didn't know security's number, or the number of anyone in the complex. I could, however, signal from here. I pressed the alarm button on the desk's control panel. But instead of activating, all the lights on the panel cut out. The security system had just stopped functioning.

I heard a click. Someone had blocked the study's door. I looked in that direction, but only the blonde was there, smiling. She was smiling and turning gray, then black, before disappearing completely.

Everything disappeared, as if I had gone back to the darkness of the cave.

I felt cold air, and I could hear the sound of something moving close by. *Now* I was not alone anymore. The shuffling continued, joined by the distinct sound of grinding teeth. Then came a drawn-out wheezing, like someone's final breath. Then there was silence again. I was petrified, thinking I wouldn't be able to move even if someone threw a knife at me. Only a few seconds later, however, a dim light crept from behind my back, and this made me turn as if I were on a spring.

The Wanderer was standing in the corner of the room. A gray glow spread around him like fog, yet his face and body were clearly visible. He was wearing the same clothes I had seen him in earlier. His eyes, filled with hatred and fear, were fixed on me. His lips were moving, without uttering a sound, repeating the same word: "MURDERER!"

"But you, you have all just gone too far," I mumbled.

Any moment now, I expected to hear the stupid laughter of this charade's organizers tear the darkness, but everything remained silent. Obviously, after all the lies and work they put in to set up this scene, they wanted to enjoy my torment in full, watching me from somewhere with night-vision goggles.

"Listen, Wanderer," I began but halted, because I was now so cold that all I could do was tremble.

A noise thundered in my head. I was losing my balance. I clutched at the edge of the desk and then felt a strong blow to my chest. I collapsed back into the chair. *This has happened before*, I thought. *Yesterday, in my studio . . .*

I turned my head to the Wanderer and he raised his hand, sliding a finger across his throat. The gesture was unequivocal. I felt around the desk, looking for the Capricorn sign. It was gone. I made an attempt to rise but felt another blow to my chest. I was out of breath, suffocating. The darkness was growing impenetrable again. I clenched my fists.

Then the thundering in my head subsided enough for me to hear the irregular thud of running footsteps. I heard another click.

I collapsed to the floor, hoping to avoid a new blow. I crawled sideways and then rose up. Feeling my way, I reached the door and opened it carefully. The lights in the hallway were switched on, but it was still empty. The Wanderer, along with the "parasites," as Chari had appropriately called them, had managed to hide somewhere.

Not that I was in any condition to look for them.

23.

I left Felix's villa and started limping down the driveway, toward the gate. The sound of an approaching car stopped me. The hope that I would finally get the jeep back, however, was vain. A white limousine appeared, headlights shining into my eyes. Its brakes screeched and it stopped right next to me.

Natalia jumped out with surprising agility.

"What's the matter?" she said.

"With what?"

"With Felix, of course. How is he?"

"I'll make sure that he isn't well."

She hurried toward the villa. Just at the thought that I'd have to drag myself after her, my knee ached even worse.

"Wait," I called out. "Felix's not in there. He stole my jeep."

"There is a jeep parked outside the gate," she said over her shoulder. "But if Felix stole it, why would he leave it there?"

"I don't know. Why are you here?"

"He called me. Told me he's not feeling well."

"Well, he lied to us both," I said. "Where's Maggie? Don't you two live together? Why didn't she come with you?"

"She's at the café and likely won't be back before midnight. She's become quite obsessed with billiards recently," Natalia said as she moved closer to me. "I see. I've got it now."

"You do?"

"Why, yes! Felix knows that you are one of my favorite artists so he decided to make me a present by arranging a meeting between us."

"I am rather inclined to think that his present was intended for me."

She impulsively raised a hand to arrange her hair. She had no makeup on and was dressed in a sports outfit that didn't sit well on her. Illuminated by the car's headlights, her face looked unnaturally white, and her eyes were contrastingly black, deep set in shadows. Also deep in the black shadows stood the former prima ballerina Natalia Shidlovskaya.

"But what are we going to do now?" she asked.

"Let's take a walk! It's a beautiful night."

"Don't," she said, pointing to my leg. "Don't offer me something that would be torture for you. Come on, I'll drive you to the jeep."

We sat in the car, but Natalia didn't start the engine right away.

"I want to help you, Rhein," she said. "I want at least to alleviate your pain and I think I can do that. As you may guess, I have substantial experience healing all kinds of traumas."

"Natalia, I know that Vanda entertained you with my story in the café yesterday. But I didn't expect you to join the charade, and in such a cheap role as the psychiatrist."

"But what are you talking about? What psychiatrist, for God's sake? I meant *physical* traumas. I saw you limping, your leg is obviously hurting."

"Aha!" was all I managed to say.

Natalia demonstrated her aristocratic manners and only nodded with a smile, as if the misunderstanding had been sorted, then she started the car. When we reached the gate I was happy to see my jeep. I got out of the limo.

"Good night, Rhein. I am sure that we will have other occasions to meet, ones much more . . . natural than this one," Natalia said softly. "Don't be mad at Felix. He is a good boy, but he doesn't always know how to express his kindness. No one taught him how to."

"Yes. I mean, I'm not mad at him," I mumbled. "Good night, Natalia."

She waved good-bye and drove away, and I got inside the jeep. But instead of heading to my villa, I drove after her. She waved at me again, this time for "hello," blinking her taillights at the same time. I laughed and suddenly felt relieved, less lonely. I liked this woman and she liked me. We had similar fates and could feel sympathy for each other. We could sit down for a drink and say, "Here we are! Not so long ago we were both at the top, and now . . . Now we are just clients of the Guaranteed Peace Agency."

We passed by gates 9 and 10; the numbers looked as if they'd been penned with embers in the darkness. The gate for villa 1, Natalia's villa, opened, and she turned into the driveway. As I followed her I saw a flicker by the fence. I looked back and saw someone's head peering from behind the bushes, a hat pulled over their eyes. I stepped on the brakes but didn't get out of the jeep; I only rolled down the window.

"Go home, Felix!" I called out at the bush. "Tell the dead man he's getting his bouquet tomorrow."

Natalia had also stopped up ahead. I caught up with her and in the rearview mirror I could see the gate closing, leaving the "good boy" locked out.

24.

"For me, dancing always meant pain as well," Natalia said. "Yet, my pain is much worse now because I don't dance anymore . . . I don't dance."

I don't paint, I thought with bitterness, *I don't paint anymore.*

We had chosen to sit outside. The sky above us was moonless but studded with stars that seemed very close. Their light was reflected in the water drops created by the burbling fountain, turning them into miniature stars, too, falling over the floating lotuses.

"We're here to rest," I said, unconvincingly. "We'll gather our strength and return to our lives. We have time, Natalia."

I gently brushed her hair. She was sitting next to me on the bench, carefully rubbing the healing lotion into my knee. Its herbal aroma was mixing with the smell of the grass.

"I am thirty-six years old, Rhein."

"See, not that old."

"True. Maya Plisetskaya danced on her eightieth birthday."

We fell silent. She bandaged my knee, pulled the trouser leg down, and stood up. She went over to the fountain and put her hands in the water. Her movements were silent and graceful, as if I was seeing them in some long-past moment, back when they were still natural to her.

"Why did you give up, Natalia?" I asked her softly. "What happened?"

"I don't know what it was about that night," she sighed. "I had played that part dozens of times, and I was in good shape. I had no reason to give in to my usual stage fright. But I couldn't overcome it. I stood behind the curtains, unable to move. What if I fell? What if my leg went numb, what if my partner dropped me, what if . . . what if . . . These possibilities had always been part of my life, but in that very moment they became utterly unbearable."

She returned to the bench but didn't sit. She remained standing, staring at the vague outlines of the villa she was renting.

"I lost my courage, Rhein, I broke down. Right then and there. Soon after, the Agency sent me its prospectus, and the charming words *oasis*, *seclusion*, and *rest* easily tempted me."

"Yes, their marketing seems to be spot-on. They got me just in time, too. I was in a deep depression when the prospectus arrived. I wonder, though, if we would be here now, if they had taken longer. Maybe we would have both dealt with our problems and continued down our paths."

"Well, we'll never know," Natalia said. "Those paths of ours, they no longer exist. They disappeared the moment we came here."

I reached for the table and took my glass. I wanted to gulp down all the wine, but I took only a few sips. Natalia picked up her glass, too.

"To the Wanderer," she said. "I didn't know him, but now I'm almost sure that he was like you and me. He wanted to return to his life and maybe that's why he committed suicide. He believed in second chances!"

"I don't understand, Natalia. What do you mean?"

"The same as you. You just said, 'return to our lives.' You are completely right. We are not living our lives here. None of us are ourselves."

"Well, yes," I said, grinning, "but in the Wanderer's case, you really stretched that metaphor."

"Metaphor? On the contrary, I was speaking literally."

I looked at her, shocked. Could it be that she was the craziest one in this complex?

"But, Natalia," I began timidly, "what second chances are you talking about? Do you mean that the Wanderer, or anyone else, would kill himself to return to his life?"

"I'm sorry, Rhein. I forgot that you're still unaware of many things."

"Is this about the Remorites again?"

"I understand your doubt. Until yesterday, I wasn't interested in them, either. But things are different now, especially after discussing the topic with some of the servants."

I poured myself some more wine and filled her glass, too. I made myself comfortable on the bench and sank into silence. I was tired of asking questions whose answers only brought more confusion.

"Do you know that all the servants are from the tribe that's been living in the oasis for millennia?" Natalia said. "Whether it's true that they are descended from the Remorites, or that the Remorites even existed in the first place, is of no concern to us. What's important is that there are people in the tribe who can still perform the ritual of connecting to them."

"Who's 'them,' Natalia? The Remorites, who, as you just said, might not have existed?"

"You misunderstood me, Rhein. The only thing I now doubt is the existence of Remorites such as *those* described in the legend."

"All right, then. What do you think the 'true' Remorites were like? Those whose existence you don't doubt. Are they vampires, or maybe ghosts?"

"Ghosts?" she said, considering the possibility. "Yes, you could say that. Ghosts, though not just of the dead, but also of the living. Of people who had the chance to achieve something great but squandered it because they didn't leave this place *on time*. Or never left, like the Wanderer. Perhaps people like us."

"Oh, I'm in no such danger," I laughed. "I don't have any money left, so the Agency will help me leave the moment my contract expires. There, by the way, is the benefit in the harm."

"Yes, Rhein," Natalia said in a serious tone, "until yesterday, I was just like you. The Remorites were nothing more than a fairy tale to me, characters of the local folklore. The fact that Maggie and Strauss believe in them seemed like some sort of lunacy to me, just as what I'm saying now seems lunatic to you. Since yesterday, though, everything has changed. I saw those creatures, Rhein! I saw them, and I am sure that they were real, not some hallucinations, like Darcy says."

I tried to think of an appropriate reply, but I couldn't. *What about me*, I asked myself, provoked by her words. Why was I so sure that those creatures in the cave were nothing more than hallucinations? And that the "faceless shadows" were also hallucinations? Or had we seen . . .

"Real ghosts?" I voiced the end of my question, quickly adding, "It's an absurd combination of words, isn't it?"

"You don't seem willing to differentiate between real and material," Natalia said. "But if I said that the canvas on which you paint is the same as the painting itself, you'd be offended, right? Right?"

"Well, yes," I mumbled before drinking my glass to the bottom.

"Rhein, I now believe, I am even convinced, that the Remorites are the bearers of the second chance. It is not important what we imagine they look like. Think of them as paintings that have deserted their canvases. Or as some strange kind of reflections. As ghosts, if that's easier for you."

"The easiest would be not to think of them at all," I said. "You should try it, too."

She smiled dreamily and sat next to me, and her eyes wandered off into the darkness.

"Tell me," she started again after a while, "if a second chance were really possible, how would you use it?"

"I don't know. First, you'd have to tell me what it is."

"It depends on the person. For example, my second chance would be to return to that night, standing there behind the curtains. So that *this time* I could go onstage! If this happened, everything else afterward would be different for me. I am sure of it. I would never have betrayed my art."

Tilting her head, she looked as if she could hear some imaginary applause.

"My second chance would be almost the same as yours. I want to go back to the day I received the prospectus, but this time, instead of giving in to the temptation I would simply throw it away and return to my studio. I would stand before the white canvas and continue my attempts to overcome my damned artist's block."

"Is that it?" she said, her voice barely audible. "Do you really want only this?"

Of course, I wanted something completely different, with all my heart.

"Does it matter?" I replied, evading her eyes. "Even if I believed in a supposed second chance, I'd still be convinced it would not do anything for me."

"What do you mean?"

"I wouldn't be able to give it to someone as a gift."

Natalia seemed to sense that we had touched upon something very personal and painful for me. She sat there with me, patient and calm, waiting for whatever came next.

"Both my conception and my birth were marked by death," I said, surprising myself. "The death of my father and then the death of my mother. They were only seventeen when for the first, and for the last, time they experienced their love. I was conceived while their boat was sailing down the river. It drifted faster and faster, and closer and closer to the waterfall. The boat fell, crashing into the rocks at the bottom of the waterfall. My father managed to push my mother to the side, to the riverbank, but he drowned. She died nine months later, while giving birth to me."

"Rhein," Natalia said. "The river was the Rhein."

"Yes. My mother, just before she passed, gave me that name. An expression of her hate for me."

"You are wrong," Natalia said, placing her hand on mine. "As a woman, I can understand her better. She loved you. To her, you were the continuation of their love. That's why she gave you that name. She was making peace with the enormous, great river."

I shook my head.

"Yes, yes!" Natalia hurried to say, before I objected. "She loved you from the beginning. Otherwise, she wouldn't have left you in her womb. She would have gotten rid of you. Do you understand? Do you understand that, Rhein?"

"I don't know. But I would give my second chance to my parents. I want them to be there, on the river again, but to sense the danger this time and stop their boat. To hold it back!"

"If you ask me, they didn't squander their first chance, so they don't need a second one. See, they have made something significant with their lives. You, Rhein."

We looked at each other, and I realized that I now saw her face somehow brighter, more clearly outlined than was possible in the darkness of the night. I drew her toward me and my lips gently touched her brow.

"Listen to me, Rhein," she whispered hastily. "You mustn't despair. You will paint again, and your paintings will be masterpieces. I know this. I am sure. You, too, are one of them. One of the Remorites I saw yesterday."

25.

The first thing that surprised me the next morning was my good mood. The second thing was the fact that it remained good even after a cold shower. I returned to the bedroom and applied the ointment Natalia had given me, although my knee wasn't hurting anymore. I put some working clothes on, went into the studio, and locked myself inside.

I quickly drained the cup of espresso I got from the coffee machine and immediately took out a large, new canvas from the drawer. I stretched it on the easel and placed the easel next to the window, which faced the rising sun. I also prepared new brushes and palettes and everything else necessary. I couldn't wait to start working on the painting, no matter what it was going to be. It was important that I paint it myself. Not the Artist in some state of trance.

I stared at the canvas—the smooth, white emptiness into which I had to breathe life. Clenching my teeth, I snuck closer to it, as if I were intending violence.

"Easy, tiger," I murmured to myself.

I dropped my arms and squinted, but instead of an idea or at least the vague outline of one, only daubery flashed through my mind. Time passed, a long time, during which I achieved nothing, besides rediscovering the fact that the emptiness was not on the canvas but inside me.

I prepared another espresso, a double one this time. It was becoming harder for me not to give in to the trance. The moments when I would lose touch with reality were becoming more and more frequent. The hands of the clock were moving in leaps before my eyes—from 7:12 to 7:16, from 7:25 to 7:41. I had the feeling that time was no longer flowing but patching itself up, after someone had cut away minutes from it.

I stood up, having no memory of sitting down, and went to the door, not knowing why. I opened it and Chari, followed by his dog, rushed into the studio.

"You're doing the right thing," he told me.

"Am I?" His statement surprised me even more than his invasion.

"Of course. No matter how absentminded you are, you haven't forgotten to lock yourself in, which means you realize that the young lady is dangerous for you."

He immediately went to the coffee machine, while the dog lay down by the easel, somewhat too familiarly. I remained standing by the door.

"Come on," Chari urged me. "Lock up again."

I did.

"You want some, too?" he asked me.

"Want what?"

"Chocolate, buddy. Hot chocolate."

"No," I said, glancing at the empty cup in my hand. "I have already finished my coffee."

"Aha!" Chari said, turning to the canvas. "Are you starting a new painting? Congratulations!"

"Why are you here? How did you get into the villa?"

He choked. I quickly went over and patted him on the back. The dog leapt and snarled, baring his adze-like fangs at me.

"Easy, Hector," Chari wheezed and continued coughing, but seemingly on purpose now.

I waited for him to sit down.

"How did you get in?" I repeated.

"Why, I flew. Just like that. I picked up Hector and flew over."

"Enough nonsense!"

"Is your question full of sense, Ray? Can't you guess that Vanda let me in? By the way, I never thought you would be so heartless. I am still in shock. I haven't slept all night."

"Why?"

"Because I'm a child, that's why. But even if I were a hundred years old, I wouldn't have been able to sleep. I've been seeing him since yesterday. Falling, without making any sound at all. He had been mute, for real, and we all thought he was pretending. We treated him badly."

I could tell he was trying his best not to burst into tears. I looked at him more carefully and only now noticed how pale his face was. I felt my legs failing me and sat down. It was true; I hadn't been lied to. The Wanderer was dead, and what I saw in Felix's study . . . What was that? A Remorite?

"God," I moaned.

"Not God, but I will help you," said Chari.

"Yes. Help me. Tell me the legend right now."

"Right, you still don't know it. Now is not the time."

"Tell me!"

He raised his eyes to the ceiling and began: "A long, long time ago, these people were on their way back to their village, when they were caught by a storm, which forced them off their path. This is how they came to this oasis. They knew that they shouldn't stop here because the place was cursed, but the abundance of water, fruit, and game lured them. So they settled and relaxed here, taking their time, enjoying their carefree rest, forgetting that their relatives were waiting for them on the other side of the desert. When they finally decided to set out again, they realized that they were late. The oasis, which was really a living demon, had torn them out of their present. He had lifted them into timelessness. He took off, Ray, just as he did with us the other day."

"Yeah, right, a demon, with engines. You're trying to trick me into believing one of your fantasies."

"Fantasies? Better ask yourself why Vanda couldn't leave the oasis! Besides, the legend uses the word *demon*, but it's pretty obvious that it's actually a time machine. A natural one, Ray, a natural time machine, not one created by some creatures from the future, as Maggie imagines. So by 'engines,' I mean energies."

"Chari, stick to the legend, and the Remorites in particular. What happened to them?"

"When they at last returned to their village, they were shocked to discover that everything there was completely unfamiliar to them. They asked around the village, and it turned out that a hundred years had passed outside the oasis! The parents and the children of the travelers had died. Know what they did?"

"You're asking me?"

"They dug their relatives out from their graves and carried them to the oasis," Chari said, a wide smile on his face. "Makes sense, doesn't it? If the demon had managed to take them a hundred years into the future, then it could take their relatives a hundred years into the past. That was their reasoning. So they prayed to him and performed all kinds of rituals and sacrifices. But what mercy is to be expected from a demon? None! He lectured them, saying, 'Pathetic, vile little humans! You spent all your time here eating and drinking and doing nothing while your loved ones starved to death in that poor village, waiting for you, sick with worry for you. Now you're bringing their bones here and want me to bring them back to life for you!'"

"Keep it short," I said.

"He made a deal with them, Ray, a cruel deal. In order for them to have their relatives back, these people had to give up light forever. The demon banished them to the caves and told them to remain there until they died. So they moved down there with the bones of their parents, wives, and children. They watched how, shrouded in the misty halo of resurrection, these bones were gradually covered by flesh, how the skulls gradually filled with brains, with eyes . . ."

The river, I said to myself, as if dreaming. *They all remained there, by that underground river. It satiated their thirst, their hunger . . .*

". . . and they made love to their until-recently dead women, and more children were born from that love, growing up together with the resurrected ones. They grew like fresh sprouts in the heavy darkness, listening to tales about the sun."

Chari fell silent and stared at me.

"Until these children set out," I said. "They crawled up and went out into the light of the oasis and became the tribe we know now."

"Exactly, and the poor ones down there continued carrying the burden of their past delay. Even death didn't release them from it. They are still carrying it."

"Is that all?"

"Isn't that enough, man? What more do you want?" Chari jumped to his feet and stepped toward me, an angry expression on his face. "Is it that hard to make the connection between those Remorites and *your* Remorite? Can't you feel that he is now wandering in the darkness?"

"Don't mix the elements of a legend with reality."

With a theatrical gesture, he thrust his hand into his pocket and took out his medical bracelet, waving it in front of my face before saying, "Here is something from reality."

Now I saw that his bracelet was actually on his wrist. He was holding mine.

"Who did you get it from?" I asked.

"*Where* did I get it from? This would be the correct question, to which my reply would be: You know very well."

"Yes. But how did you know it would be there? How did you find it? When?"

"I won't tell you how I knew. I will also spare you the details about how I found it, and the when is not important at all. Concentrate on the fact that I beat the security guys to it. Relax, be happy and thankful."

I took the bracelet from him, put it on my wrist, and, under his insistent gaze, said, "I am grateful."

"You should be," he said. "I've saved you from being accused of murder."

"Wasn't it supposed to be a suicide?"

"Yes, but the murderer wanted to fool us, and succeeded to an extent. Maggie and Strauss believed him. But not me. I am sure that the Wanderer didn't jump of his own free will. He was standing there, close to the edge, throwing stones to draw our attention. He wanted to warn us about something. He was gesticulating. It was obvious that he was frightened. But we read his behavior the wrong way, because we still thought he was only pretending to be mute. Only when he silently flew down did we realize . . ."

Chari threw himself onto the chair and hid his face. He seemed sincere, but I was already quite familiar with his skills of manipulation.

"Someone pushed him, Ray. From behind, probably crouching so that we wouldn't see. If they found your bracelet during the investigation all suspicions would have fallen on you."

"Well, thank you once again," I said jokingly. "It is a great consolation to me that you don't suspect me."

"Remember, this is all secret," he quickly blurted out. "We must tell no one that we know the truth. It was suicide and that's that. Otherwise, the murderer would come after us. Me, especially! I was a witness, you know?"

"Relax, I won't tell anything to anyone. But, Chari, you do suspect me, eh?"

He wouldn't look at me. He was silent.

"Come on. Answer me."

"Yes," he said.

"Yes what?"

"I won't lie to you, Ray. I took the risk of coming here and I am honest with you because I hope that you are innocent. But I am not entirely sure. I can't be."

He rose, called Hector, and, after spreading his arms somehow guiltily, left the studio.

26.

I snuck out of the villa so quietly that even I couldn't hear anything. Vanda, however, did.

"Rhein," she called from her window. "Where are you going?"

She was wearing a nightgown, but she didn't have the look of someone who just woke up, and her hair looked like a swallow's nest.

"Where are you going?" she repeated.

"I don't know."

"What about lunch?"

"Don't wait for me."

She seemed happy with that answer. She nodded from above and waved good-bye.

Before going to the garage I stopped by the storeroom at the rear of the villa. I pulled out a folding ladder and fastened it to the jeep's roof rack. Then I drove off.

On my way, I managed to get both my thoughts and my feelings under control, but stopping in front of the Wanderer's gate, I was overcome with such rage that all my thoughts were obliterated in an instant. I shot out of the jeep like a torpedo and buzzed with my fist.

A minute passed and I thought, *If he is really dead, he wouldn't be able to open the gate.*

I stopped ringing. I took the ladder off the rack, unfolded it, and used it to climb over the fence. After finding steady purchase on top of the fence, I pulled up the ladder and slowly dropped it over the other side. My knee didn't hurt, even when I climbed down.

For the time being, I had no intention of going to his villa. I walked straight through his park, choosing the direction by intuition. I'd made the right choice—I found the cave's exit. The door was not locked. The lock was hanging above the door handle with no key in sight. I searched for it, presuming it was thrown away somewhere nearby, but I couldn't find it. The plastic bag and the chloroform spray can were nowhere to be found, either. The broken flashlight, however, was right where I had dropped it. I picked it up and hung it around my neck. Hopefully now I'd at least avoid dealing with a police interrogation. If there was going to be any interrogation at all. I still very much doubted that the Wanderer had killed himself or been murdered.

In fact, I doubted everything, so instead of delving deeper into guesses, I started through the park again. Here and there on the grass, I could see traces of someone's footsteps, and, following them, I soon reached the infamous precipice. I stepped close to the edge and looked down.

What I saw didn't impress me. It was a precipice like any other. I couldn't see why people talked about it so much. It was narrow and long and was girdled by almost vertical rocks that were monotonously gray, as if saturated with centuries-old boredom. Its depth was not what they had described to me. It didn't look anywhere near as deep as they made it sound. The bottom was covered with rocks of different sizes, all smooth, from which I concluded that a river once flowed there. The underground river from the legend. And my dreams!

"No, it's impossible," I said to myself.

But I was already sure that the river I had dreamt of so many times was not actually the Rhein. It was *this* river, whose waters now flowed somewhere in the darkness, deep beneath my feet, rushing and splashing against the walls of the concrete tunnel, trying, with blind doggedness, to return through the precipice now run dry.

A mystic fear washed over me. When and from where had I learned of the river's existence in the first place? More questions with no answers, leading to answers I didn't want to find out.

I stepped back. It was high time I got out of here, but my eyes landed on the lonely bush growing near the edge of the precipice. I noticed something glinting by its roots and went over to have a better look. It was a plain gardening rake. There was nothing to rake here on this rocky terrain. Unless it had been used for another purpose.

"*Someone pushed him, Ray. From behind . . .*" Yes, someone was standing behind him and pushed him with this rake.

I returned to the edge of the precipice, lay down on my stomach, and stared at the stones on the bottom. In vain, of course, since, even if there were bloodstains, I wouldn't be able to spot them from this distance. I had to climb down there. I cursed this idiotic development of the "case." I stood up and steadied the rake on the edge with the help of a few stones, its handle protruding over the precipice, so that I could see it from below.

I went toward the end of the precipice where a few balding palm trees struggled for their lives. It was clear that the Wanderer probably used this spot to climb down and bother Maggie. My assumption was proved correct when I found a climbing rope tied around one of the palm trunks.

Ten minutes later, I had reached the bottom. The cavity through which the river had once run was only a few steps away. It had been a powerful, deep river, and its centuries-old presence could still be felt. But where was it now? Could the tunnel used by the Agency to divert the river be close by?

I went to the dry riverbed and listened for an underground roar. I heard nothing, but I could smell grass burning. I stepped in a little more. The floor here was covered with flat limestone blocks and led steeply up to the narrowing mouth of the cave. To the left, there was a wide, vertical crack, and as soon as I looked at it, I saw wisps of smoke weaving around it like spiderwebs in the darkness.

I tiptoed toward it, and someone on the other side began to *sing*. I thought Maggie and Strauss had come here for another one of their excursions. The singing became louder. It was in an unknown language with vibrating intonations that told me I was wrong. Neither Maggie nor Strauss could summon something like this from their throats. When I reached the crack I peeked in warily. In the middle of a small dome-like gallery, a fire was burning, and around it, holding hands, some strange creatures were murmuring and swaying. There were about ten of them, their faces painted bright red, their bodies covered down to their toes in something like cocoons. The song, however, was not coming from them.

In the dusk at the other end stood another individual. He was naked, save for the cloth around his loins. His long, gray hair hid his face, and on the floor before him, placed on a pile of sticks, an elongated white object stood out. Stooping uncomfortably, the individual was singing to the object, touching it with the tips of his widespread fingers.

It was some sort of tribal ritual and I watched with interest. Eventually, the singing man, likely the shaman, lifted the object and carried it to the fire. When the flames illuminated him, I saw that he was holding a wooden doll with a shirt pulled over its head. But the shirt was light blue, with short sleeves and bloodstains. It was the Wanderer's shirt!

The shaman threw the doll into the fire, and his ten companions, as if on command, slipped out of their cocoons and threw them into the fire, too. A heavy, intoxicating smell filled the air. I coughed. They heard me and ran screaming toward one of the gallery's side exits. I rushed toward the shaman. He went around me and dashed through the crack where I had entered. I followed him, staggering as if drunk. I was still coughing, gasping for air, but I somehow made it out of the gallery just in time to redirect him away from the mouth of the cave and toward the precipice. As soon as he got there he stopped. He turned to me and only then I saw that his face was also painted red. It wasn't a very pleasant view.

"Easy, pal," I said. "Come, let's talk."

He looked over his shoulder at the abyss. Then he issued a short yet despairing moan and rushed right at me. I stepped aside, as if I were making way for him, and when he was passing by I stuck out my leg and tripped him. I stopped him from falling down by grabbing him by the hair. The irreverent shaman began tossing around, making guttural sounds.

"Calm down, man," I shouted.

"Death, death!" he screamed.

"Did you kill him? Or did you just take his shirt for your ritual?"

His eyes rolled back, leaving only the white of the eyeballs, and he seemed to be losing consciousness. I let go of his hair and tried to hold him by his waist, but his body proved as slippery as a fish's. He collapsed and remained motionless on the limestone floor. I absently wiped my hands on my pants. This guy had covered himself in foul-smelling oils. I leaned over him. I had to get him out of here quickly, because I was already dizzy from the stink of the oils and the smoke from the fire.

A new series of screams erupted as the rest of the congregants poured through the crack and started walking toward me. Their threatening grimaces perfectly fit their red faces. I began moving away from the shaman, whom they picked up and took back through the crack with them.

"I hope you sing in hell!"

When I turned around I couldn't believe my eyes. Everything was white now. Brightly, blindingly white. I stepped forward as if hypnotized. *The spirit of the river has returned* was what I thought and it made me happy. I walked over the white stones and next to me, reflected by the white rocky wall, it was *him*, my Artist. We moved shoulder to shoulder, reaching farther into the white spirit of the river.

"Nonsense, nonsense," I heard myself whisper. "You are walking by yourself at the bottom of the precipice."

Yes, but the sun shone on it and I remembered Strauss telling me that in such moments everything here became different. He was convinced that *they* would reveal themselves in this light.

"Come on," I urged them.

"Come on," he urged them in turn.

But who are they? Who is he? I looked around. Of course, I saw no one, and the truth finally crystallized in my mind. The burning cocoons of the tribesmen had drugged me. As a result, the sun's daily illumination of this space had become mystical to me. As the sun continued its arc everything would fade back to gray. Even that shadow over there would disappear completely.

It was a *human* shadow. But it wasn't standing up. It was floating, swaying over a hollow in the rocks, and from that hollow, thousands of gray threads drifted up, weaving into the shadow, making it grow larger, darker, and somewhat woolly. It looked like a man-shaped cloud.

Despite my reluctance, I moved toward it, as if the threads were weaving into me as well. They pulled me to show me what was in the hollow—the Wanderer's body.

27.

I was feeling exactly like who I was: a recluse snatched away from his seclusion and hurled into some diabolical maelstrom of events. I sat in front of the Butler's screen, unable to decide what to do. Part of me wanted to just keep my mouth shut, but on the other hand, a man had been murdered and his body had been left rotting beneath the precipice.

"Butler, connect me to security," I finally said. "No visualization!"

"I'm listening," an energetic male voice answered.

I introduced myself and gave my villa's number.

"Major Liotta."

"I'd like to know if you've received a signal for the death of anyone."

"Let's keep calling him the Wanderer."

"If you got the signal, why haven't you collected his body?"

"We will collect it, when the time is right."

"When do you think that will be?"

"I have no idea. The tribe's high shaman will give us a sign."

"Is that so?"

"You don't expect us to deny the man his second chance, do you?"

"Well, no, but . . ."

"But what, sir?"

"He did not commit suicide," I said. "I think he was murdered."

"Oh, *you* think? We, on the other hand, know for sure."

"You know for sure, but you have made no attempt to find the murderer?"

"Exactly."

"Why?"

"Because we have already established who did it."

"Have you arrested him?"

"In a sense, yes."

"What does that mean?"

"You will find out soon, especially if you make an effort to recall certain things."

"Damn it, Major," I yelled. "It is your duty to inform me. What are these riddles?"

"Make an effort," he said. "Search deeper into your memory and you will find out."

"Find out what? What?"

"Well, sir, for example, that it suits *you* the least to pretend you give a damn about the dead bodies in this complex."

The major cut the connection without waiting for my reply, but I nevertheless continued wondering how to answer him.

"Vanda," I said through clenched teeth, storming out of the study.

She was in the kitchen, cooking again. She was startled by my rushing in and grabbed one of the pans, glancing at her watch at the same time.

"Ah!" I laughed spitefully. "Checking who's here, are you? It's no use. The Artist no longer follows his working schedule. He appears when and where it pleases him!"

"Rhein," she said, "that's not funny at all."

"But the other day in the café it was, wasn't it?"

"Why would you think so?"

"Oh, come on! You babbled on and on, entertaining the crowd at my expense. Now I'm a suspect in a murder."

I hoped that she would at least pretend to be surprised, but all she did was nod calmly.

"I expected that, although not so soon. But it's not my fault at all. I didn't say a word about your split personality."

"I don't believe you."

"I have a recording of the entire conversation in the café."

"You made a recording?"

"Secretly, of course. I met with those eccentric millionaires to gather some spicy stories I could attach to the published facsimiles of your diary."

I sat on the nearest chair and clutched at my head. Vanda also sat down, but she kept gripping the pan. I could tell she would hit me at the slightest provocation, or maybe even none at all.

"We're in a terrible situation," she said. "That's why we have to be efficient. Do you understand?"

"Vanda, Vanda, I'm telling you that I'm a suspect and you're talking about efficiency."

"Exactly. They suspect you, but they don't have the evidence to charge you. If you take care they never find the body—"

"Ha! Now that everyone knows it's under the precipice you want me to take it and bury it. Is that what you're suggesting?"

She dropped the pan.

"From the precipice?" she mumbled. "So the Wanderer . . ."

"His body is still there. Those idiots from security left him there for the other idiots in the tribe, so their shaman can give him a second chance through some stupid ritual. Can you imagine?"

She stared at me with growing horror in her eyes, and her face became as pale as dough. Which reminded me to turn off the oven.

"Whatever you're cooking is not yet burnt," I told her.

She started crying. I headed for the door.

"Rhein, where are you going?"

"I will order a helicopter for you. Prepare your luggage."

"No! Please! No, no, no."

I went back, poured her a glass of water, and handed it to her. She drank it.

"Vanda, I can't stand it anymore," I said. "What's the matter with you? What do you want?"

"I don't know, I'm confused," she said, wiping away her tears and resolutely tightening her lips. "But I will get a grip on myself, Rhein, I promise. We're in trouble. We have to help each other. Come."

We went into the living room and each had a glass of whiskey. Then we sat in the armchairs and remained silent for quite a while, staring at the beautiful view outside.

"You lied to Maggie and Strauss yesterday," Vanda said in a low voice. "You didn't walk around the Center. You got out of the cave and met the Wanderer. Right?"

"I met him because I couldn't leave the cave. I was lost and I found a passage, which led me to his park. But the exit was locked. He came by, seemingly to unlock it, but he drugged me with chloroform."

"What happened after that?"

"I don't know. When I came to, I was outside . . . Yes," I said, slapping my brow. "I remember now. I stood in front of the camera at his gate and threatened him. I threatened the Wanderer but he was already dead. That's why the major said something about my memory. Obviously, his theory is that I blocked out my memory of pushing the man over the precipice, or that I forgot about it because when I pushed him I was still under the influence of the chloroform. You see?"

"What about you? Do you see that it was not the chloroform that caused your memory to go blank?"

"Of course. When I left the park I wasn't exactly me, I was the Artist."

"Who, before giving you back your identity, killed the Wanderer?"

"That's absurd!"

"Why?" Vanda said, narrowing her eyes. "Why would that be absurd? In your diary you admit that you don't remember anything that happens to you in a trance. The Artist goes mad in normal circumstances, so it's even more likely that he went mad under the influence of the chloroform."

"What are you talking about? What do you mean by that?"

She stood up, went to the bar, and slowly began preparing cocktails. I knew that she had said something I wasn't supposed to hear. But then she was seized by panic again, which made her leave the cocktails as she rushed out of the living room, moaning. So she fled the room, but why was she unwilling to flee the oasis?

Unfortunately, other, more pressing mysteries weighed heavily on my mind. I threw a farewell look at the sunlight outside and made for the study, and for the dark passages of my subconscious where, under completely "normal circumstances," my mad Artist painted and painted his madness.

28.

The studio's storeroom was empty. Completely, utterly empty. The thirty paintings were gone.

Now, this was way more than I could handle. I blinked a few times, but the sight remained unchanged. Did I really expect a miracle? Did I hope that the paintings would reappear just because I stood there blinking?

"Did I?" I asked myself again, aloud, and felt weak in the knees. I leaned on the wall. I knew that I was on the edge, staring at the abyss of my own madness, unable to step back. It was probably the Artist dragging me down, where it would be easy for him to destroy me, swallowing the last remnants of my personality.

"Bastard," I whispered.

"Son of a bitch!" I screamed.

My voice didn't echo as it should have in the empty storeroom, which was different now. It was no longer empty. On the contrary, it was stuffed with things, similar-looking things. Or more precisely, things stuffed in boxes. *I see*, I told myself. More patches in my time.

I made an effort to focus and recognized the place: the villa's basement. But for what purpose had I come here? For the paintings, of course; it was quite likely that the Artist had hidden them here. When I'd seen them packed the previous day I should have guessed that he'd want to move the paintings. They were probably dangerous for him.

"One can tell they were painted by a psychopath."

What if he had really pushed the Wanderer? How should I act then? How would I be able to move on with my life?

These questions panicked me, but then I realized that I still knew nothing for certain. I needed to find the paintings and analyze them.

I looked about the storeroom. There were at least twenty sealed boxes, all filled with various new kitchen appliances and other spare objects judging by the labels. In order to hide the paintings here the Artist would have had to take them out of their frames and roll them up. But if that were the case, why had he wasted time packing them that morning?

"Well, because he's an idiot," I said.

I got down to opening the boxes, as well as checking their contents. I did this for quite a while, before realizing that the idiot was in fact me.

"God," I whispered in shock. "How could he have hidden the paintings inside without unsealing the boxes?"

I sat on top of a box and tried to gather my thoughts for the same reason a shepherd gathers his flock—not because all the sheep together would do something smarter than grazing and bleating, but because he would be able to see them all.

So, once again I had proven to myself that I couldn't rely on myself. The concepts of common sense and logic had regularly lost their meaning for me. But here in the oasis, I couldn't count on reality, either. Here, absurdity had won the right to exist and manifested itself in all kinds of ways, becoming the rule rather than the exception. Some Remorites were wandering about the place in the form of ghosts, shadows, and even my own self. Back in the cave, these Remorites, I now thought, had really "borrowed" the dog's eyes. Earlier I had seen—maybe through their eyes—death, disguised as a cloud, leaving the Wanderer's corpse.

But, fine, fine. Let's say I succeeded in grasping all this nonsense *and* the fact that I seemed to remember the underground river, plus parts of the legend I had never heard of before. Fine! But how could I also accept the fact that last night a dead man had left wild but true statements about me and my Artist all over another person's computer screen, and later appeared before me in person, accusing me of murdering him?

And how could I swallow this present moment, sitting here wondering whether the Artist had hidden the paintings because they revealed the truth? I asked myself how much more time I had left before becoming utterly and completely mad during this "guaranteed peace" of mine.

"Well, not much," I said to myself in all honesty. "As for the Artist, he hasn't hidden the paintings. He has destroyed them!"

Before realizing that this was just another guess, I had started to shiver. I left the storeroom and went upstairs, unable to shake off the disgusting image of myself, deep in a trance, scratching, cutting, and tearing at the paintings, throwing them into the disintegrator one after the other, dooming myself to never seeing them again.

"Never." I repeated the word with such horror as I had never known, not even in the company of hundreds of ghosts and vengeful dead men. *Never?*

I entered the study loudly enough to give Vanda an idea of where I was, so that she could save us another chance meeting. I collapsed on the chair in front of the Butler and, with a rattling heart, asked him for the data on the disintegrator in the studio over the last couple of days. His check came up with only three cases of its activation, each lasting no longer than a few seconds. Besides coffee cups, it hadn't swallowed anything.

Vanda came in.

"I came to tell you that I took care of your paintings, Rhein. I sent them to my father."

I was speechless.

"Today, after you left," she continued, "I ordered a helicopter and four servants, who carried the paintings and loaded them. Please understand, I didn't want to take any risks. You know that you flip from time to time, and when you're like that, you could damage them. Or even destroy them!"

"I understand," I sighed, not sure if I was happy or not. "I understand your worry. But tell me, Vanda, did you see at least one?"

"I wanted to look but you could have returned at any moment. By the way, I also sent your diary to my father."

"Get out!" I yelled.

She complied, and I immediately called the control station of the complex.

"Earlier today a helicopter took off from sector number five, but there was a mistake, a misunderstanding. It was carrying things that it shouldn't have . . . things I need . . ."

"Just tell me what you want," the controller advised me.

"I want you to bring the helicopter back!"

"I am sorry, but this is impossible. The cargo has now been transferred to the plane and is on its way to the addressee."

"Are you telling me that the helicopter reached the airport in less than two hours, that it was immediately unloaded, while at the same moment there happened to be a plane there, whose destination was the same as the package's shipping address?"

"Yes, that is what I am telling you, sir. And now I am saying goodbye and have a nice day."

I tried to figure out the best way to wade through my conflicting emotions. On one hand, it was good that the paintings were safe. But they were not with me, and neither was my diary, so I couldn't know what they might reveal.

"What a nightmare," I said.

"Your entire diary is a chronicle of whining," Vanda had told me. Now her father was going to read it. My humiliation was so tangible that I could feel it going through my soul like a drill. "It's a good thing you started writing in your diary before you went crazy," Vanda had also said. "You can see how much your handwriting has changed."

"Changed," I said, opening my desk drawer and pulling out my will. I took it out of the envelope, but consciously didn't look at it. I laid it aside, took a blank piece of paper, and wrote several lines on it with approximately the same text. Then I put the sheet of paper and the will next to each other and noticed that, indeed, my handwriting was now very different from before—something that had been obvious in the diary, too, but which I somehow hadn't noticed.

Well, that was it. As it turned out, back then, on the day of my failed suicide attempt, I had also lost my handwriting. The Artist had taken it away with him.

29.

The gate to number 8 was still open, as it was yesterday when Natalia and I had left Felix's park. I reached the villa and saw that the second-floor window was also still open, as was the front door. Could it be that Felix was still away? Or that he had been so high that he forgot to close the door behind him?

I called his name several times and went in, after getting no reply. I walked through the hallway of my twisted reflections and pressed the button at the end of the anteroom. Then I headed upstairs.

Walking down the corridor with the zodiacal signs hanging from the ceiling, I called Felix's name again and the sinister silence absorbed my voice. I reached the study door and held my breath. This was where I had seen the Wanderer last night, although now I knew that when I'd seen him his body was beneath the precipice. What was I to expect now? Maybe another meeting with the dead man?

I took a good look around the study but saw no signs that someone had been there after I left. The Renegade poster I had taken down was still on the floor where I had thrown it, and the portrait of Felix was still hanging on the wall. My eyes met his tortured gaze, and my concern for him grew.

I stepped closer to the computer and saw that it had been turned off, probably by the villa's Butler. I turned it back on. I searched for the file that was closed last, and when I opened it I saw that it only contained a medical article copied from the Internet two days ago. *Someone deleted the other file from last night*, I said to myself. But when I checked the computer I was surprised to discover that the last time it had been turned off was two days ago.

Before falling too deep into trying to figure out this puzzle I was interrupted by the growing wail of someone's car horn. I went to the window and saw Maggie's car coming to a stop in front of the villa.

"Are you people deaf?" she angrily exclaimed, getting out of the car.

She stormed into the villa and a minute later she rushed into the study.

"We've been calling for hours," she said, looking around. "Where's Felix?"

"I don't know."

"What do you mean?"

"Just what I said."

"You don't know where he is, yet you're here. Who opened the gate and the door for you, if I may ask?"

"Nobody. They were open."

Maggie walked around the study, paying special attention to the Renegade poster.

"Why is this on the floor?" she asked me.

"It came down last night."

"Did you and Felix have a fight?"

"Unfortunately, no."

"Strange," Maggie said, sitting in the chair facing the computer and turning to me reproachfully. "Rhein, now is not the time to joke. Natalia and I are very worried about Felix. We've been trying to contact him since early morning but to no avail. Tell me what happened between you two yesterday."

"I already told Natalia."

"Yes, but I want to know what *actually* happened, not what you told her."

"Last evening, he called me and asked for help. He was scared. He said that the Wanderer was with him."

I paused to give Maggie time to express her astonishment, but she only nodded with understanding, astonishing me instead.

"I thought he was high and hallucinating. That's why I came. I really wanted to help him. Before he opened the gate for me, he yammered on about some mystical scary stuff, and he sounded hysterical. When I stopped in front of the villa, the entrance door was open and the lights in this study went off. I came up here but Felix was gone. Then I saw him taking off with my jeep."

"He took off with it, but then left it by the gate," Maggie said. "Doesn't make sense to me."

"Nothing makes sense."

"His mother is a psychic, and a very popular one at that. She made a lot of money with her 'gift,' which makes me think she is actually a big fake. Felix, though, believes her, and he got it into his head that he was also psychic. So when we told him about the Wanderer's suicide, he conjured up his psychic spirit, and, as usual, fell victim to his own fantasies."

"So, he's done this before?"

"Yes, and Strauss instigates it. The two of them do experiments from time to time. When it comes to this, they're both unstoppable."

"Felix's parents aren't blameless, either," I said. "These crooked mirrors and the writings all over the villa could do a lot of damage to a boy with such a fragile mind."

"They could and do, no doubt about it. Luckily, Felix thought of covering most of them with his posters. He takes them down when his parents come for their short, *very* short, visits. All in all, it's tough for our Felix. That's why Natalia and I are trying to support him whenever we can."

"I will be helping him, too, from now on," I mumbled.

"Tell me about the mystical scary stuff he unloaded on you before opening the gate."

I opened my mouth to give the answer but knew that the truth would only generate a slew of more uncomfortable questions.

"I don't remember. The poor boy wasn't himself."

Maggie reached for the control panel and pressed two of the buttons. "Rhein, is that you?" It was Felix's voice, and the display of the outside camera lit up and showed me staring angrily at its eye. "Yes, it's me."

"Come on in!"

"Come on in?" I said, shocked. "But he didn't say that. He said a great deal more before opening the gate. Someone has edited this."

"Someone? Why do you think it wasn't Felix?"

"No, no! That's not what I meant."

"Does that happen to you often?"

"What?"

"Talking without thinking," Maggie said, as she cued the control panel to watch the recording again. "No one has cut or edited anything, Rhein. Come take a look and you'll see that the camera's timer is factory set."

I looked and broke into a sweat.

"As I already told you," Maggie said, "Felix is an unhappy boy. But he is fighting his drug addiction like a man and doesn't deserve anyone's scorn. It was ugly of you to attribute to him *your* fantasies about the Wanderer."

She took out her mobile and called someone. A mix of bewilderment and excitement appeared on her face as she took the phone from her ear and started listening for something. I strained my ears, too, and heard a muted melody.

We looked at each other. Then we quickly went out into the hallway and heard the melody more clearly. It was coming from the adjacent room.

30.

The dry bloodstain stood out clearly on the pale green carpet. Felix was lying there on his back, his eyes wide open, his gaze fixed on the ceiling; something jutted out of his chest. It was the Capricorn. The same Capricorn I had taken as a defense weapon last night, before entering the study.

I clutched at my head, pressing my hands against my ears. Chopped into intervals, that melody—playful trills imitating a bird's warble—still crept from the boy's pocket.

"Stop it," I said.

But Maggie just stood there petrified, her face devoid of any thought.

I took it from her hand and switched it off, and Felix's phone stopped ringing at last. But then Maggie screamed. I took her out of the room and we returned to the study, where I helped her to the desk chair. She cried but I was completely, abnormally, calm. The two shocks—Felix's death and the weapon he was murdered with—seemed to have cancelled each other out in my mind.

"I will call security," Maggie said, barely audibly, pressing the alarm button.

No reply came.

"Butler, connect me to security immediately," she said, raising her voice.

Again, no result.

"Now what? What should we do?"

Maggie was already dialing her phone.

"Gregg, I'm calling from Felix's place. I'm here with Rhein. We found him. Felix. He's dead. He was murdered!" After listening to Gregg's reaction, she said, "My mind can barely grasp the magnitude of their irresponsibility . . . That's right . . . Go to the Center, find them, bring them here. Hurry, please."

As soon as she was done talking, Maggie turned to me, an insisting, questioning look in her eyes. She was right: I had a lot more explaining to do about what had happened last night in this damned villa. But even if I'd wanted to, I could explain nothing to her. I no longer knew what had happened, and the worst part was I didn't know what had *not* happened in reality.

"Who is Gregg?" I asked, evading her eyes.

"Gromov, Chari's father," she said. "Rhein, I believe you, despite how you distorted the story, but I have no doubt that you came here last night because Felix had told you those tall tales."

We fell silent, both of us staring at the huge photograph of Felix. "HERE HE IS AS HE USED TO BE—ONE HAPPY CHILD!"

"Those people must have been blind," I said.

"His parents are blind to everything concerning their son. It's much easier this way, more convenient," Maggie said, looking me in the eye. "The same as I believe you, I believe Felix, too. He truly believed he had seen the Wanderer. I am not surprised that he reached out to you and not to me or Natalia. After all, we would've immediately thought that he was back on drugs."

"But who was supplying him with drugs? Where do you get them here?"

"Sometimes, when her old trauma awakens, Natalia takes painkillers. Recently some of them disappeared. No one but Felix could have taken them. If the investigation proves that he was on drugs before his death, his parents will blame Natalia. It would be better for her if there were no autopsy, and that, to a large degree, depends on you."

"What does it have to do with me?"

"Just don't tell anyone about all the nonsense Felix said. Stick to the version of Felix being afraid of something and calling you, and when you arrived you couldn't find him. Or have you already told *everything* to someone? Maybe to Vanda?"

"No. No one but you knows the details. Let's leave it like that."

Maggie called Natalia. She lied to her about Felix not coming home yet, cutting the conversation short with tears in her eyes.

"I have to be with her when she finds out. It will be very hard for her. For us all."

She was probably right. But it didn't look like it was very hard for Gromov and Darcy, who showed up just then. On the contrary, they seemed like they didn't care at all.

"We found no one from security," Gromov said.

"But how is that possible?" Maggie said. "Where are they?"

"Ah, women's logic," Darcy said, grinning. "If we knew where they were we would have found them by now."

"In that case we're calling the city police," Maggie said.

"We already tried that," Gromov said. "No connection with town for now; even the Internet is down."

"Due to some magnetic anomaly," Darcy added, waving his hand impatiently. "Come on, tell us how the boy was murdered."

"Go into the next room and see for yourself," Maggie snapped at him.

Knitting his brow, Gromov went in that direction and Darcy followed him with enthusiasm. When they came back, Gromov was pale, while Darcy appeared quite lively, as if he had just seen a "perfectly shot" animal.

"An antelope, for example," I said aloud.

"What?" the three of them said.

"Nothing."

"Did you notice that his bracelet is gone?" Gromov asked.

"Yes," Maggie sighed. "I've been trying to warn you from the beginning that these creatures know everything. They are very dangerous."

"Unfortunately, you've been right all this time," Gromov said. "But resorting to murder . . ."

"Wait, are you talking about the servants?" I asked. "You think they killed him?"

"Of course," Darcy said, "only they have a motive."

"What motive?"

"Where are you coming from? Mars?"

"Enough, Darcy," Maggie said. "Rhein is not supposed to know everything. Only a few days ago he was completely isolated from us."

"Ah, yes," Darcy said, making a mocking grimace. "The reclusive artist."

This time I paid him no attention. At the moment, nothing could break through the relief that ran through my whole body. I crossed my arms and leaned on the wall next to the window. I breathed deeply. *It wasn't the Artist that killed him*, I told myself.

"What a mess," I said.

"No, it's not a mess, Rhein," Maggie said. "Felix really went too far and made the whole tribe his enemy. But the only one to blame is Strauss."

"Stop it. I don't want to hear about this paranormal bullshit anymore," Darcy said. "You'll tell it to him some other time, when I'm not present."

"Maggie, you must be exhausted," Gromov said. "Go home, get some rest. No need to stay here."

She smiled at him with gratitude and, almost running, left the study. I was envious. I wanted to run away, too, anywhere, but for the time being I had to restrain myself. From the window I watched Maggie drive away, and then another car approached the villa. Funny. While still alive, Felix had probably never had so many visitors as now, when they were of no value to him.

The newcomer was Ludo. He entered the house, but it took him quite a while to join us. We greeted him in silence.

"I was . . . there," he said in a low voice. "Damn! He was a good boy. The murderer has to be punished."

"He will be." Darcy's eyes had a brooding expression. "They will all be. By me, personally. I will get the rifle and the moment I see a tribesman I'll blast his head off. I'll crush it like an egg."

"You're sick," I burst out.

"Shut your mouth, Darcy," Gromov said, banging the desk with his fist. "You don't seem to understand that we're in a deviously serious situation."

"*Deviously* is an appropriate word," Ludo said, raising his eyes to the ceiling and crossing himself.

To me, this showy display of piety seemed dubious, somehow incongruent with the gladiator frame of his body.

"Death has come as a guest," he continued. "It is haunting the complex. Now we have to ask ourselves if the Wanderer truly killed himself or was murdered, too."

"Murdered, of course," Darcy said. "The people of the tribe hated him, too. It had been like that for a long time."

"Let's establish the facts about Felix first," Gromov suggested. "Rhein, tell us what happened yesterday."

I gave them the edited version, adding only Natalia's appearance.

"I can say for sure that he was murdered after midnight," I said. "Because I saw him just before. He was hiding in the bushes by Natalia's gate."

"No," Ludo said, shaking his head. "You didn't see him. It was me."

"You?"

"Of course," Darcy said. "He is the volunteering bodyguard of the *ex*-prima ballerina, and it seems that one does need a bodyguard around here, especially since she's so close to her servants, and so informal."

"Not informal. Humane," Ludo said, barely containing his anger. "She treats them like human beings."

"Trust me, they will kill us all," Darcy said. "Unless we kill them first."

"I am sorry that I called you," Gromov shouted. "Both of you are good for nothing save quarreling and haggling."

"Well, Gregg, it's clear that we are no good as detectives," Ludo said. "The most reasonable thing to do would be to continue looking for those who are supposed to be here by now, doing their job."

31.

The thought of wandering around the complex looking for the security guards was too much for me, so I went back to my villa. I wanted some alone time with a bottle of vodka. If you ask me, getting drunk was not only desirable, but also advisable, considering the situation. Vanda, however, thought otherwise, as a note left on the refrigerator informed me:

> *Rhein, I heard about what happened to the poor boy.*
> *Maggie told me everything. It is a HORRIBLE fact that*
> *you were at his place last night, but DO NOT drink!!!*
> *And don't despair, because there's a chance the servants*
> *might have done it. That's what I think after watching*
> *the recording Maggie brought. Take a look at it—it's in*
> *the study.*

I went to the study and found a CD on the desk. I put it in the computer and a small meadow appeared on the screen, with about ten people from the tribe sitting in a circle, dressed only in loincloths. The familiar bright red paint colored their faces, and their eyes stood out, just like the eyes of the people I'd seen. They all were seated in the same position—legs stretched out, hands raised and clutching a rope, or maybe a fiber, that was long enough to connect the entire circle. In the center of the circle were the gray ashes of a dead fire, and over it stood a shallow piece of pottery, resembling a baking dish.

The picture remained on the screen for a considerable time until I saw a butterfly flutter through the frame and realized that it was a video. It was amazing how they sat absolutely motionless, as if not even breathing. They looked like sculptures, not living people.

After a couple of minutes, a stooping, skinny boy entered the frame, dressed in shorts. He crawled beneath the rope and stopped at the ashes. It was Felix.

He leaned over the dish, with both hands scooped up whatever was in it, and smudged it all over his face, until it became the same red as the others' faces. Next, he found a spot between two of them and sat down. He stretched his legs forward, raised his hands, and grabbed the rope. He was straining to remain in the position but failed. His hands soon started shaking. The shaking gradually took over his entire body, grew stronger, and transformed into weird, rhythmic convulsions. The taut rope was now vibrating along its entire length, but the tribesmen didn't seem to feel it. A moment later, they didn't seem to hear Felix's screaming.

The camera zoomed in on his face. It was something grotesque. Half of it was his gaping mouth. His screams suddenly merged into something like a howl. His eyes were blinking faster and faster, becoming now black, now white, while the red paint trickled down, dripping on his chest, like blood.

I looked away, but it didn't help me get rid of the haunting thought of someone stabbing that very same chest with the Capricorn until real blood gushed forth. But who? Only they had a motive, Darcy had said about the tribe. But what if the murderer were a psychopath? He would have needed no motive.

I looked at the screen again. Felix was no longer howling. The convulsions, the shaking, the blinking ceased abruptly. He froze just like the others, joining in their trance. *Only then* did they sense him. They reacted simultaneously, as if they were a single organism. They dropped the rope, jumped up, and gathered around Felix. They started shaking him, pulling him, but he gave no signs that he felt any of it.

Now Strauss appeared, too. Shaking fists, yelling, "Leave him alone, let go of him," and running toward the angry tribesmen, one of whom dashed for the camera. His silhouette eclipsed it and then must have pushed it from the tripod, because the camera spun once and showed only the sky. Then everything turned black and the recording ended.

The date said it was shot about a month ago. The revenge of the tribe? Felix interrupted their ritual and they waited for the perfect moment to punish him? I didn't believe that story. If they were the murderers, their motive should have been different, significantly more serious.

"Butler, connect me to Gunther Strauss," I ordered.

I waited, repeated my words, and waited again, but the Butler had gone deaf, like the one in Felix's villa. It seemed that the anomaly mentioned by Darcy had a truly deteriorating influence on the complex's IT. I checked the Internet—still disconnected. For some reason, however, our mobile phones were only partially affected. They still functioned but their range was now only within the limits of the oasis.

I called Gromov.

"Did you find the security guards?" I asked.

"No. No sign of them anywhere."

"Call me as soon as you find them."

"You're right," Gromov said. "But if we don't find them before the night comes, we'll have to take care of the body and put it in one of the freezers."

There was nothing more to say. I hung up and stood there, facing my image obscurely reflected in the monitor's screen, feeling my thoughts creeping toward some terrible revelation. I had no strength to stop or divert them. *In the freezer, in the freezer,* I was repeating to myself, trapped in some idiotic circle of mine. *We'll have to take care of the body and put it in the freezers.*

I saw that I had stood up and was now walking, treading like a sleepwalker. I realized where I was headed only after I reached the garage. I opened the tool cabinet. I reached for one of the finer screwdrivers, but then realized that I wouldn't have the patience for precise manipulations, so I decided on a hammer as big as my fist. I grabbed it, rushed out of the garage, and dashed back to the villa. I stopped and took some time to regain my composure. All in vain. Vanda was peeking from her bedroom window again and I could tell that the sight of me had very much upset her.

"All's fine," I called to her, making another mistake, because I waved with the hand clutching the hammer.

She shut the window and moved out of sight. It was becoming harder and harder for us to live together. In a few minutes, it was probably going to become unbearable.

I went inside and headed straight for the corner room by the kitchen. Here, though, my courage disappeared. I stopped in front of the freezer next to which I had found Vanda after her unfortunate departure and her even more unfortunate return. Alas, now everything strange about her behavior seemed quite explicable. I could see logic in her actions, and, even worse, I could see the relation between them and the torturous dragging sound that had woken me.

I tried to open the freezer but it didn't budge. Vanda had locked it so that I wouldn't find whatever she had hidden in there.

But I don't want to find it.

I stood like that for a while, staring at the freezer as at a sphinx. Then I left the hammer on top of it, gripped it with both hands, and shook it. There was something inside, something big.

I picked up the hammer again and smashed the electronic lock. I heard a crunching sound, as if I had broken an ostrich's egg. I struck it several more times, despite knowing that there was no need to. The truth is, it felt good.

Finally, I stopped and jerked it open. Folded into a fetal position was the frozen corpse of a man I did not recognize.

"Well?" Vanda's voice startled me. "Who is he?"

Standing there in the doorway, she was extremely pale but didn't look frightened. Her face showed the apathy of someone who didn't have anything more to lose.

"I don't know," I mumbled. "I've never seen him before."

"You've seen him at least once."

"When?"

"When you killed him."

32.

The sun was setting, but the evening brought no coolness. We sat on the terrace, sweating, silent, scowling at each other. Each of us was waiting for the other to speak first.

"I'm broke," I said finally. "I paid the monstrous rent to be in this villa, and now I feel sick just at the thought of going back in. Because you've turned it into a cemetery."

"Only because you turned it into a slaughterhouse."

"The man was slaughtered?"

"No. You strangled him. I was speaking metaphorically."

"Watch your words, Vanda. It's the third time you've accused me of murder."

"I know, I know. You want evidence. How about this: I found the body in the studio's storeroom."

"Someone could have put it there."

"No, that's not possible," Vanda said firmly. "Don't forget that the room you're using as a studio is in fact designed to be like a vault."

"It's designed to ward off insolent guests like you."

She nodded and looked at me, as if to say, *Come on, you can piece it all together now.* Unfortunately, she was right. The other day, at about ten in the morning, I locked the studio door using my fingerprint and unlocked it in the afternoon, after agreeing to let Vanda see the paintings.

"The body could have been there before I locked it," I said.

"The man was murdered after I returned from the café. You strangled him while I was packing, Rhein. I should have known something was wrong with you, the way you just passed out on the chaise longue. Your trances aren't right."

"So tell me, why do you think I killed him?"

"Before running away I checked his pulse. There was none, but his body was warm, much warmer than the temperature of the storeroom. So the murder happened not very long before that."

"But it proves nothing about me being the murderer. It's true that I fell asleep in a peculiar manner. You exhausted me with your ideas for selling my diary and paintings. But that doesn't mean that the Artist . . . Damn it, Vanda! There's got to be another explanation."

"Like what?"

"Like, like . . . I can't think of anything at the moment," I said, floundering. "First we need to find out the dead man's identity."

"He's one of the staff."

"A servant?"

"Good Lord, Rhein! Think! You just saw that he's not a tribesman."

"One of the guards? A medic?"

"I have no idea who he was. The Agency logo is stitched to his shirt, and there are no personal belongings in his pockets. I suppose you—I mean the Artist—hid them somewhere."

"Enough!" I said. "We're done with the guesswork. Now I want you to tell me why you're here. Why stay with me if you think I'm a murderer?"

"They brought me back against my will!"

"Who? The faceless shadows?"

Vanda laughed at how seriously I asked the question.

"Don't tell me you fell for that?"

"I fell for nothing. That's why I insist that you tell me what *actually* happened after you ran away from here."

"The helicopter landed on a rocky spot in the desert and its hatch opened, as if someone was prompting me to get out. When I did, the hatch closed. I was left outside in the horrendous heat. I panicked, began wandering about, fell down, lost consciousness. When I came to, the hatch was open. I went back into the helicopter and it took off, returning me here."

"What was the time?"

"I don't know. The servants were outside, setting up the barbecue. I told them to take my bags to my room, I dragged after them, and the helicopter took off. I knew that you hadn't heard it because you were in the bathroom, so I decided not to show up. Not before hiding the body."

"How clever of you, hiding the victim from the murderer."

"Rhein, from the beginning, I knew that you wouldn't remember what you had done. Otherwise, you wouldn't have let me in the studio. Am I right?"

I said nothing.

"I waited until the guests and the servants had all left. Then I waited an hour more to make sure you had fallen asleep. Next, I dragged the body from the storeroom, and since I knew that the freezer was empty . . ."

"Yes, yes. I know that part of your adventure. So when I appeared, to justify your presence there, you performed that spectacle. Is that right?"

"It wasn't spectacle, Rhein. I was really scared. I had no choice. I had to play it disoriented. I had to act as if I believed I was in the kitchen, hungry, after spending three days in the helicopter, and so on. Otherwise, you would've suspected that I had hidden something in the freezer. You would've opened it, seen the body."

"And after seeing it, strangle you, too?"

"Yes."

"Vanda, Vanda, you're not even trying," I said, laughing. "You can do better. Try harder and you'll come up with a better lie."

"Everything I just told you is the truth, Rhein."

"If that's so, then you have to be afraid of me now. I've seen the body."

"It's different now. You know that I won't tell on you. I've had many chances to do it, but I didn't."

"What's stopping you?"

"There are many reasons."

"We're in a vicious circle, Vanda. Let me tell you what, according to me, is the truth. In the studio, you gave in to panic after seeing the body, but after that, in the helicopter, you were overcome by greed. You returned here to steal my paintings, the prices for which would skyrocket once people found out they were painted by a murderer."

"By a psychopathic serial killer. You killed the Wanderer and Felix."

"Let's suppose you're right. I still can't understand why you have stayed. Why didn't you just board the helicopter you used to send the paintings?"

"Stop it! The first helicopter really landed in the desert. But there was nothing wrong with it. They did it on purpose to scare me."

"Who are 'they'?"

"The Agency people. It was a warning, telling me, unequivocally, that should I make another attempt to leave the oasis they would kill me. They'll just leave me in the desert to die."

"But why, Vanda? Why?"

"I don't know. But here's my theory: Their man comes to you, for a reason only the devil knows, and then disappears. At the same time, I rush out of the villa and jump into the helicopter, screaming hysterically about leaving right away. They realized that you killed one of their men and that I had stumbled upon his body. Think, what would happen to the Guaranteed Peace Agency if this information leaked out? It would bankrupt them. Do you see?"

I thought of the conversation I had with Major Liotta, and, no, I didn't see. "It suits *you* the least to pretend you give a damn about the dead bodies in this complex," he'd said before hanging up on me. A few hours later he, too, had disappeared, along with his subordinates.

33.

It was almost impossible for the paintings to have reached Kort by now, but despite that I dialed his number as soon as I woke up. But the range of the mobile phones was still limited and there was still no Internet. I checked the Butler, who turned out to be only partially functioning; he still managed the villa's basic functions but did not grant any of my requests. All in all, it was clear that yesterday's "anomaly" was today's reality at the oasis.

I got into the jeep and drove in the direction of the Center. I saw none of the servants but this didn't surprise me. Before any of this madness, I knew their orders were to be as inconspicuous as possible. I hit the horn once, not entirely sure why I was doing it. Then I took the Agency's prospectus out of the glove box and followed the map to the so-called combined building. It was only three stories high, although large, with a control tower protruding from its roof. From this tower one was supposed to be able to see the landing platform for the pilot-free helicopters.

I crossed the empty lounge, got into the lift, and went up—straight to the tower. There was no one there, either, and there was not a single helicopter. The computers were on so I sat at the nearest one. I preferred finding the necessary information by myself, instead of relying on those who were obliged to supply me with it. I now had reason enough to doubt their honesty.

Soon, however, I found myself doubting the honesty of their computers. First, looking into the helicopter Vanda had requested three days ago, I got an answer stating that it had arrived without problems in the town where its passenger had left it, after which it had returned to the complex, all right on schedule. Then it turned out that there was no date in relation to Vanda's second request for the helicopter that had transported my paintings. Finally, the cherry on top, the computer confirmed for me that all three helicopters were currently available. I glanced at the empty platform and, once again, bewilderment blanketed my mind.

I waited for about ten minutes, but no one showed up. I left the tower, taking the stairs to the third floor. I was hoping to find at least one person to explain the absence of everyone else. I found nobody. The administrative wing of the building was completely deserted. Before moving to the wing with the personnel's living quarters, I decided to visit the security office.

I had to switch on a computer here but then it was easy to search the information they had about me in the database. I skipped the biographical data, the electronic copy of my contract with the Agency, as well as the details concerning my arrival. I activated the "Current information" link, and the first thing that appeared was a picture of the man who was now in my freezer.

At the bottom of the picture it said: "Gaston Fouchet, first category expert. Server administrator," and further down, in the style of official documents, there followed a description of how Fouchet had received a signal regarding a glitch in the communication network, and after tracing its source to villa number 5, mine, had gone to fix it by physically replacing a router.

Gone, never to return. Disappeared. The date marked was four days ago.

I left the security office feeling dizzy and headed toward the living quarters. I knew I'd find no one there, but I was still hoping. For what, I didn't know. I guess I was hoping to continue hoping. I had experienced so many horrors recently that according to the laws of probability something good was bound to happen to me.

I reached the common dining room and entered. Scanning the tables, I saw that four of them were empty, but there were two plates full of barely touched food and glasses with juice in them.

I stepped back and closed the door. No use looking at the apartments. I knew what I would find. There had been some sort of alert and everyone had rushed to the helicopters. They had left the oasis. They had run away from something that was about to happen.

34.

"Were you sleeping in there or reading a novel?" Chari said, catching me off guard as I exited the building. "I've been waiting for you for half an hour."

He had on a checkered cowboy shirt, a sleeveless leather vest with fringe, and a sombrero; the handle of a water gun stuck out from his belt.

"Chari," I said, pulling him toward me as if I could protect him with my arms.

"Get a grip," he said, pushing me away. "What do you think is going to happen? An explosion, a fire, a flood? Or all three simultaneously?"

I didn't answer. I didn't want to scare him. Plus I truly had no clue what I expected to happen.

"Call Hercules," I said. "We have to go."

"You call Hercules. Let's see if he comes."

I closed my eyes, suddenly dizzy. This kid had an uncanny knack for making me feel like an idiot.

"Hector," he said. "My dog's called Hector. But he's not with me."

"Let's go," I said, helping him into the jeep.

I jumped behind the wheel and slammed my foot on the gas.

"Drive more economically, Ray. You won't find any more gas around."

"Oh, yeah?" I said.

"The gas station's empty."

I hit the brakes.

"Early this morning, Darcy called my father. He went hunting and on his way stopped to refuel. But he couldn't. My father and I and Ludo also went there. Nothing, Ray, not a drop of fuel, although according to the computers both reserves were full until yesterday."

"So someone drained them on purpose?"

"No, Ray. We checked. No signs of spilled fuel around. It's a mystery, I'm telling you. The fact is, we're trapped here now. The refueling of the helicopters used to happen in town, which means that we have no aviation fuel, either."

"Doesn't matter," I said. "The helicopters are gone."

"I know." Chari nodded. "Something is happening to us here, and it is more horrible than any emergency because it will keep us imprisoned in this trap even after our death."

"Kiddo, don't start with your fantasies again, and don't be so dramatic. In a day or two people from the Agency will come to see why we're disconnected."

"My dad and Ludo have the same hope. Unlike them, though, I warned you the other day so you shouldn't waste your time with futile hope. I put it quite clearly, Ray. The oasis will take off! It will carry us away into a timeless dimension."

"Where is your father? I'll leave you with him."

"How should I know? I don't have a crystal ball."

"But you have a phone. Call him."

"You call him! He'll tell you all about how they stuffed Felix's body in some freezer last night. Those freezers come in handy, don't they, Ray?" Chari said this as he was trying hard not to cry. "I really liked Felix."

I gave him a reassuring hug, but I wasn't trying to find comforting words. Something else absorbed my entire attention.

"Since when have you been eavesdropping on me?" I said.

He blushed, opening his mouth to deny it before gathering his courage.

"For a long time," he said.

"Since when, exactly?"

"I gave myself away by mentioning the damned freezers, didn't I?"

"How long have you been eavesdropping on me? Tell me!"

"All right, all right," he yelled. "From the day you tried to kill yourself!"

"You . . . you saved me?" I said, my eyes blurring. "You bandaged my arm?"

"Do you know how horrible it was with all the blood in the bathtub? I was afraid you might try it again so I placed another bug into your bracelet. I had it from before and have used it a lot here. But because of you, I gave up my other investigations."

"But how did you end up with me at that moment? How did you enter my villa?"

"I can enter wherever I want to," Chari said proudly. "I hacked the files of those bums in the medical station on our second day here. I had to check something, but I didn't miss the opportunity to steal their access code, which is universal."

"You are dangerous. A hacker! But I still find it hard to believe that you came to my place just at the right moment at six in the morning."

"It wasn't by chance. Back then my mother was still living with us and I could only sneak out when she was sleeping, between midnight and ten in the morning. I used to visit you in the early hours, when you would drag your exhausted self to the studio. You know you have the habit of talking to yourself, Ray?"

"You've had good fun at my expense," I said bitterly.

"Not at all. I could tell you were deeply depressed. That's why I watched you as closely as possible. I was worried about you, especially after reading your diary."

"Good God!"

"God or no God, that's how things are. Since all the cards are on the table now let's keep it that way until the end."

I wiped my brow with my sleeve. I was sweating despite the air conditioner.

"Take it easy, Ray," Chari said, patting me on the shoulder. "As you can see, I'm not afraid of you, and I don't hate you. Why do you think that is?"

"Why indeed?"

"Because I am sure that you have killed no one. As for the Artist, I've always been sure about him."

"You visit my studio while he paints?"

"I visit him almost every morning. We chat. It's nice for both of us. Yesterday, though, you asked me how I had entered the villa and I realized it was you and not him. It's good you're such a naïve fellow to believe that Vanda let me in."

"Naïve" sounded flattering next to what I would have called myself.

"The legend," I said. "You told it to the Artist. I was wondering how I could vaguely remember it, given that I had never heard it before."

"It's the reason I made that psychological move in the cave. You see now? Had such memories come to you there, you would've probably thought that the Remorites had transmitted their legend to you. Of course, it didn't happen like that because you weren't willing to concentrate enough."

"Guilty as charged. Sorry for not letting you shock me there also!"

"Wrong again, Ray. My goal was not to shock you, but to push you toward the truth."

"An interesting method," I said, "pushing me toward the truth with the help of lies."

"Why not? Considering you wouldn't have believed me if I had told the truth."

"You can try now. I might even believe you."

"I'll try, but not until the end of our conversation. Once you hear me out you will want to be alone, wallowing in your dismay."

"How did you learn to be such an effective manipulator?"

"Until this morning I also thought of myself as a manipulator, but, to my chagrin, now I see that it is not so. My predictions are coming true!"

"Don't play the prophet," I said, waving dismissively. "Only the personnel have taken off, not the oasis."

"You really are dumb. We're no longer in the present time of our own world. We're not in the now. We have disappeared from our own world. We are present there maybe only as bones and ashes! Is it really that hard for you to understand?"

"But, Chari . . ."

We rode in silence until reaching the Center. He looked at me questioningly and then jumped out of the jeep.

"Very soon you will be looking for me, Ray. You will start looking for me the moment you realize that you failed to ask the right questions."

35.

The kid walked away with his usual strut. He knew I was watching, and he was intelligent enough to know that this gait fitted him the least, making his disproportionate body look like a grotesque caricature.

"My mother and father hate me, Ray. They think I'm a disgrace."

"If they do, then this means they never knew you, Chari. I would've been proud to have a son like you. I would have loved him very, very much."

"You're saying it, but you don't mean it."

I had meant it, I thought. *Because . . . because I had been the Artist then, and now . . .*

"I don't want to think about this now!" I said out loud.

When I heard my voice, I immediately remembered the bug in my bracelet. I drove after Chari, who was just entering the café. When I entered he already held a large chocolate bar, broken in two. He gave me half. I took it, and we looked at each other hopefully.

"Yes," he whispered to me, despite the fact that the café was empty. "The Artist and I are used to sharing all the nice things. We're friends, Ray. I am the link between you two."

I smiled at him; he smiled back. It was a pleasant moment, but also an odd one. It was as if the Artist was giving me a present of the kid, along with his own love for him.

We crossed the café and sat by one of the windows. We began to eat our chocolate.

"I was sure you'd follow me," Chari said.

"You forgot your bug. That's why I came after you."

I took off the bracelet and gave it to him.

"You're not a practical man, Ray," he mumbled as he began to dismantle the listening device. "Otherwise you would've been happy about the bug. After all, thanks to the bug I found your bracelet in the Wanderer's park. I got there before the security guards and denied them the opportunity to put a noose around your neck. Don't you realize how much better it will be for you if I continue to keep an eye on you?"

"You're offering to continue spying on me, only this time with my consent. Is that supposed to be better?"

"Of course," he said and, perhaps sensing that he had crossed the line, he dropped the spying device in his shirt pocket, put the bracelet back together, and handed it to me. I clasped it on my wrist out of habit, but now with the medics gone, it was of no use at all.

"The medics," I said. "If their access code is universal, then it could be used to wipe out the fingerprint codes!"

"Of course," Chari said. "That's why Vanda's theory that the Artist is the murderer is worth nothing. Anyone on the security crew could have snuck into your studio and from there into the storeroom. I bet it's one of them."

"But it could be one of the clients. Someone who used their hacking skills, just like you."

"I don't know. But I am sure of one thing," Chari said. "Whoever it was, his goal was to draw all doubting eyes to you. You're the scapegoat, Ray. But this no longer matters because they are gone and we're here.

And we will be here forever, a bunch of wretches, disappeared from their present, immersed in the swamp of timelessness."

"Don't start again. Just focus on the fact that if we're right, there'll be no more murders here. Don't worry about the rest."

It was good advice, which, unfortunately, I was unable to follow. How could I not worry when there was a dead body waiting in my freezer, and in another freezer there was another dead body, with the Capricorn, my fingerprints on it, sticking out of its chest? And what about the Wanderer? He'd somehow accused me of killing him. But then it hit me. Chari had told someone about my double, the gossip had spread, and the murderer had arranged everything around this information.

"Chari," I said, looking at him very seriously, "you've told someone about my split personality, haven't you? Be honest, please! It's very important."

"What's important is that you start thinking. Ask yourself, would you, in my place, have boasted about something that might reveal that you eavesdropped and read other people's diaries?"

"Good point. I believe you."

"Do you believe yourself, Ray? Do you believe all these tales about your double?"

"You're right," I sighed. "There is no me during those hours of trance. The Artist throws me out of my own mind."

"He does this in order to paint," Chari said. "Where fear and faint-heartedness dwell, no great ideas can be born."

"So that's my personality: fainthearted and fearful?"

"I don't mean to offend you, Ray, but consider the way you're acting now. It's been an hour and you're still afraid to ask the question that's been torturing you for almost a year!"

I felt the color drain from my face.

"I'm sorry," he said. "I shouldn't have kept you in suspense for that long. It was completely unnecessary because I have no idea what the paintings look like. He never agreed to show me any of them."

"You've been in the storeroom, you've seen them. Tell me the truth!"

"No, that's not true. From the very beginning I promised him that I would never go in there, and I never broke my word. I told you, we're friends, Ray. I would never lie to him."

"To me, on the other hand, you lie as you please. You see us two quite differently. You seem to have forgotten that we're the same person."

"Ray," Chari said, waving his hands before my face. "Wake up. Come to your senses! What kind of logic is this? Just listen to yourself. You and the Artist are the same person, but this doesn't stop you from suspecting that he's a psychopath and a murderer, so he couldn't have put anything less than a monstrosity on the canvas. You're toying with the idea that the paintings might be monstrous, but actually you are afraid that they might be simply bad. Well? Tell me why I shouldn't see a difference, a *big* difference, between you two?"

I was silent.

"Still, you're not schizophrenic," he said. "You're also not some other kind of madman. Your tragedy lies in the fact that you're not the one you think you are."

Now it was time for Chari to be silent for a moment.

"So?" I said, when I couldn't take it any longer. "What do you mean?"

"If only you had believed us in the cave, that the Remorites truly existed, you wouldn't have asked me this question. Because your spiritual sight would have become clearer, allowing you to see some of them or at least him. The Artist! You would have seen him and realized that *you are not Rhein.*"

Chari stood. He put his hands on the table and leaned toward me.

"He is the real Rhein. Not you!"

36.

Shots rang out from somewhere outside. Or were they just in my head? I threw a quizzical glance at Chari, but after seeing nothing but an empty chair, I remembered that he had left—to leave me alone with my shock. Whether I was truly shocked or not, I could not remember. I couldn't remember what was supposed to shock me.

In front of me on the table there was also an empty plate. I waved a hand in the direction of the kitchen, and much to my surprise a waiter shot out of there like a champagne cork.

"What was this?" I asked him.

Staring at me, blinking dumbly, he looked as if he hadn't understood me.

"What did I just eat?"

His eyes grew dark, if such an expression could be used for eyes as black as his. I concentrated and realized that the man had taken my words for some sort of mockery.

"My tribe is in the oasis," he said in very good English. "There're not many of us left. What about you? You no longer know how many of you are left. But you're not many and you're alone."

"Can you at least tell me when the boy left?"

"About an hour ago."

"Damned Artist. Stealing precious time again."

"I am not an artist."

I heard another shot.

"So it's not just in my head," I said, jumping to my feet and unintentionally bumping the servant. "Sorry."

He only hissed at me like a wild cat as I rushed outside, where I came across an appalling scene.

One of the swans was thrashing about in the lake, splashing blood all around it. These chaotic movements rocked the body of a dead swan to and fro. The rest of the swans were crying, fluttering their wings in ungraceful attempts to fly away before dropping back into the lake.

I ran toward the bank, where Darcy stood, rifle raised over his head, next to Strauss, who was jumping, arms outstretched, trying to reach the rifle.

"No, Darcy, don't, no."

"Darcy, stop!" I yelled, but this only made things worse.

Seeing me running toward them, Darcy pushed Strauss, who fell on his side and immediately tried to clutch at Darcy's leg. Darcy kicked him, aimed his rifle, and took another shot at the swans. The bullet popped a bird's head off.

"I have paid to hunt," Darcy roared at me. "I'm not going to set off on foot around the oasis because there's no damned fuel."

As I got closer to him he aimed his rifle at me. Strauss moaned and made another attempt to clutch at Darcy's leg. When Darcy focused on kicking Strauss again I lunged at him. A bullet whizzed past my ear as I brought Darcy down to the sand and punched him in the nose. It brought me great joy. But that didn't last long because he was still holding the rifle and now managed to bang me in the head with its butt. My ears started ringing and for a few seconds everything went dark. When I came to, Darcy was back up on his feet. He kicked me right in the belly, knocking the wind out of me. While fighting for my breath,

I caught a glimpse of the servants standing in a tidy group in front of the café, watching us with curiosity.

"Ahaaa! There's the game!" Darcy shouted, his voice hoarse.

He shot. A window broke. Luckily for them, the servants had gone back into hiding.

My normal breathing returned, and I managed to stand up. Darcy was running like a mad horse toward the café. Panting, Strauss was limping after him. I rushed after him, too.

"Stay here," I told Strauss, running past him.

I reached the café only thirty seconds after Darcy, but the chaos I found inside made it seem as if he had been on a rampage for hours. Chairs and tables were turned upside down, a huge planter had been toppled over, and under it someone moaned. It was one of the servants. I tried to move the heavy wrought iron object.

A shot rang out from one of the back rooms.

"God," Strauss moaned behind me.

"I told you not to come," I yelled.

We rescued the tribesman. Strauss immediately leaned over him, and I grabbed a crystal vase on my way into the back room. Darcy was standing with his back to me, firing his rifle. I threw the vase at him but missed. To my surprise, one of the servants crawled out from under a counter and began gathering the broken pieces.

Darcy was hastily loading his rifle. I lunged at him, clutching his hair as my knee hit his waist. He went down, and with a single jerk I turned him on his belly. I mounted him and pressed his arms with my knees, still pulling at his hair. In a moment he realized that resistance was futile and he calmed down. But then the servant who had collected the pieces of the vase began gathering the bullet casings on the floor around us before picking up the rifle.

"Rhein, this man is not well," Strauss shouted from the café salon. "Not well at all!"

I released Darcy from my grip, and we both stood up. I stepped toward the man holding the rifle.

"Give it to me," I said.

"His ribs are broken," Strauss shouted again. "His lungs could be punctured."

Now the servants left their hiding place and quickly moved toward the salon. There were six of them, each holding a sharp or heavy object in his hand. The man with the rifle followed them, making a threatening gesture at Darcy on his way.

"Sons of bitches," Darcy grunted.

"Shut your mouth, dumbass," I said.

"I don't think they'll be able to help him," Strauss said, joining us. "I think he's going to die."

"He won't die," Darcy said. "These creatures are tough like crabgrass."

"I hope you're right," I said, "because otherwise we're in deep trouble, especially you."

"Nonsense! They're just servants."

"Yes, you are sick," Strauss said.

"And you're quite normal, eh?" Darcy said. "How are your Remorite friends? Are you done trying to fit them into your hypothesis, Mr. Wannabe Einstein?"

"Go away!" I said, clenching my fists.

This time he didn't object. He summoned an arrogant facial expression and walked toward the salon. Strauss and I followed him. The servants did not react to our appearance. The wounded one had their full attention, and Darcy was able to leave the unfortunate café without problems.

"How can I help?" I asked the wounded man. "Our medics are gone but I could bring one of your healers. Or take the man to your village?"

"No!" The word rattled in his throat.

I stepped closer to him. His face was ashen, and his pain made him grimace in a very odd way, now twisting his features, now making him look like someone very calm, someone from beyond. I couldn't help thinking that this man was dying and coming back to life, dying and coming back to life, as if in the grip of a hyperaccelerated passing of time.

"No," he repeated.

"Come on," Strauss said, pulling me away. "We're only getting in their way."

I turned hesitatingly to the servants, and they immediately began nodding. There was no need to press things further. I followed Strauss outside. The surface of the lake was smooth, but its undercurrents had already washed the murdered swans onto the bank.

"It's my fault," Strauss said, his voice shaking. "If I hadn't fed them so much they would have been able to fly away."

"I doubt that. The swans belong to the Agency and that's why they can't fly away. They are here to make the place pretty, Strauss."

"You think they were disabled on purpose so they always would be on the lake?"

"Yes," I said.

"All right," he whispered.

37.

Unfortunately, Vanda and Maggie had become friends again. As I pulled up to the villa I could see they were sunbathing by the pool. They were wearing bathing suits and hats the size of baking dishes. They'd covered their faces with cream that made them look like geishas, though their bodies were shiny with oil.

"Why are you punishing me, God?" I asked as I got out of the car.

Besides not looking good, the two ladies were giggling, which I guessed was a consequence of the empty beer bottles scattered all around the pool.

"Rhein," they shouted simultaneously.

"Take a shower and get dressed," I said. "Drink some coffee."

Another burst of laughter followed as I hurried inside. I took a few beers from the kitchen refrigerator and headed straight to my room, closing the door behind me. I sat on the bed and drank one of the beers. My head hurt for many reasons, the main one being the bump from the rifle butt. I needed at least an hour's rest, during which I had to obliterate from my mind the dying man and the dead swans, the missing personnel, the mysterious anomaly, the corpses in the freezers, the corpse below the precipice, the Remorite ghosts, the helicopters, the codes, the bugs.

I went to the window and opened it so that at least I could hear the two women if they started to drown. I saw them lying by the pool and calmed down a bit. I set the air conditioning to fast cooling and jumped in bed. It felt more comfortable than ever. I instantly grew sleepy—a perfect time for a short nap.

Was it going to be a short one, though? Or a nap, even? Was the Artist going to play another trick on me, disposing of my life, while I sank, not into a dream, but into nonexistence?

I decided to stay awake. I opened another beer and drank it, but when reaching out for the next one, I told myself no.

"Yes, you're right," I agreed with myself.

But then I realized that my *no* had not been about beer. It was about the times when the Artist ruled my life and how I remained connected to him, which rendered my theory about my sinking into nonexistence entirely erroneous. How could I remember parts of the legend and his conversations with Chari if I wasn't there? How could I feel his love for this boy and sometimes even hear the sounds he heard?

"Stop," I told myself.

So I sensed things. But how come I never saw anything when the Artist worked? Was I blind during a trance? Or maybe he borrows my eyes to look through them? Because for him not a single place is the same as it is for me. No person is as I see him or her. Because he is the Artist and his world is different, incomparably richer, more colorful, more meaningful than mine.

His world is what my world used to be, before I gave in to my faintheartedness, which in the end brought me here.

"If that's so, then Chari is right. The Artist is the real Rhein. He is, and not me!"

I started shaking. Shock? Oh, no, this was pure hell. I was losing everything, losing even the meaning of the most basic of words: *I.* I am not Rhein. But who am I? What am I?

I stood up and headed for the studio, oddly confident that all the answers to my questions were waiting for me there. But I didn't check if I was right, because when I stopped in front of the door I didn't dare open it. I didn't go in. I walked down the hallway and then down the stairs.

I went out onto the terrace, relaxing in my chaise longue and closing my eyes. "Enough, enough of this," I repeated. I didn't want to find out who I was, what I was . . . But I already had.

A fragment. That's what I was. A pathetic remnant of the person I had been. The person that was now the Artist, to whom I was connected by ever-thinning threads, and these were breaking, one after the other, and he, not me, was sinking for longer and longer periods into nonexistence, coming back ever more rarely. Until the day he wouldn't return at all. He would leave me forever, and with him, I would lose everything I held dear, everything I had.

"Don't," I begged him softly. "Don't leave me."

Or at least forgive me, before leaving forever, I implored him in my thoughts. I had been unfair to him. I had been accusing him of stealing my gift, of stealing my time, my life, of taking even my handwriting away from me. But how obvious it had been all this time. How did I miss it? Such things could never be stolen! They were all very personal and could belong only . . . only to him now.

But what belongs to me, what is left for me? Probably only memories. Here they are now, returning slowly, coming to me like a passing breeze from my past, with its gift of comfort and tranquility. I remember myself, and this means that I know the Artist very well, too. I am sure that he would not sneak behind the Wanderer's back to push him off the precipice. Or stab Felix with that Capricorn. And he would never strangle someone for no reason.

Through the fog of dreams, I heard my phone. How long had it been ringing? I took it out from my pants pocket and saw Kort's name!

"Kort!"

"Hello," he replied joyfully.

"Listen to me and don't interrupt, please." I started talking quickly. "There is some anomaly here and the connection could break down any moment. Call the Agency immediately. Tell them to send people here, a rescue party."

"Rescue party? What's going on?"

"I don't know. But it is crucial that I return immediately to his world . . . I mean, mine. I am losing so much here . . . I'm going to lose everything, if I don't leave this hellish place right away."

"But why? You have a whole year left, you've paid an outrageous sum of money."

"I don't care about the rent! I only care about the Artist now," I said. "Did you get the paintings?"

"You've sent them, eh? When was that?"

"Not me, Vanda did. Yesterday morning."

"What?"

"They will get there, don't worry."

"Rhein, did you just say 'yesterday'?"

"Yes. She ordered a helicopter . . ."

"Shut up and listen to me. Vanda could not have sent the paintings yesterday. She came back from the oasis the day before that."

"Kort, this is not the time for jokes. Vanda is here."

"Vanda returned the day before yesterday," he said. "In fact, she made me call you. She's worried, says you acted really weird during her stay. She's here with me now."

"Stop it, Kort."

"Hello?" It was Vanda's voice! "I am so mad at you. Still, I'm not telling anybody."

"No, oh, no," I cried.

"Go to the storeroom, Ray," Vanda said from thousands of miles away as she was lounging here by the pool, only a stone's throw from me. "Now, do you remember what you've hidden behind the largest painting?"

"Vanda!" I screamed, jumping from the chaise longue.

"Yes?" said both Vandas.

The one by the pool rubbed her eyes sleepily and, seeing me with a phone in my hand, asked, "Who are you talking to, Rhein?"

"You," I replied.

Bored, she turned to the just-awakened Maggie and they started talking.

The other Vanda hung up.

38.

The lake was slowly blending into the dusk, as quiet now as it would be in an hour when filled by the darkness. It would be as tranquil tomorrow, under the golden glimmer of the day, and later, too, when the bloody streams of sunset would trickle onto its surface.

"Such tranquility," I whispered.

Strauss nodded in agreement.

We were sitting on the beach, watching the swans that would never fly away. Their fattened bodies floated on the water—white creatures with their beaks tucked under their wings, making them appear headless.

"They are sleeping, too," Strauss said, turning in the direction of the three mounds at our side. The black earth was still wet where we'd buried the birds Darcy had killed. "Sleeping," Strauss said. "Felix also. But he will get his second chance. He will wake up, I am sure. You will wake up, too, Rhein."

His old man's hand touched mine encouragingly. There was a peculiar sparkle in his eyes while he stared at the lake. I hadn't told him about the two Vandas and the ghost Wanderer, but I'd told him all about the Artist, even how I had seen him in the cave. I told him how

I had hit rock bottom after finding out that I was no longer myself. It was no wonder he compared me to Felix. After all, his dream probably hadn't been much different from mine. Now my real life belonged to the Artist. My Remorite.

"Strauss, explain your theory to me," I said. "Could the Remorites truly exist?"

"And could they *not* exist?" he said, smiling. "What about the possible, Ray? Does it exist?"

I shrugged.

"Answer me," he insisted.

"Well, if something is only possible, that means that it doesn't exist. Not yet."

"Meaning it's not here now, but could be at some point later. Do you see the contradiction?"

"Do you mean that everything that is possible has to exist now as well?"

"Exactly! Otherwise we would have to admit that at the moment it is nothing, and nothing, Rhein, never and under no circumstances can become something."

"All right," I said. "It is indisputable that the future is contained in the present, but—"

"It is contained, but how? In what shape?" Strauss said, impatiently raising his hand and leaning in closer to me. "In the shape of information, of course. This information, my friend, is not only about the things that might happen, but also about those that, for one reason or another, remain unrealized. Since information is never lost, the question is: *Where* does it go?"

"You think it stays in the past, where the Remorites are. Right?"

"Yes. That's why we call them Remorites. It means 'latecomers.' But you're wrong when you speak about the past, and about time in general, as if it is some sort of abstraction. There is no information without a material body, Rhein. This is a fact that has given me grounds to reach two astonishing conclusions. First, if time is a carrier of information, then it must be material in nature. Second, as any other matter, time is also embedded in space. So our Remorites are somewhere out there. They are there *now!*"

The silence that followed soon felt like a burden.

"They are there, now," I mumbled, skeptically. "But what the hell are they? Are they ghosts?"

"Yes. To us they are ghosts, just as we are to them," Strauss said, seeing the doubt on my face. "I know you're thinking that from an old Einstein look-alike maniac like me only something crazy could come out. That's why you don't believe me."

"On the contrary, I would believe in it only if it were crazy enough. After all that has happened to me here, my criteria for truth have changed."

"So," Strauss said, nodding approvingly, "we have to start from further back. It is a complex hypothesis. I can't explain it in a few sentences, what with it being related to quantum physics, which itself is full of complex and seemingly paradoxical phenomena. Do you know what the terms *superposition* and *decoherence* mean?"

"Not at all."

"Don't worry," he said kindly. "First I'll tell you about one of the most notorious and controversial experiments in physics. In a nutshell, it was conducted by directing photons at a screen with two slits, behind which there was a photographic plate. The photons were directed one by one, not in a bundle, so that, according to common sense, each of them would have been able to pass either through the left or the right slit. But that's not how it happened. The experiment has been repeated thousands of times, and it has been proven, beyond any doubt, that each of the photons passes *simultaneously* through both slits. The same thing happens when electrons are used instead of photons, as well as whole atoms, and even molecules."

Many questions ran through my mind in a very short time, but none of them was sensible enough to ask aloud.

"It was this multiplied manifestation of microparticles that led scientists to the conclusion that, before being registered by the equipment, every particle is simultaneously in all possible states. Or in other words, it is in a quantum state called superposition."

"But since everything in this world is made of microparticles, this means that the superposition in question should be ubiquitous."

"It should be, and, if you ask me, it *really* is. I think it is absurd to claim that between the micro and the macro worlds there is some kind of boundary, on one side of which the objects are in superposition, and on the other they exist in only one state. That's why I think that decoherence is an illusion we have maintained. An instant collapse, disappearance of the superposition at the moment of any type of contact, direct or indirect, between the object and the subject, is what we call decoherence."

"So, according to you, no matter how we influence an object, no collapse ever happens. In other words, the object remains in superposition permanently, but we are constituted so as to receive information about only one of its states, while all the others continue to exist outside the grasp of our perception."

I had never seen Strauss look so enthusiastic.

"I guess you could be right," I said. "After all, who doesn't sense, at least intuitively, that our perceptions reveal only a small part of reality?"

"A tiny part," Strauss emphasized. "For example, astronomical data have definitely convinced us that there is an enormous amount of matter in the universe which is invisible to us, dark matter."

"I've heard of that. But what is it really?"

"No one knows. We register it only from its gravitational effect, and its structure is still a mystery to us. Speaking in general terms, this is matter that is not dependent on light, because it doesn't take part in electromagnetic interactions. It doesn't emit, absorb, or reflect photons.

That is why, Rhein, the so-called light matter, visible and known to us, goes through dark matter like it would through empty space. Do you understand? Hardness is a quality that results from electromagnetic interactions and, more specifically, from the forces of repulsion. We owe to these the mutual impermeability of the bodies in the world visible to us. In dark matter such forces have no . . ."

"Do you think that this matter, that it is time itself? Where not only the objects are in superposition, but also all of us, the subjects? And each of us exists there in all our possible versions, simultaneously?"

"Dark matter is everywhere, Rhein," Strauss said, screwing up his eyes and digging his fingers into his wild hair. "The whole world is immersed into this strange substance, and yes, I do think that it contains time. Because I think that the information about the universe—about what has happened or could have happened, as well as about everything that happens, will happen, or could happen—is encoded in it. I also think that everything that is subject to the forces of light travels through dark matter in its own unique fashion. That's why the paths weaving through its fabric are more numerous than anyone could imagine."

"Paths through time?"

"Through the fourth dimension," Strauss said. "This is why that dimension is so different from the other three we know. We move through time in one direction, and due to this fact we harbor the illusion that time flows. However, the truth is that everything always already exists, frozen once and for all into a global, many-layered superposition. Everything there is unchangeable, static. Eternal."

"And predetermined," I added sullenly.

"Oh, no, it's not predetermined. Not for human beings, Rhein. We are endowed with free will, and this means that the path for us is not just one. We have a choice," Strauss said, making an all-encompassing gesture. "There, in the dark matter, in the form of specific quantum information, exist many versions . . . projections of ourselves. I don't know what exactly to call them. But I know, I believe, that they outline our different paths through time. When we are choosing the path to take, we are actually also choosing which of our versions to realize. In which of them we would become ourselves."

"Good God, Strauss, you're talking about us as if we're some kind of spirits."

"Ghosts," he said. "In this dark matter, that is, in time, each one of us is a ghost."

I clutched at my head. This was maddening.

"Why so surprised?" Strauss said. "I just explained to you that light matter passes through the other without meeting any resistance."

"Aaah, yes," I mumbled.

"Yes, yes," Strauss mumbled, too, leaning back to lie on the sandy ground and placing his hands under his head.

His face was lit up by his thoughts, his eyes staring at the sky flickering above us with countless faraway stars. When he started talking again, it was in a muted and somewhat patient voice.

"We travel endlessly down our winding paths through time, and they are always before us: our possible versions," he said. "Dark shapes woven into dark matter, carrying no life or spirit, or perception. Yet all amazingly different, with different human potential. Designed so as to be able to change us if only we illuminate them with our souls, if only we put our hearts into their silent chests. If only we choose them. And those we pass by? Nothing. They remain the same as they have always been; they remain eternal and immutable in the memory of time."

Strauss rose a bit.

"Not all of them, however. Sometimes it happens that we give up, Rhein, we collapse. Then our Remorites are born, animated by our own losses, by what we have been before. They start to follow us, sometimes catching up, so that they could return to us what we have lost, before leaving us again. Look," he said, pointing at the small burial mounds we had made for the dead swans.

No. He was pointing at the tiny lights wandering above them. Chills ran down my spine. In my mystical haze it took me a few very long seconds until I realized they were just fireflies. I looked around and saw many of them flying around us.

"The Remorites are just like fireflies," Strauss said in a barely audible whisper. "They shine on and go off, they shine on and go off, off into the darkness. Such is your Artist, Rhein. Such is he now."

39.

"Morons!"

It was Darcy, approaching from behind us, a rifle slung across his shoulder and a cartridge belt around his waist. I stood up instantly.

"You're sitting here in the dusk," he said, "gazing at the lake while the killers are roaming the place."

"You are the killer," Strauss said, as he also stood up.

"Nonsense. That servant will live."

"Yes, he will," Strauss said. "But I—"

"But you, old man, dare to call me a murderer because of some lousy swans that look like hens," Darcy said and roared with laughter.

I lunged at Darcy, he jumped back and bared his teeth at me, and Strauss put himself between us, swearing.

"Damn you, my lord." Someone else was cursing, too.

It was Ludo. He and Gromov were coming down the path from the café and soon joined us. I saw that both of them had their revolvers tucked into their belts. Darcy laughed again.

"I brought them with me, Rhein, to protect me," Darcy said. "Because you're one really ferocious artist. Who knows what terrifying things you draw in your spare time when you're not busy beating up peaceful citizens."

"Are you done?" Gromov asked before turning to us. "It's time to discuss the situation. Come with me."

We set off after him and followed him into a glazed gazebo not far from the lake. It was cool inside and it would have been quite comfortable if not for the feeling that we had entered an aquarium. Fine golden sand covered the floor, the chairs were in the shape of seashells, and the table looked like a sea turtle. Artificial seaweed hung from the walls, swaying with the air conditioner, as if with a water current.

"Interesting décor," I said.

"Indeed," Ludo said. "But tonight the café is not at our disposal."

"It won't be even after those savages have gone from there," Darcy said. "The nasty stink from their weeds will remain."

"Those are healing herbs," Strauss said. "They helped save the man you wounded. But instead of thanking them, you call them savages!"

Darcy opened his mouth to respond but he met Gromov's eyes and restrained himself. Meanwhile, Ludo had taken out a bottle of vodka from the liquor cabinet and was now sitting at the table, a glass in his hand. The rest of us helped ourselves, too.

"You are wrong to think that the tribe had a motive to kill Felix," Strauss said once we'd all settled at the table. "It's true that he interrupted their ritual, but as you can see from the recording they sensed him immediately, the moment his mind crossed the barrier. This means that he saw nothing, that he was still blind when they drove him away."

"But they could have murdered him as revenge," Ludo suggested. "Him and the Wanderer."

"Impossible," Strauss said. "According to their faith, murder is not revenge, since those who die a violent death get their second chance automatically. Such people don't even have to fight for it."

"Wow, it's so kind of you to tell us all of this," Darcy said, clapping his hands loudly. "We thought that our servants were evil, while all they've been trying to do is reward us by murdering us. They have nothing but good intentions, sparing us all from having to fight for a second chance. I wonder, why don't they grab their axes and start killing each other?"

Ludo and Gromov laughed, but my solemn expression showed that I sided with Strauss.

"Their motives probably have nothing to do with the ones you imagine," Gromov said a moment later, his face serious again. "But now, if you ask me, there's no doubt that they are the murderers."

This time Strauss only objected with a wave of his hand. I didn't object, either, despite having reasons to do so. Alas, these reasons were not something to share with other people. Now was not the time to bring up the third murdered body in my freezer.

"I don't think it's them," I said.

"Why's that?" Gromov said, looking at me suspiciously. "Do you know something that is still a secret to us?"

"What about you?" Strauss said. "What do you know?"

"The same as you," Gromov replied. "But now I think that their superstitions are at the bottom of these murders. As you well know, according to them this oasis is a living entity, a demon or something of the sort. They probably interpret the anomaly as a sign from it. A call for sacrifices, say. Do you understand?"

"But if that's the case," Ludo said, knitting his brow, "then they should have sensed the anomaly much earlier than us, before it became strong enough to influence the complex's electronics. More importantly, this anomaly should be something familiar, something that has happened before."

"You are absolutely right," Gromov said. "Since Natalia is close with them, we'll ask her to make some inquiries."

"No," Ludo said, baring his teeth and bristling like an angry dog. "Don't involve her in this! She has to stay out of this, I'm warning you."

"OK, OK, Ludo. Anyway, it's not Natalia, but the two A's who are closest to the servants," Darcy said, turning to me. "Listen, Rhein, yesterday we had a fight with the A's, and now you're the only one who could get to them. Go to their villa tomorrow, ask them a question or two. These simple peasants plow their gardens shoulder to shoulder with the savages, so they might have heard some bits of information about previous anomalies, provided such have occurred, of course."

"They are in villa number 10," Strauss said.

"I will go," I said.

We poured ourselves another round of drinks and asked Gromov what he thought.

"I think that it is no coincidence that the security people disappeared the day after the murders," he said. "I think that they found out the identity of the murderer, or murderers, and paid for it with their lives. The other personnel guessed what awaited them and hurried to get out of here, before the anomaly took down the electronics and the helicopters."

"Well, at least Hans and Wilma must have gotten lucky," Ludo said. "They must have been somewhere nearby and the personnel took them."

"You think so?" Darcy said. "Did it happen like that or have they also become victims of the sacrificial rituals?"

"Many questions remain," Gromov said through a smile, though his gray eyes remained cold and staring pressingly at me. "For example, why is there still no rescue crew? What happened to all the fuel? Maybe the Oasis-Demon, eh, Rhein? Or have you got another guess?"

He didn't pretend to wait for an answer. He just stood up and left, followed by Ludo and Darcy. They shut the door, but the lights in the gazebo were soft enough for me and Strauss to see their silhouettes through the glass wall. None of them looked around. They headed for the small forest ahead of them and disappeared in it together.

40.

When I got back to the villa, I found two notes. The first one, on the kitchen table, was from Vanda, who informed me that she was going to spend the night with Maggie and Natalia. I found the second one on my pillow in the bedroom; it was from Chari:

> *Go into the bathroom and open the cabinet by the mirror. Keep in mind that I found those things in your garage, where—according to DELETED data in the Butler—someone was at 11:46 pm the night Felix was killed! Think about the conclusions you can draw from this. I will come tomorrow to compare notes.*

I undressed, got into bed, and turned off the lamp. To a certain extent, I had gotten used to the kid's tricks, but playing with me from a distance via written instructions was too much.

For five minutes I tossed and turned like a lunatic. I got up, went into the bathroom, and opened the cabinet. There was a black plastic bag and inside it, a spray can of chloroform, a key, and something wrapped in a special absorbent towel, just like the ones I used in the studio.

I put these unpleasant objects on the table. For a moment or two, my eyes remained fixed on my reflection in the mirror. I felt sick. The look in my eyes was devoid of intelligence, and there was an idiotic smile on my face. I spent some time trying to summon a more normal expression, but then I forgot to check if I had succeeded. I leaned over the towel and unwrapped it carefully, afraid that I might find something terrible inside. The friendly face of Gaston Fouchet was looking at me from his ID card.

The towel also contained a phone, a miniature flashlight, aspirin in a plastic blister, and packs of chewing gum and mints. These were all probably from Fouchet's pockets. It was obvious why the murderer had taken them out, wrapped them in a towel picked from the studio, and hidden them in my garage. But why had he put them in the black plastic bag, along with the chloroform and the key?

I sat down on the stool by the mirror and started thinking. When the connection with my bracelet had been restored, the murderer must have found out where I was. Then he decided to take advantage of the situation and eliminate the Wanderer, making sure all the evidence led back to me. He took the can and the bag and went to the Wanderer's villa, using the universal code to get inside—proving that he is someone from the staff, most likely a medic or a guard. He threatens the Wanderer and forces him to the cave. Once they're both there, he has the Wanderer unlock the door for me, while he himself stands out of sight. The Wanderer, however, does not obey, and even tries to warn me.

When I went back for the broken flashlight, the murderer unlocks the door. He remains hidden at the exit, waiting for me, but loses control over the Wanderer, who dashes toward the precipice. The murderer, however, does not run after him, at least not immediately. When I emerge he puts the damned black bag over my head, waits for the chloroform to kick in, takes my bracelet, and then heads for the precipice. He sees the Wanderer there, standing at the edge, throwing stones, trying to alert Maggie, Strauss, and Chari that something terrible is happening. The murderer seizes the opportunity to push the Wanderer over the edge, before dragging me out of the park, and, finally, throwing my bracelet somewhere near the cave, in order for the security people to find it and draw their conclusions. Luckily for me, though, Chari found it before they did.

I stood up, splashed cold water on my face, and sat back down.

As for the key, I supposedly found it at the cave entrance, unlocked the metal door, but then, out of sheer absentmindedness, dropped it into my pocket, so later on I had had to hide it, along with the other pieces of evidence. But what kind of evidence were the can and the bag? After all, they were not used *by* me, but *on* me.

He used them on Felix, too, I realized, horrified. He made Felix call me and ask for my help by telling me all the nonsense about the Wanderer. He also made him write more such nonsense on his computer. By the time I arrived he had drugged the poor boy using the chloroform. He must have taken the jeep to the gate to keep me in the villa longer. While I was waiting for Felix to return the car, the boy was actually lying unconscious in the next room. Unconscious, but alive. I could have saved him, had I just looked around, instead of sleeping in the study. That's why I hadn't heard the murderer entering and taking the Capricorn from the desk. He killed the boy with it, and then he staged the appearance of the ghoulish Wanderer. That was the one detail that didn't quite fit, but all the rest of it made sense when looked at from this angle.

As for the murder of Gaston Fouchet, well, it was self-evident.

I took his phone and, unsurprisingly, there was not a single number in it, or a text message or any other information that could tell me something about his communication with other people. Everything had been erased.

I dropped the phone and the other objects back into the bag and went to the disintegrator. In a moment, I heard the muted clanking of the grinder down there, somewhere in the villa's basement.

I returned to the bedroom and collapsed on the bed. If there was anything positive about Chari's little present for me it was that I hadn't been thinking about Remorites, the Vandas, and all the other mysteries. I was extremely tired, so I fell asleep right away, as if I had been knocked out with a hammer.

41.

Alvaro and Adela turned out to be a nice couple, who, despite being past middle age, had well-toned bodies, lively smiles, and more energy than most teenagers. They looked like each other, like so many couples do after they've been together for a long time, working and living for similar interests and aims. Their aims, at least in my opinion, were not to be underestimated. I knew that the moment we started walking along the perfectly aligned rows of vegetables and other plants, the result not only of hard work, but also of scientific knowledge. During our walk I saw many beautiful flowers, whose colors managed to partially bring back to life my artistic sensibility. In Alvaro and Adela's garden, I found myself in another world, one that was contrary to the world outside, in which so many terrible and mysterious events happened. Here, even the servants looked different—dressed in motley clothes, loud spoken, smiling wide, working happily, and with the feeling that no one underestimated them or treated them like servants.

"We now have test fields around their village, too," Adela told me. "The land in the oasis is—"

"Ideal," Alvaro said enthusiastically. "We used to live in a harsh and miserly climate before, but here everything is generous."

"Our dream has come true," Adela said. "We have always wanted to put our ideas into practice, but we never hoped for such an opportunity. Yet here we are. Chance, in the shape of a piece of paper, has given us everything we ever wanted!"

"Hey, don't call our luck a piece of paper," Alvaro said. "No, it was a lottery ticket."

"I see you've hired many helping hands," I said.

"They are our friends," Adela answered. "We've been working together for three years. We're really close now."

"Just imagine that some people think their tribe has something to do with the murders," I said.

Alvaro and Adela exchanged glances, and their faces grew solemn.

"I'm sorry," I said.

"We guessed you hadn't come here because of the onions and the pumpkins," Alvaro said. "Come, let's talk."

We walked to the house and sat at a large table on the roof terrace. Adela went in to make some tea, while Alvaro and I tried to return to the casual tone with which we had begun our acquaintance. We exchanged a series of pleasantries until he waved his hand, indicating there was no need to keep beating around the bush.

"I know some people believe the tribe to be murderers. But we think that's a story invented by the actual murderer. We think it is Darcy."

"But we have no proof," Adela said, joining us again with a tray in her hands. "It is true that he has a terrible temper, but this is not enough to accuse him of murder. That's why we shouldn't talk about him any further. The tribe, however, we should discuss, because we know them better than anyone."

"You don't have to defend them. I don't believe they had anything to do with the murders."

"Let's hope it's true," Adela said.

"What?" I said.

"That you don't suspect the tribe," Adela said. "Rhein, they told us about how you unequivocally showed them that you do suspect them of murdering the Wanderer. All they ever felt for that man was pure gratitude."

"They had dressed a doll in his bloody shirt. Then they threw it in the fire, dancing and singing at the same time. All this was happening while the Wanderer's corpse was rotting among the rocks. Is this any way to express gratitude?"

"It's not rotting anymore," Alvaro said. "They burned that, too."

"On a funeral pyre," Adela said. "It wasn't easy for them to make such a decision. They knew that they risked being accused of his murder, yet they followed all the steps of the ritual. They wanted to quicken the transition to his second chance."

"You seem to take their superstitions quite seriously," I said.

"No, not entirely," Alvaro said. "But what's important in this case is that they take them seriously, which only proves that their actions have been all in good faith."

"Yes," Adela said. "As I already told you, they were grateful to the Wanderer. Some time ago, there was a fire in their village and he helped them put it out. He saved the life of an old woman by taking her out of her hut, risking his own life. He always treated them well."

"Uh-huh," I mumbled, putting an end to the discussion.

I drank my tea, and the richness of its aroma restored the peacefulness and serenity that I felt surrounded everything in this place. I sighed and closed my eyes. When I opened them, I saw that Alvaro and Adela were looking at me with understanding and concern, somewhat like parents. I sighed again. No one had ever looked at me in that way.

"It's nice, your place is very nice," I said, genuinely moved.

"You should come more often," Alvaro suggested.

"You are always welcome," Adela said.

"Tell me, what will you do once your contract with the Agency expires?"

"Oh, we have a whole year to go," Alvaro said. "Then we'll stay for a while with the tribe. They have an electric generator now so we'll be able to install our laboratory there."

"We used the rest of the jackpot to invest in the laboratory, and now we're almost broke," Adela said.

"Yes, but you've created all kinds of valuable seeds," I said. "Can't you sell them?"

"We'll get rich again," she said optimistically, "and we'll return to this place here, creating more valuable seeds."

They laughed, and I laughed with them. Then I remembered the main question I had to ask them.

"Have you discussed the anomaly with the tribe?"

"Yes," Alvaro said, "but they don't think there is an anomaly in the oasis. They are quite adamant about it, but they might be wrong."

"They are," I said, despite thinking the opposite.

42.

"They are here! They are here again . . . I can see them . . ." Natalia's voice faded away.

"Hello, hello," I said. "Natalia, I can't hear you. Where are you?"

"I'm in my villa . . . in the hall . . . Rhein, you are here, too!"

"No, no, I'm in the car," I said, hitting the gas. "I'm coming! Just stay calm!"

Natalia's gate was open. I sped up to her villa and jumped out of the jeep. I ran into the house, where Natalia greeted me with a happy smile and a zombie stare.

"It's all true, Rhein. There is no doubt anymore."

"You think so?" I said, looking around but unable to see anything out of the ordinary. "That's wonderful."

"Isn't it?"

"Of course," I said, slowly walking toward her, summoning a serene expression on my face so as not to scare her.

She looked at me and then turned her eyes to something on my left.

"Oh, how different you are," she said, pointing at a lantern. "God! You don't look like each other at all!"

"It's not surprising that I look nothing like a lantern," I said, placing my arm around her waist and leading her to the sofa.

"You're not so handsome with a beard," she said, "but you're more interesting-looking, more artistic."

"You're right. I've been focusing on being handsome recently, so I shaved off the beard."

A sleeping pill. I had to give her a sleeping pill, but then an entirely different thought crossed my mind. My whole body broke out in a cold sweat. She had never seen me with a beard. So how did she know about it? Was she pointing at the lantern or at *somebody* standing next to it? The Artist?

I stared at the lantern so hard that tears welled up in my eyes. But no, I didn't see him. I felt both disappointed and relieved. *From Vanda,* I thought suddenly. *She must have heard about my beard from Vanda.*

"How was last night?" I asked cheerfully. "Vanda left a note saying she was spending the night here. Seems like the gossip kept you up. I bet you have sleeping pills. Just tell me where you keep them, and I'll bring you one right away."

"They are going away," she said with sad, faraway eyes. "You're going away, too. But I . . . I stay!"

I took out my phone and made several hectic attempts to get in touch with Maggie, none of them successful.

"Natalia," I said, "we have to get out of here. Right now. Listen, you are hallucinating. Don't believe your eyes, trust your mind."

"I am getting on the stage," she said, rising up and bowing before her imaginary audience. "I haven't given up. It was only a dream in some distant oasis."

She bowed again, and set off with dancing steps toward the middle of the room, where there was furniture. Her face was illuminated by joy. I opened my mouth to tell her another sobering truth, but stopped myself. She was happy. Why should I bring her back to reality?

I leaned back, resigned. I waited for her to live her hallucinations to the end, wishing they would continue for longer. Dressed in a light-green silk robe, she began moving to the rhythm of the music only she could hear. The once prima ballerina Natalia Shidlovskaya.

Her dance was becoming more and more energetic. She took off her slippers, kicking them aside. Her heavy body swirled in a whirl-wind of heightened tempo, her robe now fluttering, disclosing the pale flesh of her thighs, now twisting around them. Her bare feet with pearly pink toenails were making swift, tiny steps. Their complexity at moments impeded her balance, making her sway.

I wanted to turn my eyes away, but didn't have the courage to. I was afraid that Natalia, even in this state, could somehow sense the feelings her lumbering dance evoked in me. I sat there, watching her, with the false expression of keen interest on my face, and with a lump stuck in my throat.

The light coming from the windows spilled over the opposite wall, lending a strange brilliance to the dark picture hanging there. When Natalia would move close to it, a violet shadow would fall on her face—a reflection of the light coming off the picture. Then only the moon on the canvas would remain clear and bright, enveloped in the magnificence of its halo.

A Full Moon. My painting. I had painted it ten years ago, and here it was now, the background for an ex-ballerina's dance. She was danc-ing between day and night.

I heard vulgar laughter. It came from somewhere nearby, but Natalia didn't hear it. I stood up. She didn't see me. I moved behind her and dashed for the just-shut door. I went out in the hallway, shak-ing with anger. The laughter echoed again, this time from a greater distance. I followed the sound. *I'll kill whoever it is,* I said to myself. Or was it the Artist who said that?

"Ha-ha-ha!" This time I heard my own laughter.

Then came other noises that led me to the door at the end of the hallway. It was ajar and I could hear muted whispering. There was more than one person. The whispering was joined by soft giggling, which simply drove me mad. I stopped thinking, kicked open the door, and stormed into the room. Spacious, half-dark, it smelled of staleness and dust.

I turned on the lights. There were many pieces of gym equipment behind which the nasty freaks could be hiding. Though now the whispering had been replaced by heavy breathing.

"You're scared?" I called. "Come out! Show yourself."

They did not. They were lurking, panting, as if not lungs but bellows exhaled. A sense of danger finally made its way through my brain, and lodged itself between my anger and my puzzlement. I pulled an iron bar from the weights stand. The smell of staleness hit my nose, and just then I noticed that one of the windows was open, while all the rest were closed, with the blinds rolled down. *Someone must have opened it just a moment ago.*

The heavy breathing still wheezed from behind a ramp of some kind, which was nestled into the corner. I moved in that direction with silent, preying steps, clutching the bar in my hand, asking myself whether it was possible at all for a human being to breathe in such a monstrous manner.

I reached the ramp and stopped in front of it.

"Come out," I said with determination that I didn't feel.

I waited. I made a few steps to the side and kicked the ramp. It fell down. I jumped back. At first, I didn't see anything but the empty corner. Then I saw a small iPod-like device on the floor. It was breathing loudly.

"A recording," I whispered to myself.

Terrified, I turned my head to the open window. I understood—I understood everything.

43.

Natalia was sitting on the sofa, her head drooping, her hands resting on her knees. She looked like a woman lost in thought, or a woman remembering something extremely sad. But Natalia wasn't thinking or remembering anything now; she was dead. Blood dripped from her smashed skull and onto her lap, staining her white, forever-resting hands. A statuette was on the floor behind the sofa, its white marble flecked with blood.

I wanted to rush after the killer, but I knew that I would never find him and that this would only amount to an escape on my part. It would be my excuse for the cowardice of leaving this woman without even touching her, without even looking her in the face, without even sitting next to her as a friend to lend her support at the start of her breathless, eternal meeting with Death.

I gently raised her head. Her frozen expression told me more than she herself would have been able to tell me had she been alive. On it, like a stamp, was sealed the pain of humiliation. Yes, she had heard the vulgar laughter. She had realized how pathetic her dance was. She had seen herself through my eyes. But she had managed to stay calm—she had tried to keep her dignity, at least a little, by pretending to still hear only the imaginary applause, under the exalted eyes of her former admirers.

"I'm sorry, I'm sorry," I whispered meekly, sitting next to her. "Remember, Natalia, despite everything, you came to the end of your life as a prima ballerina. You continued to dance!"

"Stand up!"

The cold muzzle of a revolver pressed against my temple.

"Get up!"

I did not stand up or even move. An inexpressible, overwhelming exhaustion came over me. The revolver's muzzle moved away. What followed was the sound of shuffling feet going around the sofa. It was Ludo. His gladiator's frame stood between me and the open window. His hair, so blond it was almost white, glimmered around his head as if electrified. His face was expressionless. The revolver, however, was shaking in his hand so hard that its muzzle at moments pointed at Natalia, instead of me.

"Be careful," I said.

"Stand up," he repeated.

I had no intention of obeying him. I decided to follow one of my own desires, probably my last one. I rose to my feet and went to my painting. I stood facing it and saw, remembered actually, that it was not as dark as it looked from a distance. I also remembered those precious moments when I had had the feeling that the moon itself was painting, that it was drawing on the canvas the fine, golden contours, pushing the darkness, little by little, out of this empty, rocky beach.

I turned to Ludo.

"Slowly," he told me. "I will kill you very slowly."

"Why?"

"To bring back the memories of the good times."

"You, too?"

"No," he said, stepping back. "You're trying to provoke me to kill you quickly, but it won't happen."

He stared at me with unblinking, glassy eyes, clearly trying hard to keep his composure. But he couldn't—the expressionless mask of a thug cracked and fell apart. He turned his head to Natalia and from his throat came a long sound—something that was both a roar and a moan.

I lunged at him, knocking the gun from his hand. He came to his senses immediately. We both jumped for the weapon, but I reached it first. We stood there, facing each other.

"I didn't kill her," I said. "I have never killed anyone. Understand?"

"I don't believe you. She called me, told me to come. She was scared. She said that you were here."

"She called me, too. She was hallucinating. She told me she could see the Remorites again, and among them she had identified my image."

"Stop it! Don't lie!"

"The murderer fooled me. He made me leave the hall. I left her alone."

I threw the revolver at his feet.

"Shoot, if you really don't believe me."

He reached for the revolver with hesitation, but did not pick it up. Instead he fell on his knees before the dead woman.

44.

I drove back to the villa in a strange dreamlike state. As soon as I passed through the gate, I hid the jeep behind a tufty shrub off the driveway. I got out and set off stealthily in the direction of the house, using the landscaping as cover. The branches scratched my skin and tore my trousers. I stepped dangerously close to a hornet's nest. But at least I was sure that I had taken all the precautions not to be seen by Vanda. I didn't want to be the one to break the news about Natalia, which was just one reason I had to avoid her company. But whose company was I trying to avoid, anyway? Maybe that of a vampire, while the real Vanda was sipping coffee with her father thousands of miles away from here.

I felt truly sick. All I wanted was to stop dealing with this nightmare, but seeing Chari's dog tied up to one of the palm trees by the pool meant that it would all just continue along. I hesitated for a moment and decided that before showing myself, I'd better change the torn trousers, if nothing else. I snuck into the villa and could hear that Chari and Vanda were in the kitchen, talking and laughing. I made for the dining room and peeked into the kitchen. The scene there was almost blissful. Her sleeves rolled up, Vanda—or "Vanda"?—was fussing about Chari, who was sitting at the table, eating with such gusto that it made me envious. She produced a richly ornamented cake from the fridge and the kid greeted it with joy as spontaneous as her contentment at finally being appreciated as a good housewife. They ate the cake before Vanda announced it was time to check on Hector.

As soon as they went out with treats for the dog I ran upstairs and managed to take a very quick shower. I put on my bathrobe and went straight into the bedroom. I looked through the window and saw that they were still outside. How normal it all looked.

My phone began to ring. It was Kort. I took a deep breath, trying to gather my senses. This time I had to explain the situation in a formal, convincing tone.

"Hello, Kort. Listen—"

"Rhein? No! How is this possible?"

"What?"

"Hello? Who's there?" Kort said, his voice bordering on hysteria. "Who's calling?"

"What do you mean? You called me."

"I didn't call. Wasn't it you who called me? It really does sound like you. Is it you, Rhein?"

"No. I mean, it wasn't me who called. You called me, Kort. But, yes, this is me. I am Rhein."

"This is impossible!"

"What is?"

"Where are you calling from?"

"I am calling from hell," I said. "I've got a place reserved just for you!"

I expected him to laugh or tell me off but instead he sounded like he'd been kicked by a horse.

"Listen, Kort, get yourself together. We have to talk."

"Rhein, where are you?" he screamed.

"I am at the oasis. What's wrong with you, man?"

"OK, I'll calm down. Wait just a moment."

I waited, for quite a while. The strain on my nerves was enormous, because the connection could cut out at any moment now, and such pathological behavior from a stable and calm person like Kort could mean nothing good.

"Rhein, I was at the oasis," he said finally. "I came back from there only a week ago."

"You were here, without even stopping to see me? Why didn't you say anything yesterday?"

"What do you mean, 'yesterday'?"

"When we spoke on the phone."

"Rhein," he said, bursting into tears. "Last time you and I talked was ten days ago. Do you hear me? Ten days ago! You told me you needed help. I came, but I was too late."

"You were late for what? What happened?"

He fell silent, in a very peculiar way, as if he could not muster the courage to utter the horrible truth.

"Speak," I said, shaking. "Kort, tell me."

"I was late," he said. "I found . . . your . . . corpse. You had killed yourself, Rhein. You were dead. You looked terrible! I am telling you, we last talked ten days ago, but your dead body was at least a year old. I don't understand, I don't."

"Me, neither."

"But I saw you with my own eyes, no doubt about that. It was you. In the bathtub. There could be no doubt."

His voice was fading. I heard crackling on the line.

"Kort! Kort, what about my paintings? Did you receive the paintings?"

"Yes."

"Have you looked at them? What are they like, Kort?"

"They are nothing, my friend. I received thirty blank white canvases wrapped in paper."

45.

I don't know what I did for that next hour after my conversation with Kort. I didn't care. "I received thirty blank white canvases." Only these words mattered to me. Only they stood out, bright against the blurry, muddy stream of my consciousness. This would probably have gone on for quite a while, if not for the banging and shuffling noises of things being dragged across the floor downstairs.

Then the loud sounds stopped and my phone rang again. This time it was Vanda. But which one?

"Yes?" I whispered.

"Rhein, where are you?"

"I am at Guaranteed Peace, of course! Where are you?"

"At your villa, waiting for you with the child."

"I am not a child," Chari shouted.

"Maggie called just now," Vanda said. "She told me about Natalia. When are you coming back?"

"Don't worry," I said. "Don't wait for me, I won't be back before this evening."

"Are you sure?"

"Yes, I am absolutely sure, Vanda. Bye," I said and then hung up.

Their noisy activities continued and I heard them heading outside. I went to the window and watched them hauling out a large, long object stuffed in a black garbage bag. They crossed the driveway and made for the farthest end of the park. The dog, still tied to the palm tree by the pool, howled after them.

"So, this is how things are," I said as the pieces of this entire disgusting puzzle were arranging themselves in my head.

I smoothed down my hair and dressed tidily. I went down to the first floor and checked the room with the freezers, confirming what I already knew: the deeply frozen Gaston Fouchet was now gone.

Having nowhere to hurry off to, I drank a cup of coffee and made a sandwich in the kitchen. But I wasn't able to swallow even a bite. I drank some water and went out. I felt no need to sneak around. The two of them were busy digging somewhere. I found them without trouble and moved closer, without being noticed. I casually leaned against a tree and crossed my arms.

Their work was going smoothly, as they had chosen a crumbly, sandy spot for the grave. They were not talking. Vanda was so carried away by what she was doing that she threw some soil on the body, which startled her. She actually took the time to brush it off, as if he wouldn't be entirely covered by it in a moment. It was only then, when she raised her head, that I saw her face clearly. Tears were trickling down her cheeks.

"What a brilliant special effect," I shouted, clapping my hands. "The vampire's tears, am I right?"

Neither she nor Chari was as surprised to see me as they should have been. They leaned on their shovels and stared at me with something like tedium in their eyes.

"This is it," I said maliciously. "I will not come home in the evening because I am already here. I was in my bedroom when you called. That's where I talked with you, Vanda, just to see how far you would go in your scheming."

They were still silent.

"You have nothing to say, Vanda? You have no excuse?" I said, pointing an accusatory finger at her. "On top of it all, you lure the boy into your wicked game."

"I insisted that we bury him," Chari said. "She didn't want to."

"Why would she? She wanted him to be found in my freezer. I know, Vanda, I know everything now!" I said, stepping up to the unfinished grave. "Here is the whole story. You arrive here, instead of your father, and you find me in a state of spiritual and mental decline. You read my diary. 'Schizophrenia,' you say to yourself, happily devising your satanic plan. You kill this poor guy in the bag with the idea of framing me to increase the price of my paintings, which you had already decided to steal. But then you give in to panic and fly away with the helicopter. On the way, though, your cold, calculating self wins over your fear, and you come back."

"Rhein, come to your senses," she said, crying.

"Don't interrupt me!" I roared. "You come back to my place. You get in touch with your father and make that recording, which he would later play to me over the phone to drive me entirely crazy, making me believe there're two of you. You arrange another call from him during which he tells me that he has received blank canvases. Oh, and by the way, he found my corpse, which had been rotting away in the bathtub for almost a year."

Vanda climbed out of the shallow grave, holding the shovel.

"Stop right there," I warned her. "You also killed the Wanderer, Felix, and even Natalia today. But you set it all up to lead the cops straight to me. The psychopathic serial killer! This is the image you have carefully and purposefully been creating for me since the moment you arrived. You're hoping to make me try to kill myself again, because your father has already forged some documents to claim that I sold you my paintings . . . which . . . which probably are sublime, true masterpieces, and they are mine. They are my paintings!"

I swayed, feeling dizzy.

"Ray," Chari said, in a quiet voice, "whoever called you, it wasn't her father. It's impossible. Absolutely no one outside the oasis could get in touch with you. With us, I mean."

"Oh, come on," I said, panting. "There is no anomaly."

"Of course there isn't," Chari said, climbing out of the grave. "But the murderer, he is manipulating you."

"He? You mean she! She! Her! The vampire!"

I burst into uncontrollable laughter through which I vaguely felt Vanda slapping me.

46.

I was on the sofa in the living room, a wet towel on my brow. Vanda and Chari were sitting on stools opposite me, looking very worried and torturing me with their silence. They had insisted on hearing everything I had been through. Now, my story finished, they looked as if they wanted to let it pass without comment.

Chari stood up and removed the towel. He handed it to Vanda and she soaked it in the bowl of cold water on the table. She wrung it out and handed it back to him so he could reapply it to my forehead.

"Don't worry," I said, smiling wearily. "I am fine now."

"No, you're not fine," Vanda said. "Actually, you're okay. Any other person in your place would be in much worse shape."

"Any other person in his place would have gone mad by now," Chari said. "You've managed to resist, even on the verge of madness."

"You're right," I said. "It's amazing that my mind has survived these nightmares."

"It is one nightmare," Chari said, "and it is called ignorance."

"He's right, Rhein," Vanda said. "It's unacceptable that an educated man should believe such nonsense. The fact that you are an artist is not an excuse."

"You think that everything I have just told you is a figment of my imagination or some delirious nonsense?"

"No," she said. "We believe that what happened to you was real. But your interpretation . . . Why, it's primitive, Rhein, barbaric."

"That's it," I said, throwing the towel and sitting up. "Get out of here, leave me alone."

"Easy, Ray," Chari said, patting me on the shoulder and sitting next to me. "Voice synthesis, that's the answer. The technology to imitate any person's voice with a computer already exists. The recording of a single sentence is the only thing you need to make an analysis of the person's speech patterns, and then, via virtual simulation of the vocal cords, to create a voice sounding just like that person's."

"You understand, don't you?" Vanda said. "Before the mobile connections were interrupted, I spoke with my father a couple of times. The murderer somehow recorded his voice, along with his phone number."

"The murderer is also a computer genius," Chari said. "Yesterday I managed to break deeper into the complex's server and made a few checks."

"What checks?" I asked. "Are they connected to the anomaly?"

"Some of them, yes. But, as even you have already guessed, there is no anomaly, really. The killer has simply blocked our access to certain modules of the server, preventing us from making contact with the outside world. He also emptied the fuel reserves. He's been able to manipulate everything in order to murder us all without much effort. He's treating us like mice caught in a trap."

"But we're not mice," Vanda said.

"You're right, of course," Chari said, lowering his head. "I'm ashamed to admit it, but all of his actions, including the murders, were made possible, to a considerable extent, by me."

"You?" I said.

"Sadly, yes, Ray. There is no doubt that the murderer is quite familiar with your problems."

"How?" I said.

"He must have tapped into the signals emitted from the bug I installed in your bracelet. So he would have heard everything. That's why he decided on a series of murders staged to be traced back to the 'schizophrenic artist who has problems with his memory.'"

"First category expert, server administrator," I said. "That was Fouchet's job title on the missing person report. So by killing him the murderer gained complete control over the server, and through it, over the entire complex."

"He even linked to the server using your Butler," Chari said. "It was easy for him to make it look like Gaston Fouchet came to your villa to fix some router and you trapped him there and forced him to participate in your weird psycho activities."

"To ensure the plausibility of his story," Vanda said, "he decided to really drive you crazy with all the staged performances, using manipulated recordings of everyone's voices to lure you from one murder scene to the next."

"So today, he called Ludo while impersonating Natalia," I said. "He even impersonated the dispatcher who lied to me about the helicopter carrying my paintings, and Major Liotta, too."

"He's meddled with all of the complex's communication systems," Chari said.

"The murderer was the one who brought me back here with the helicopter," Vanda said.

"At least he brought you back here," Chari said. "He probably won't be that kind to the personnel."

"What?" she said.

"What do you mean by that?" I said.

"Don't tell me you still think that all those people reached the city? Don't you realize that the murderer fooled them with the emergency evacuation signal? My guess is that he simply got rid of them."

"Wait," Vanda said. "Fouchet could not have been the only person with such responsibilities. He must have had at least one fellow administrator."

"He must have," Chari said. "Quite possibly the murderer himself. But, of course, it could have been anyone from the personnel, or one of the tenants."

"I don't believe any of the tenants is a computer genius," I said.

"We can't exclude anyone from our list of suspects," Chari said. "We have to be constantly on alert. Yesterday I made a mistake by supposing that the murderer had left with the personnel. Today he proved me wrong by killing Natalia."

"I still can't believe she's dead," Vanda said. "We were together last night, talking. We became really close."

"Vanda," I said. "I know this will sound like a crazy question to ask, but please answer it. Did you tell Natalia that I had a beard until recently?"

"No, Rhein. Who would care about that?"

"I haven't mentioned it to anyone, either," Chari said.

"We are discussing such serious and horrible matters, and you ask about your beard?" Vanda said, casting paranoid eyes around the room. "What if the murderer has heard us, what if he's listening to us right now?"

"He is clever, sly, and cautious," Chari said. "He would never risk leaving bugs in the villa of the one person he is trying to turn into the main suspect."

"You're right," I said. "If the cops found bugs here it would derail the murderer's whole scheme."

"But there are no cops on the horizon," Vanda said. "No rescue on the way. What are we going to do?"

"Something could always go wrong—this is a wisdom the murderer respects. That's why he's trying to foresee even the least likely outcomes. There is one thing he is unable to foresee, however," Chari said.

"What is it?" I said.

"What the murderer can never foresee is my part in the game. I am his fatal element. I am his nemesis. I and no other!"

47.

After his grand statement, Chari rushed out. It was only at the end of the park that I managed to catch up with him. I reached out, clutched at his shirt collar, and did not let go, despite Hector's warning growl.

"What's the matter with you, Chari?" I said, fighting for breath. "Why did you leave so suddenly?"

"Listen, Ray, didn't you notice I'm in a hurry?" Chari said, slipping out of my grip and setting off again.

I followed him. I had no choice. But when we reached the spot where I had hidden the jeep, I took the dog's leash and led him into the vehicle.

"You're playing with fire," Chari grunted, but just as I expected he joined us.

"You can't wander the complex all by yourself," I said.

"Damn it," Chari said. "We used to have so much fun, me and the Artist."

"I'm sure it was fun," I sighed. "Too bad I don't remember."

"You will remember, Ray. The Artist is not one of those who remain Remorites forever."

"Enough, enough already. Haven't we settled this? The Remorites do not exist."

"Seems like you haven't really grasped Strauss's hypothesis."

"I got it but didn't think it was very convincing."

"It is extremely convincing. Thing is, to people like you and me, Strauss explains it only in the most basic manner. He has developed his theory with exceptional scientific precision. With equations, formulas, and all the other stuff that comes straight from the heart of quantum physics. And more precisely, from the phenomenon known as super-position and from Heidelberg's principle."

"Heisenberg," I said. "You mean Heisenberg."

"Maybe. But first of all, Ray, I mean Strauss. Gunther Strauss! He has a degree in theoretical physics. We should trust him! The Remorites do exist and he has proven it, beyond doubt. How can you deny it after all you've been through?"

"I've been mostly through my own stupidity," I said bitterly.

"True, but there are also facts that have nothing to do with your stupidity or with the murderer's tricks. In the cave, for example, you really saw the Artist, and the other Remorite ghosts. You saw the death cloud hover over the Wanderer's body. The question is what exactly you saw in Felix's study," Chari said, before contemplating the thought for a moment. "Drive to his villa, Ray."

"I'll drive. But I'll take you to your father and tell him to keep an eye on you."

"Do you want me to find out who the murderer is?"

"I don't want the murderer to find you, Chari. I worry about you. You hacked the server, acquired information that might lead to identi-fying the murderer, and you probably left some traces that could lead him to you. Maybe he has already found out it was you."

"He would have to perform some really tough checks to get to me. But what makes this information so dangerous to him? Nothing! After all, his entire set of tricks would eventually be attributed to Fouchet and, in the end, to you."

"So that's why you buried Fouchet. If he remained in the freezer, then even the best specialists would never have been able to determine the day of his death."

"Exactly, now the degree of decomposition will serve as evidence against the murderer."

"Only if he continues to use Fouchet's account."

"He will, no doubt about that. How else would he enter the server—by using his own account?"

"Of course not. I meant that he has already achieved his goal by isolating us here, and now there's no need to mess with the server anymore."

"You're wrong," Chari said. "He has to keep in touch with the bosses at the Agency on Fouchet's behalf and fool them into thinking that everything is okay here. Otherwise, they'd immediately dispatch a rescue crew."

"Yet," I mumbled, "it's still very possible that you made some mistakes."

"Mistakes, no. Risky moves, yes, like the one I'm about to make. I need to hack the passwords for Fouchet's account. Once I get them we'll get in touch with the Agency, and that will be it. Everything will be all right."

48.

It was early afternoon, but Felix's study looked as if night had already fallen. We just stood there, next to each other, in the frame of the open door. We felt no particular desire to enter. Finally, I clutched harder at the knife I had taken from the kitchen downstairs, and stepped forward. The lights automatically went on. I looked around. The blinds were rolled down on every window, the computer and the security system control panel were turned off, and the poster with the Renegade was put back in its place, hiding the enormous picture of Felix the "happy child." It seemed like whoever put his body into the freezer tried to freeze everything around here, as well.

Chari went in, too, followed by Hector.

"There are crooked mirrors behind most of these posters," he said softly, closing the door.

"I know."

"Not behind Spiderman, though. That was his favorite superhero, the only one that would remain on the wall during his parents' visits. Once his father tried to tear it down but Felix managed to stop him. They almost had a fight. Can you imagine?"

"Did they come here often?" I asked.

"Not more than three or four times in the year and a half he was here. I'm sure they won't mourn for him much. Just like my parents."

"Yours won't mourn for you because you're going to be alive and well for many, many years ahead."

"I will be alive and well, Ray, but only after I die and get my second chance."

I went to one of the windows and opened it. I rested my elbows on the windowsill and looked outside, reaching up to stroke my nonexistent Neanderthal beard. This reminded me of Natalia and her hallucinations. Could it be that she really had been seeing both me and the Artist at the same time? "Here." Chari's voice startled me. "He was here, wasn't he?"

I turned around to find Chari standing in the corner where the dead Wanderer had appeared.

"But how," I said, "how did you know?"

"I noticed that the Butler is turned slightly in the direction of this corner."

"What does that matter?"

"The murderer set it this way to use it for the remote activation of the device."

"The device with which he simply projected some hologram?"

"Yes."

"Son of a bitch," I growled. "Another joke at my expense."

"All he had to do was connect to the Butler and there he is, your vampire Wanderer."

Sensing my dark mood, Hector whined. Chari patted him and led him to the desk. The dog settled there, and the boy sat in front of Felix's computer, turned it on, and started searching. The chance of stumbling upon something truly important was almost nonexistent, but not completely null, so I let him peck away at ease—if one could speak of "ease" in my presence. But no, one couldn't really, because the murderer was in his element in my presence. So, besides everything else, he had put me in the humiliating position of being a man able to protect people only when removed as far from them as possible.

I realized that I had been clutching the large, sharp kitchen knife tighter than necessary. I imagined driving it deep into the murderer's body, screwing it ever deeper and deeper, reaching all the way to his cold heart.

Chari seemed petrified before the computer. He was staring at me, unblinking, with empty, lifeless eyes. A dark stream trickled down his chin—he had bitten his lower lip and drawn blood. The absurd thought that he had somehow seen my fantasies about killing the killer flashed through my mind, and I made to say something, but then realized that his eyes were actually not directed at me, but at something above me.

"Chari, what's wrong?"

"Stop!" he yelled, feverishly clicking the mouse.

"What are you doing?" I asked.

Looking up at me, he bit his lip again and sucked at the blood. I took a paper napkin from my pocket and leaned over him. His eyes, engulfed in my shadow, seemed like holes, dark holes drilled into the hollows of his eye sockets. Now his face, deformed by the perspective, looked absolutely unfamiliar to me. Old. Sick.

I started to soak up the blood that was now flowing down his neck. My hand was trembling, and the other one was still clutching the knife.

"Are you feeling sick? What's the matter?" I heard myself whispering.

"I deleted it," he said. "Felix . . . He had a secret."

"This secret was that shocking to you?"

"Yes," he screamed. "Get away, stay away from me with that knife!"

I began stepping back, nodding in as reassuring a manner as I could muster.

As soon as I had moved away, he jumped to his feet, rushed to the door, and, before I knew it, slammed it behind his back. I rushed after him, but it was too late. I heard the familiar click. He had locked the door from outside. Or had the murderer done it?

"Chari," I shouted, suffocating on terror. "Watch out. Be careful!"

I listened for his footfalls and any other noise coming from the hallway, but at the same moment the dog started barking and whining deafeningly, scratching at the door.

I yelled at Hector to shut up but he continued barking, this time at me. I resorted to reasoning with the animal, explaining that we needed to figure out how to get out of the room to make sure Chari was safe. That quieted him right up. I still didn't hear anything in the hallway so I went to the open window. Chari was probably still in the villa, but I figured he'd be out soon.

My mind was a chaotic swarm of guesses, suggestions, suspicions, and questions. What had shocked Chari? What kind of secret could have caused him to panic so much that he left his dog behind? Or did the secret have to do with me somehow? Or was it related to Chari, who only a moment ago seemed a complete stranger to me, as if in the moment of panic he had forgotten his role and showed me his true face?

The face of the murderer? Someone who could sneak into any place thanks to the universal access code? Who was a computer genius. Who had read my diary and knew everything about me, about the Artist, about my trances. Who was filled with hatred for everything and everyone because he was unhappy and lonely?

He had run because he was afraid that I would guess the contents of the file he deleted.

"Am I right?" I said, my voice hoarse.

Why was he still in the villa? What was he doing? What was he planning on doing?

Several more minutes passed, during which I could not decide on how to get out of the study. I kept wondering whether to break the door or to concentrate on the lock. Or maybe, despite the risk, I could jump from the corner window onto the balcony next door? Simpler, I could call someone with my phone and wait for them to come and unlock the door. However, when they came, the mastermind behind all of this madness might spring an ambush and kill them, acting as if it were me doing it.

The dog whimpered again and scratched at the door, which, following the sound of being unlocked, began to slowly, slowly open. Chari came in and his disproportionate figure stood out before me. A large head, muscular arms, a broad chest, and the hips narrow and thin, like the sticks he had for legs. His face was so pale it was almost blue, as if someone had just drained all the blood from it. But it was still the face of a nice kid, streaked with traces of dried tears.

"Look," he said almost inaudibly.

In his raised hand he held the Capricorn. He must have drawn it out of Felix's frozen chest slowly, really slowly. This was what he had been doing while in my mind I'd made him out to be a freak, a twisted creature, a murderer. But he had done this for me because my fingerprints were on it.

He went to the disintegrator and threw the Capricorn down with a sharp movement. He came close to me and his wounded lips curved in an attempt at an encouraging smile.

"Come on, Ray, there's nothing more to do here."

49.

The café had reverted back to its previous look of order and luxury. Only the weak smell of the healing herbs served as a reminder of Darcy's excesses and the wounded tribesman. I joined Strauss, Maggie, Ludo, and Darcy.

"If you want something to drink, you'll have to get it yourself," Maggie said. "There are no more servants in the complex."

"The rats have fled the sinking ship," Darcy said.

"Come on, let's not waste time," I said. "Why did you call me here?"

"We've prepared an elaborate exposition of the matter," Darcy said.

"Which matter?" I asked.

"Asking you to finally stop with the murders. There have been too many already."

"As usual, Darcy, no one finds your jokes funny," Strauss said.

"If you jiggle your professorial brain a little, you might grasp the fact that I am not joking," Darcy said. "While he was living like a recluse there was life for us all. Since he crawled out into the light, however, the eternal darkness has started swallowing us one by one."

"It will spit you out, don't you worry," Ludo said. "The darkness will."

"I'm talking about Rhein," Darcy snapped. "I wonder why you, Ludovic, harbor no doubts about him, especially after seeing him at the crime scene this morning. Furthermore, today's victim had also seen him at Felix's. Do I need to mention how he disappeared from the cave and vanished into thin air, just at the moment the Wanderer was murdered? You can't tell me you really buy the story about the iPod luring him away from Natalia."

"How do you know about the iPod?"

"I know from Vanda," Maggie said. "I called to see how she was, and she told me your story, which I just told all of them. What I don't understand, though, is why you didn't take the iPod with you if it could corroborate your statements? Why did you leave it in the room, where, by the way, I was not able to find it?"

"What did you expect—that the murderer would just leave it there?" Strauss said.

"My question is why Rhein didn't pick it up," Maggie said, looking at me. "So?"

"It didn't occur to me, that's why. I forgot about the stupid iPod the second I realized the murderer had used it to get me away from Natalia."

Just then Gromov entered the café. But Chari wasn't with him.

"Where's the kid?" I said. "You promised to keep an eye on him."

"Relax," he said, smiling. "Right now my son is out of danger."

"What makes you think so?" I said.

"For one, you're here," Darcy said.

Gromov sat with us and stared at me with a penetrating look.

"Listen," I said coldly, "I am not in the mood for your accusations. If you have something else to say to me, go on. If not, I'll leave you to discuss me in my absence."

"I am not accusing anyone," Gromov said, still staring at me. "But now that the members of the tribe are no longer suspects, and with the two A's never having been under suspicion, we have to face the truth and admit that the murderer could only be one of us."

"Oh, no," Maggie said, shaking her head. "Strauss and I watched the Wanderer fall. Don't count us. It could only be one of you four."

"You are right," Gromov said.

"Actually, I have never suspected the tribe," I said. "But I'd like you to explain why you no longer consider them suspects."

"There are several reasons," Gromov said. "First, after Natalia's murder, the tribe panicked and left the complex, despite the fact that by doing so they will have to pay the Agency. Second, yesterday Darcy and I managed to get into the server and found out that the so-called anomaly is in fact the result of a hack that no one from the tribe would be able to pull off."

"Third, and the most important reason," Strauss said, "is that they had agreed to perform the ritual for Natalia, and also that they had performed the same ritual for the Wanderer."

"More to the point," Darcy said, "today, after the servants left the complex together, one of the people present here performed yet another of his computer tricks."

"What trick?" Gromov said, looking startled.

"Denying us access to the server."

"Isn't it reasonable to suppose that this person is one of the qualified personnel?" I asked. "Someone who did not leave with the others?"

"No," Gromov said. "According to the boarding information, all twenty-three people from the personnel, together with Wilma and Hans, left on the helicopters."

"Twenty-three?" Maggie said. "Didn't the prospectus say that the qualified personnel consisted of twenty-four people?"

Gromov lowered his eyes again, deliberating whether to answer her.

"It's not the time to play it delicate," Darcy said. "Yes, there were twenty-four of them. Why are you trying to conceal the fact that we found in the file information about one Gaston Fouchet, who went to Rhein's villa and never came back?"

"I am telling you again and with absolute certainty," Ludo said, staring at Darcy with an icy look, "Rhein is not the murderer."

"Who is, then? Maybe you?" Darcy said, baring his teeth in a horse's smile. "The honest, pious mafioso."

"Darcy, stop it," Maggie said. "You know that he would never do anything of the kind to Natalia."

"On the contrary, Maggie, on the contrary," Darcy shouted. "He could have come to the oasis only to murder her, all the other murders nothing more than elaborate camouflage. We are sitting here, wondering which one of us might be the killer. It is this man, the man who eliminated so many people in his life that if he gathered them all in one place he could form an army. The army of the dead, isn't that right, Ludo? What do you say?"

"Yes," said Ludo.

"Yes?" Strauss asked. "Yes what?"

"Yes everything, old man," Darcy said, patting Strauss on the cheek. "Ludovic, the ex–hit man, just made a confession. He zapped the ex–prima ballerina because he loves his country. He would never allow the idol, the pride of the nation, the beautiful prima ballerina Natalia Shidlovskaya, to leave this place and reveal to the world her flabby matronly look. What a disgrace to Mother Russia. What do you say, Ludo?"

"You're on the right track, my lord," Ludo said before finishing his drink and standing up.

His voice conveyed no menace. He delivered the words with the even tone of a man who was simply stating an insignificant fact. Shivers crept down my spine. The others around the table had frozen in something like hypnotic expectation. Only Darcy was still talking.

"Yeah, right! A colossus on feet of clay," Darcy went on. "This is what your *batushka . . . matushka Rossiya* is! Hee-hee—"

The movement with which Ludo took out his revolver was so quick it was almost imperceptible.

"—hee!"

Darcy finished just as a tiny hole appeared right in the middle of his forehead.

50.

None of us was shocked, surprised, or scared by what had happened. No one tried to express even the slightest regret, or even fake sadness over Darcy's death. His face against the table did not even look scary. He looked like a man who had passed out after a night of heavy drinking.

"We saw," Gromov spoke first. "We all saw that this was in self-defense, right?"

"Yes," Maggie said without hesitation.

"I have to go," Ludo said, glancing at his watch.

He turned his back to us and suddenly in a hurry, as if late for a meeting, left the café.

"I am sorry," Maggie sighed. "Natalia was a friend of mine, but I can't . . . I don't want to go there. After all, this is not a funeral, it's a barbaric ritual."

"No, it's not barbaric," Strauss said. "The ritual is of great significance, and because she knew it, Natalia had asked the tribe to perform it for her."

"It's as if she had a premonition that her end was near," Gromov said as he turned his head to the window and watched Ludo disappear in the distance. "Poor guy. He's out of gas and will have to walk to the village. In this heat."

I rose and impulsively made for the exit.

"Where are you going?" Maggie shouted after me.

I turned to answer her, but from where I stood, I saw Darcy in another light. I saw his narrow back, his vertebrae jutting up beneath the T-shirt, their knotty file going all the way up his bare neck and ending at the line of his perfectly cut dark hair. He had cut his hair today, by himself, because the servants were gone. I could see he had done his best. He hadn't put on his usual hunting hat. He had wanted us to notice his new haircut. No one had noticed it, however.

"And now we can't even notice his death," I said out loud.

Maggie and Gromov looked at me as if I were a puzzle, but Strauss understood what I'd said, because he looked as embarrassed as I was.

"Our souls have gone callous much too soon," he mumbled.

I wanted to say something nice about Darcy, but only stupid things came to mind. So I hurried to leave the café.

Driving, I caught up with Ludo and I made a sign for him to get in. He sat down next to me and we were soon out of the complex. We were in the "free" oasis, a place I'd never been before.

The road to the tribal village was clearly visible. I drove down at a reasonable speed, not saying a word to Ludo for about ten minutes. He was still absorbed in his ghastly apathy, and I was absorbed in oppressive thoughts. There was nothing I could focus my mind on to avoid them. Even the exotic landscape looked depressing to me now. I was seeing it only with my eyes, and not with my soul. Strauss had said our souls had grown callous. Mine seemed to have gone blind.

I felt hot. I turned up the air conditioning, took two bottles of mineral water from the cooler bag, and handed one to Ludo. We drank as if for the last time. I poured what remained of mine over my head. This distracted me so much that I drove past one of the tribe who was standing by the road, making a sign for us to stop. I came to a stop and backed up until the jeep was in front of him. I rolled down the window and told him to get in.

"Get out," he said. "We won't be able to get there by car."

His clothes were not typical of the tribe and showed complete disregard for the heat: a black suit, a white shirt with a thin black tie, black shoes resembling boots, black felt hat.

"What are you doing here, Arlos?" Ludo asked, after we stepped out of the jeep.

"I was waiting for you, to take you to her."

"But why on foot?" I said. "Won't the ritual take place in the village?"

"Never!" Arlos exclaimed. "There will never be such a ritual in our village! Ne-ver!"

"All right, all right," I said.

"We, Arlos, insist on nothing," Ludo said in a tired voice. "Just take us to the place you've chosen."

Arlos's hesitation was evident, but it was even clearer that I was the cause of whatever was bothering him. Finally, he seemed to have made up his mind, and we cut through the tall bushes on the left side of the road.

"Still, Arlos," I said, staring at his back, "you have to explain to us . . ."

"I used to work for Natalia," he said without even turning.

"Yes, I got that, but . . ."

"I respected her," he said. "She respected you. That is why I am going to ask the shaman to let you watch the ritual, despite everything."

"Despite what?"

"You witnessed the ritual for the Wanderer," Ludo said from behind me. "I guess that's what he means. Am I right, Arlos?"

"Yes."

"I stumbled upon it by accident and saw only a part of it."

"Yes, but you saw Death," Arlos said in a choked voice. "You stepped toward it, you stood close to it, and it did not possess you. How come?"

"Maybe it didn't like me."

"Oh, no! It likes everyone. But why do you like it?" Arlos said, finally throwing a glance back at me. "Why aren't you afraid of it?"

"You think I became an ally with Death, is that it? You suspect that I want the ritual to be in your village so that Death, with my help, could possess you all at the same time. Am I right? Tell me, Arlos!"

"Yes, you are, yes," Ludo said.

We quickened our pace and when the shrubs thinned out, I saw that we were walking toward a rocky area ending in a chain of tall, gray rocks. We approached them, entering the coolness of their shade. Ludo and I kept stumbling over stones, but Arlos, despite his uncomfortable shoes, moved nimbly. The man was in his own territory.

This was also the end of the oasis, the border beyond which the desert began—it was illuminated by the low sun and white, brilliantly white, just as the rocks were in this light.

"Is it far?" I asked Arlos.

"No."

After another ten minutes we entered a recess between the rocks, where we saw a familiar scene. In the middle of the recess there was a fire, and around it, dressed in their traditional "cocoons," with their faces painted red, sat a dozen members of the tribe, swaying back and forth, staring at the flames. The shaman stood by the fire, only a loincloth on him. Judging from the way his body glistened, he had been generous with the paints and potions. His face, peeking through the locks of gray hair, was still the normal human skin color, but in his eyes, which he had turned toward me, I could not see anything I could call human. I greeted him with a nod.

"Where is she?" Ludo whispered.

"Not anywhere near," Arlos answered. "We will go to her only if her shadow manages to catch up with her. Now wait here."

Arlos approached the shaman, bowing before discussing something. Sighing, Ludo took a pack of cigarettes from his pocket, lit one, and sucked in deeply.

"She was intelligent, Rhein. It is beyond me how she suddenly started believing in these . . . things. She even hallucinated," Ludo said.

"She started believing in these things after the hallucinations began. The question is actually how come she started having these particular hallucinations."

Like the ones I had started having, I thought. *It all started when the murders began.*

"You can stay, but you cannot participate," Arlos said, coming toward us with quick steps.

He led us to the farthest part of the recess and urged us to sit there, on an old, ragged mat. We sat down and he remained standing.

"Are they already drugged?" I asked Arlos, nodding in the direction of the tribe members swaying around the fire.

"No, they are only preparing."

"I watched a recording of another ritual, but it was different," I said. "The whole atmosphere was more . . . It was nicer, under the open sky, on a meadow, without the shaman."

"That was a ritual for the living," Arlos said. "You don't think that only dead men have shadows that remain after them, do you?"

"What shadows are you talking about?"

"The latecomers. Those you call . . . I don't remember the word."

"Remorites," Ludo said, extinguishing his cigarette on the sole of his shoe. "We call them Remorites. Damn them and those who made them up!"

"So, with that other type of ritual the living wait for their Remorites?" I said.

"Yes, and they can do it without the shaman's help, precisely because they are alive." After a short pause, Arlos thrust his chest forward and added with pride, "My shadow, however, has never lagged behind me, that's why I have never participated in such rituals. All that I know I have learned from the others, and it is not much."

The shaman had painted his face red and started to chant.

"Woha, woha, uy rudum!" he began chanting, stepping toward the sticks heaped in a corner of the recess and leaning over the object lying there. He touched it with the tips of his fingers, never stopping the chant: *"Woha, woha, uy rudum . . ."*

"What does it mean?" I asked Arlos, but he only shushed me.

When the shaman raised the object I saw that it was a wooden doll dressed in a silken robe—pale green in color, stained with blood. Natalia's robe.

Ludo let out a low moan. At the same time, the shaman, following exactly the same ritual as the one for the Wanderer, threw the doll into the fire. The others crawled out of their cocoons, throwing them in the fire, too. The heavy, dizzying aroma spread all over the place. I felt it rushing into my lungs.

51.

"Woha, woha, uy rudum, uyr rur dur dum," we all sang together.

The tribe was dancing their whirlwind dance around the shaman, who was jumping with upraised arms. Arlos, his legs bent under his body sprawled on the mat, was shaking his head rhythmically, and Ludo and I looked curiously at each other every now and again, but we kept singing, *"Woha, woha, uy rudum,"* like drunken sailors. At some point, I tried to shut my mouth with my hand, but it didn't help; it only made me sing even more out of tune.

Out of nowhere the shaman screamed. It was a startling, piercing, shrill scream, like the whistle of a train. Everything became silent. The tribe froze in their dancing positions, and the shaman lowered his head, listened around, and finally said something unintelligible, with palpable terror in his voice. He pronounced the words again, and then dashed to the exit of the recess, stumbled over something, and bumped into the rocky wall. His loincloth caught on its edge and dropped to the ground, but he didn't stop to pick it up. He continued running as naked as a newborn baby, and disappeared outside.

Several seconds passed. Everyone remained petrified. Then they began moving simultaneously, as if parts of a single organism, and rushed in the direction of the exit, bumping up against each other.

"What is going on?" Ludo rumbled, standing up and grabbing Arlos by the neck.

"Let's run," Arlos whined, wriggling to free himself. "We have to run. He is here!"

"Who?" Ludo said, shaking him.

The answer was a long word in their language, and it took Arlos a panicked few moments to find the right words in English.

"None. None is here," he said. "He has never come here, but now . . . he has found his way to freedom. HE IS HERE!"

I rose, too. We were the only ones remaining in the recess. We wobbled toward the exit, Ludo still clutching Arlos. We went outside, hoping that he would feel better there and explain what was happening. We stood in the bright white light, which made us dizzier than the drugs had, and blinked dumbly after the tribesmen, who were running in a tight group toward the end of the rocks. Arlos started tossing about to escape from Ludo's grip.

"Where is she?" Ludo said, shaking him again. "Where is Natalia?"

"No! We cannot be safe around her before a month has passed."

"You want us to leave her wherever it is you dragged her to?"

Like an enraged madman, Arlos pulled himself away with such force that his jacket tore and remained hanging in Ludo's hands. Ludo threw it aside. Arlos ran like a rabbit.

"Stop," Ludo shouted as he pulled out his revolver.

He aimed at the man's legs, but I pushed him and he missed. I grabbed his arm, and the revolver fired again.

"Let me go," Ludo yelled. "He has to tell me where she is!"

"I will tell you," a soft voice said from somewhere nearby. "I will show you where she is."

We looked around but since there was not a soul anywhere to be seen, I thought we were experiencing aural hallucinations. I was just about to ask Ludo if he had heard anything, when one of the tribe appeared before us, springing out like a mushroom from between the rocks.

Startled, I cursed but then my eyes met his, and to my astonishment, a wide smile spread across my face. I turned to Ludo. He was also smiling. But why? I had never met such a bland-looking fellow in my life. He lacked any particular individuality, so much so that he looked unfinished—as if God had created him in the broadest strokes only and was still considering whether to shape him in the image of a young man or an old one, whether to endow him with beauty or punish him with ugliness, whether to highlight his masculine features or transform them into feminine ones. Even his color seemed to have remained a question—his skin was unevenly gray, as if only a primer had been applied, but not the final coat.

"What's the matter with you?" I asked Ludo with a smile.

"What's the matter with you?" he said, smiling back.

"I gave you peacefulness," our new friend informed us.

Indeed, I was feeling unusually calm, a fact that by itself should have made me anxious. What kind of a man was this? What kind of power did he possess, giving peacefulness with such ease?

"Why didn't you calm down your fellow tribesmen?" I asked. "Are you that . . . What did Arlos call you?"

"None," Ludo said. "Maybe this isn't who they were talking about."

"They were talking about me, and they were scared of me, me and no one else. I terrify them because he who is everywhere is actually nowhere. I am None, because he who has many faces has none, none at all. So, yes, I am None, No-one."

Suddenly, Ludo and None were only two tiny specks in the distance. It seemed like my sense of time had taken a long break. I chased after them.

"I thought you had given up," Ludo called over his shoulder as I caught up.

The three of us walked on in a line, None in the lead, Ludo in the middle, and me at the rear. There were moments, however, when I thought None was floating in the air.

"Rhein," Ludo whispered to me, "I wonder why None has such a good command of Russian."

"Russian?"

"He's been speaking Russian the whole time."

"No, no," I said, also whispering. "It's English. He's been speaking only in English."

"I've been speaking in all and in none kinds of ways," None shouted. "I told you already: I am None!"

Ludo and I both stopped and stared at None. I could see him only vaguely, as if he were shrouded by mist, despite the fact that he was only a few feet away from us. He seemed to be disappearing gradually, swallowed by the whiteness of the rocks he was now walking toward. Yes, his grayish skin was becoming whiter. His hair, also.

"Keep calm, keep calm!" None said, sounding as if his voice were coming from inside the rock.

Ludo and I arrived at the spot where None had been absorbed, which was actually a spacious room carved into the rock. In its center, on a pyre, was Natalia, illuminated by the rays of the low sun shining on her like spotlights. She was covered with white flowers. The opposite wall was also white and so smooth that it reflected the pyre like glass. Our faceless dark reflections also flickered on this wall.

None was waiting for us, sitting on a rock outside the light's path. His skin was grayish again, and his hair was back to its indeterminate earthy color. I looked around. The other walls were rough and stained black by smoke. It was obvious that many pyres had burned here. Many dead men had turned to ashes while their flames danced in their reflections over the white wall.

"What's the meaning of this?" I whispered.

"The meaning is there," None replied, pointing straight at Ludo's heart. "It is there because he wants to take the death of this woman."

"Yes, I want to take it," Ludo said with longing in his voice. "I want to."

"You want to, and you will, if I help you," None said, staring at him with eyes that were so colorless as to look transparent. "I'll help you, believe me, you have to believe, have faith."

Ludo started nodding and each nod was slower than the previous, and dreamier.

"Ludo, pull yourself together," I said.

"I will believe, believe, believe."

"Good," None said before looking at me and ordering me to leave.

I obeyed like a robot, but after going out I stopped and looked back. None was standing up, leaning over Ludo, whose head was drooping so low that it touched his knees.

52.

I was walking down the stony path between the white rocks and the white desert. I was moving away from the ritual room, from its sooty, death-covered walls. Death's sanctuary. Where what happened during the rituals was always unforeseeable because death could not be the same for everyone.

What had Natalia's life been for the last few years? Nothing. An empty shell she had abandoned long before the murderer dealt his blow. Death had started to accumulate in her body a long time ago. In her soul. That's why now it was so terrifying, so dangerous.

Yet Ludo remained there.

I tried to stop, but couldn't. I hastened my pace, realizing that I was shaking like a jellyfish in the tides of an uncontrollable, panicking fear. *Get out, get out, get out!* None's voice kept repeating in my head. I started running. What about Ludo? I didn't care! He deserved whatever it was that was happening to him now.

I screamed and this time managed to stop. I turned around and swiftly set off in the opposite direction. I was still shaking, only now it was with anger.

I stormed into the sanctuary. The smell of burning grass hit my nostrils. The fire was not in the pyre. Something was burning far away from it and close to Ludo, who was still sitting on the rock, petrified, his hair thrown back and face turned toward the smooth, mirrorlike wall. None was sitting next to him, chanting, his hand gliding over Ludo's brow.

I stepped over the burning grass and grabbed Ludo by the shoulders and tried to shake him, but he didn't budge.

"It's too late," None told me through his laughter. "He's with her now."

"Where, where, you savage?" I said, meeting his eyes, where I saw everything but savagery. "What do you want from this man? How do you intend to use his grief?"

"No, not his grief. His love," None said. "I intend to use his love for the dead woman. This man is willing to do anything for her. If he manages to free her shadow from dark death, I will use her. I will take the power of her flame and then I won't be None, because my face will be one, and one only."

I caught myself nodding at him, and stopped. I asked myself why he was talking to me with such brash sincerity. Had he somehow become taller, or had I become shorter? I searched for the answers to these questions and discovered that I wasn't standing, that I was sitting on the rock next to Ludo, that the nasty grass was still smoldering right under my nose. I tried, with all my strength, to stand up, but all I did was throw my head back. I ended up staring, just like Ludo, at the glassy wall.

"Good, good," None murmured, running his hand over my brow.

It was as cool as a gentle breeze, a fleshless touch. I felt it sinking into my head, into my brain, feeling its way with its spectral fingers.

Of course, all my experiences have been imaginary, I thought.

"No! They are not imaginary!" I was startled by Strauss's voice. *"This is None, this really is None! Get out of there immediately!"*

"God! Have you also gone mad?" Vanda exclaimed from somewhere. *"How could he get out of there, when he's here?"*

"He's here, but he's also there—where 'now' and 'then' are indistinguishable."

"Don't listen to him, Rhein! You are in your villa, only here with us."

"No, no! In the relative dimension of time, you will be here after a couple of hours. You may die, Rhein. You may die here, if you don't get out of there now!"

There was silence. Was it because they had stopped talking or because I had stopped hearing them? I couldn't tell. It was a fact, though, that I couldn't see them. I couldn't see None, either. There was nothing before my eyes, save for that wall that no longer reflected the pyre. It wasn't reflecting anything anymore, and its color had turned from white to something semitransparent and watery.

I stared at it, hypnotized, even though I wanted to look down at the ground, where I could hear someone's heavy, intermittent breathing. It was as if somebody was in agony there, only a step away from me, and I couldn't even move. Straining, I began to turn my eyes downward, feeling them cold and hard like marbles of ice. They bounced back up several times, but finally I managed to turn them down enough to see Ludo. He was crawling toward the wall, like a snail carrying a piano.

When he reached the wall he raised his head and apparently glimpsed something beyond it, which gave him the strength to stand up. He stepped back, swayed, but didn't fall. Then he ran straight to the wall, his hand reaching into it as if the wall were liquid glass. Ludo howled with pain, but pressed his forehead against the wall, his jugulars bulging from the tension, and his head gradually sank in, becoming distorted together with his shoulders. He was penetrating the wall, tearing it down with his body, and it was tearing him to pieces.

The scene was so nightmarish that it actually shook me out of my stupor. The next moment, I was standing by Ludo or by what remained of him. I tried to pull him back, but he didn't want to be liberated. He pushed toward the thing glowing dark on the other side of the wall.

"Don't stop him," None called from a distance. "Don't stand in his way!"

I recognized what Ludo was so desperately fighting for. The glow from inside the wall was Natalia's face.

"You were drugged, Rhein!" Vanda cried. *"Please, come to your senses now!"*

"I returned there because of Ludo."

"But why? He's not your friend, he's nothing to you."

"Leave him!" Strauss shouted at me. *"Get out of there!"*

Ludo was engulfed by the wall, and this time he was truly in agony. He was suffocating. Natalia's face was growing darker. I took a few steps back.

"If you cross over to the other side, you're dead," None said, standing by the pyre. "Dead! Like him, like her."

"Oh, don't write us off so easily!" I said before running into Ludo and pushing him forward.

"Such enormous resistance! As if we were trying to swim in liquid glass!"

"You're in an in-between zone!" Strauss said excitedly. *"Yes! That's the exact way one should feel there."*

"St-rauss! Lo-ok at hi-im."

"Wha-at is wro-ong with you? Rhe-in, wha-wha-at . . ."

". . . dy-i-inng . . ."

"No-no-nnno . . ."

My words were crumbling, turning into a rain of sounds that was becoming softer and softer, slipping further and further away. The resistance was unbearably powerful. Crushing. It was stealing my breath away, stealing my will to live, stealing life itself from me. I gave in and relaxed. The crushing heaviness immediately grew weaker, then disappeared.

"Hey, listen to me! This is not even scary. It's easy."

"Death is easy."

Ludo and I rise up. We look at each other. He blinks. I lift my hand, touching my beard, unshaven for almost a year. We both look around in search of Natalia's dark dead face. It is gone now. There is nothing else around us but grayness. But when we look up, we see that it is there. We've been sinking, then. Sinking.

Her face is hovering above us, and farther up, we see the sprawling body, dark gray and fibrous, swaying up there like a cloud through which fine white threads are sifting. His head thrown back, Ludo stares at the giant face, darkness still spilling out and changing its outlines, as if shifting between vile grimaces. Although the eyes are closed, darkness actually flows from them.

Ludo tears his shirt apart. He is naked to the waist and spreads his arms out in an appeal. I can see his heart beating, pulsing fast beneath the muscles and his white skin. I also see the white threads growing longer, moving downward on some strange current, reaching out for Ludo. They twist around his body, connecting him to that monstrous thing, which is now trembling, denser up there.

"Come, come, come," Ludo urges it.

The echo responds, "Come, come, come."

It seems to have heard him and answers his call by opening its dark eyes slowly, very slowly. Their darkness rushes down toward him while he waits without moving. He is waiting for her.

53.

"Come, come, come . . ."

We were facing the wall that reflected the pyre.

"Come, come, come," Ludo repeated, his hands spread out for an embrace. He was naked to the waist. He was breathing heavily, in fits and starts, as his lungs were also torn. "Come, come, come."

I nudged him, I shook him, and he finally fell silent, turning to me. His face was bloated and scratched, and when he dropped his hands I saw that they were in even worse shape. I chose not to look at my own reflection. I had the feeling that my face was no better. My hands, though, were not as badly hurt as his.

"I did it," Ludo said. "You were there and you know. You know that I did it. Right?"

No, I thought, *there was no "there."*

"Yes, yes," came None's cackle from somewhere. "You made it, and now her death is in you, along with all its darkness."

"You're right," Ludo said, turning his head to the pyre, a trembling smile on his face. "But I won't die immediately. Not before I have seen her rise, not before I have told her."

"Stupid wretch," None said, crawling out from beneath the pyre. "You hope in vain. She won't be back. It is impossible. But I will live on."

"Stay away from her," Ludo said, reaching for his revolver.

His fingers were mangled and he couldn't grab the weapon. None was walking around Natalia's body, still laughing.

"Son of a bitch!" I said.

Ludo tried moving, too, took a step or two then collapsed on the floor. His body, none of its gladiator strength left, convulsed.

"Ludo, Ludo," I said desperately, kneeling next to him, "this is some kind of hypnosis, a murderous hypnosis! Get back to your senses! Whatever it is you have seen did not happen in reality. There is no death in you, no darkness whatsoever."

"Listen to me, Rhein," Ludo wheezed, "I am sure that I dragged her out of there. I dragged her out, and now she's here and is the same as she was years ago. I am sure. I see her floating above that dead body, which . . . which is no longer hers."

He made one last attempt to stand up, which drained all of his remaining strength. The convulsions ceased, and his voice fell to a whisper.

"You have to help her. I don't know what None wants from her, but you have to get in his way. Stop him."

He fell silent. He had lost consciousness. The mocking cackle came from the pyre again. I stood up, blind with rage. None was by the pyre in an inexplicably strained position, staring at the devil knows what. Of course, there was no "previous" Natalia floating there. However, I noticed that she was not laid in the middle of the pyre. For some reason white flowers were piled up there and also covered everything but her head. Coiling into garlands, they were falling down, covering the entire pyre, from under which None had crawled out a moment ago.

Now None hissed like a wounded snake and suddenly started gesticulating over Natalia's body. I moved toward him. His gestures were becoming more and more furious and more focused. He looked as if he were trying to pull something connected to Natalia's body, or something that was still in her body?

I went back to Ludo and checked his pulse; it was weak but even. I took the lighter from his pants pocket and returned to the pyre. None had moved to the side of the pyre where there were only flowers and was thrashing about over them.

"Step back," I said, showing him the lighter. "If you don't, I'd be happy to see you singed."

He threw me a mocking look and continued gesticulating. I leaned in and the smell of the flowers rushed through my lungs, heavy and intoxicating. I took the garlands reaching the floor and pulled them away. But there was no wood there. There was nothing there. The pyre was nothing but flowers.

"What are you doing to these bodies?" I said.

"Bodies, bodies," None said. "Bodies, and the absence of bodies."

My heart sank. I turned my eyes away, only to fall on another mystery. None also looked upset. He appeared on the verge of tears, but of course, these were not tears of compassion, or of human grief. This creature who had been so blatantly insolent was now trying to conceal from me his pathetic, teary fit of fear. I had scared him, but unfortunately, I couldn't remember how and with what.

"Come on, None," I said, "explain it to me."

"None, yes, I am still None! The explanation is about to come."

"No, that's it! Enough!" I said, leaning over Natalia. "I will take her out of here. I won't let you . . ."

His heart-wrenching howl made me jump back and press my palms over my temples. None's face was twisting before me as if I had just splashed it with a bucket of hot water.

"You should not touch her," he said hastily. "That man told you the truth. Her shadow is now here, haunting this place. You can't see it, but I can. I know that its merging with the body is near, and as soon as it is done, this woman will get her second chance."

I could no longer hear him. I was watching the human fingers creeping from under the flowers, barely touching Natalia's left hand. I continued staring at them while I walked around the pyre of flowers. I stopped by the side with the empty space, which wasn't empty. Someone was lying there, also masked by the flowers, which now looked disgusting to me. I reached out and began pushing them onto the floor. I wasn't paying attention to None, who had stopped talking and was only whimpering next to me.

He was whimpering next to me, but he was also lying next to Natalia. He was an exact duplicate of None, naked, wearing only a loincloth. His loincloth, however, was different from None's, different in the most terrifying way, because it was so rotten that even a gentle touch would have made it fall apart. Its owner had put it on many, many years ago.

"He's not your twin. He's not sleeping," I shouted. "How long has he been lying here?"

"For centuries. But I am not dead! I am not entirely dead. That's why I'm everywhere, and nowhere. That's why I'm also None, neither, nor."

He turned his eyes to Natalia and laughed somewhat happily. He made a weird jump and landed on his back on that deathless body of his. He sank into it, disappeared into himself. Merged with himself.

I shaded my eyes as the aura around Natalia's body became very bright, bluish, and so charged with energy that it gave off sparks. The aura had appeared after None had "merged." Enveloped in it, Natalia also looked bluish, and her face seemed to soften, melting like a wax mask. Her features were losing their individuality, becoming plainer, more indeterminate, neither female nor male. They were beginning to resemble those of None, who was now also enveloped by Natalia's aura.

I reached out toward the aura, but the energy pushed me back. *Too late, it's too late,* he cackled in my head. *I will live on instead of her.*

He would live on and by doing so he would also rob her of her second chance!

I no longer cared whether this was happening for real or whether I had once again fallen victim to hypnotic manipulations. I sharply drove my hands into the bluish substance, and an instant before being pushed back again, I managed to clutch at None. This time the shock was much stronger, like an electric shock. It threw me back. I landed far from the pyre, and None's body hit the floor next to me.

I crawled sideways, and little by little managed to sit up. I continued with my efforts and finally stood up. Pain, vertigo, nausea—I was spared nothing, but right now it didn't matter. The substance there, over the pyre, continued to increase its energy, boiling, seething all around Natalia's body. It whirled into a horrifying, destructive tornado.

I looked at Ludo. He had come to and was watching the tornado, nodding encouragingly at it, as if he was seeing some living being in it.

"Ludo," I said, going to him. "We have to get out of here!"

I grabbed him under his arm to drag him outside.

"No! Don't be afraid," he shouted, but not at me. "Everything's fine, dear. You'll make it, I know!"

I looked up and thought that there, in the eye of the tornado, there was indeed a ballerina's figure, swirling into the wildest, most inimitable pirouette.

"Don't be afraid!" I yelled.

"Go on, go on," Ludo pleaded.

The tornado broke free from the dead body, shooting straight toward the glassy wall. There was no reflection. It sank deeper and deeper into the wall. It stormed into a different, boundless space, disappearing and reappearing, now shining, now looming dark. Like a firefly! After it disappeared completely, I closed my eyes and imagined it glowing in the invisible distance. Because all of this mysterious light was now there, in the heart of the great prima ballerina Natalia

Shidlovskaya, who was again behind the curtains, only this time instead of a step back, she moved on.

Ludo and I smiled at each other, and I saw the brightest hue of sky blue in his eyes. I helped him get up. The pyre was burning, and the ordinary orange flames were reflected by the smooth white wall. We went outside. The sun shed its dying rays over the rosy desert.

"That's all from me," Ludo said.

I understood, so I didn't try to stop him. I stayed behind, watching him until the desert engulfed him completely in the dead stillness of its sand.

54.

I was back on the sofa in the living room, a wet towel on my forehead again, accompanied by a Band-Aid on my nose as well as an abundance of regenerating cream on my cheeks and chin. I was in my pajamas, my arms were bandaged to the elbows, and there was an electric pillow under my feet, supposedly "pumping out the tension" from my head.

"You are a lucky man, Rhein," Strauss said, walking about, a dreamy expression on his face. "In the annals of history, people like you were considered chosen by God."

"Chosen, yes," Vanda said. "Only not by God but by a murderous sociopath!"

"Don't think of the murderer now, my girl," Strauss said, sitting down opposite her. "After everything Rhein told us, don't you realize that today he was part of the greatest mystery?"

"Stop confusing him with this nonsense," she snapped. "Look at him! What's so great about getting so high you lose all sense?"

"There I was with a beard," I said weakly, "and Ludo saw her."

"See," Vanda said, pointing at me. "Just listen to him."

"His Remorite has a beard. Rhein entered the in-between zone through him. Through him he also got the impression that he was swimming through the wall. Without the tribe's drug, he would have seen nothing there. It broadened his consciousness and led to a greater perceptual scope."

"He's right, Vanda," I said. "I'm telling you, None truly was a ghost. Ludo and I never would have seen him if we hadn't been drugged. The fact that we could both see him tells me that despite being a ghost, he was real."

"Speaking to you in Russian and in English simultaneously? Yeah, right," Vanda said.

"He communicated with them telepathically," Strauss said. "Also, keep in mind that None is not a Remorite. He's singular and the tribe says that his body has been lying on that pyre for ages."

"Big deal," Vanda said. "Such remains have been discovered all over the world. They don't decompose due to specific environmental conditions, such as those in deserts and caves."

"Well, according to the legend, he was one of those wretched men to whom the demon-oasis laid down the condition of having to give up light to bring back to life those whom they left behind for so long. But None didn't keep his promise. He tried to leave the darkness, so the demon cursed him. He had no choice but to become a ghost in a body that is neither living nor dead, and to spend his existence in eternal, futile attempts to leave this body."

"But after so many centuries, how did he manage to break through his undying shell today?" I asked.

"We may never find that out," Strauss said, rubbing his temples. "But there's no doubt that it had something to do with Ludo."

"He needed Ludo," I said. "He wanted to take only him to the sanctuary. I am sure that he interrupted the ritual on purpose because he needed Ludo to finish it. Because Ludo gave his fire to Natalia!"

"Come on, Rhein," Vanda sighed. "As soon as the drugs wear off Ludo will probably return to the complex."

"No, he won't be back."

We were silent, staring at the darkness beyond the open window. Vanda rose brusquely, grabbed two cans of beer, and thrust them into our hands.

"Drink," she ordered us. "Cool down your imagination. You cooked up a nice cocktail of legends, drug-addled visions, and all kinds of fantasies, and on top of it all, you seem to take it seriously."

"I take seriously what I have seen, what I have experienced. Strauss takes it seriously because it supports his hypothesis."

"Completes it, even," he said, livening up. "I can't believe I hadn't thought of it before. Of course the transition of the mind from light to dark matter could not be a sudden one. The in-between zone is necessary, and the Remorites exist independently only in this zone."

"Something like the twilight zone?" Vanda said. "These shadows of ours become independent because they are late, and have come to life?"

"Exactly," I said. "The worst thing is that sometimes they remain there even after we die. They are left there to wander eternally in the hopeless grayness between light and darkness."

"Don't get enthusiastic on me again," Vanda said, sitting next to me and digging her fingers into my knee. "Only about an hour ago we fought to bring you back to life, precisely after a moment of unreasonable enthusiasm. I thought you were going to die."

"I thought I was dying inside the rock," I said, looking right at Strauss. "But before that . . . Good Lord, I remember. I could hear your voices in the sanctuary! Snatches of our conversation, which, at that time, had been still in the future!"

"As soon as you began raving here, I guessed that you might be hearing us there," Strauss said, quite pleased. "I guessed that your mind might have had access at least to the near future by that time. In the dark matter, though, you're supposed to be completely disoriented, because in it past, present, and future become one."

"Why is that?" Vanda asked. "Why do they merge into one? How can that even happen?"

"There are no cause-and-effect connections. There are no causes to bring about effects that could later become causes for new effects. In other words, Vanda, in the dark matter this flow of constant changes to which we owe our movement through time does not exist."

"Dark matter is everywhere, Vanda," I said. "All of the information in the universe is encoded in it. It is frozen time, the eternal now. *The eternal now!* It is the memory of the universe, where, precisely because of the absence of past and future, we, as well as everything else, are in superposition. Each one of us exists there in all possible versions—eternal, indestructible . . ."

"What?" Vanda said, nudging me. "What's the matter with you now?"

"You thought of None, didn't you?" Strauss asked.

"Yes, yes." I nodded, absentmindedly. "He who is everywhere and is in fact nowhere, who has many faces, yet has none. This is what he told us about himself."

"None is a nickname," Strauss said. "The nickname of a man who roams about aware of all his possible paths through time, realizing himself in all the possible versions, yet who is incapable of turning any of them into reality."

"Seems like your None has been hearing a lot of legends and scary stories, too," Vanda said, getting up and moving to the chair across from Strauss. "As far as the possible versions are concerned, let's say they really exist in that dark matter. Why should they matter to us if they are not living beings, but only assemblages of information?"

"Oh, they do matter," he said. "They are of great importance, because without them we wouldn't have a choice, and without choice, there can be no free will."

"But didn't you say that we can only get their information if we make them real?"

"No, exactly the opposite," Strauss said. "We can make them real only if we get their information, or in other words, only if our mind goes through them. You see, acquiring information is always related to the inflow of energy, and after every inflow of energy the result is some change, and every change means movement, including through time. Because of their different informational structures, our versions have varying energy potential. This means—"

"This means," I said, "that when we screw up by making the wrong choice, we leave behind us the unrealized potential of many other, more energetic, more valuable versions of ourselves. Such as my Artist."

"Your Artist, Rhein, is your optimal version," Strauss explained. "Each Remorite is that, an optimal but unrealized version."

"Unrealized, yet living," Vanda said. "So, living like a ghost, right?"

"Yes," Strauss confirmed.

"Yes," I repeated like an echo. "Like a ghost, because he is everything I could have been. He has all that is precious to me, all that I have lost, all I keep losing."

"Enough," Vanda said, banging her fist on the table. "You'll stop losing now. You'll get back what you have lost, with the help of your strong will and your perseverance. As for the Remorites-shadows-latecomers that you think have come to life—"

"No, we're not the only ones," I said. "The tribe—"

"Oh, the tribe," Vanda said, brushing away the word. "If their fairy tales are the inspiration for your hypothesis, Professor . . ."

"No, Vanda," he said, looking offended. "I had designed it long before I was aware of them. I accidentally met one of the architects of this complex. He told me about the tribe. He was the one who told me the legend that seemed to contain some of my ideas, if only symbolically. I found this quite intriguing, and as I had received a large sum for damages from a car accident, I decided to rent one of the villas here."

"You made the right choice," I said.

"Absolutely! Before coming here, I hadn't ever thought that I would be able to prove my hypothesis because it is based on events that, in normal conditions, are invisible and imperceptible to us. In this oasis, however, there are places where the conditions are not normal . . . or are ordinary, but are combined in an unusual way. It's difficult to explain. But take the caves, for example. Some people are able to expand their perceptions even without the help of the drug."

"Did Felix see ghosts in the caves?" I asked.

"No, but he kept saying that he could feel their presence. So far, only you and Hector have had visual contact with them."

"The dog?" Vanda said.

"I spent a lot of time observing him. In the end, I found out that in the caves the focus of his eyes is displaced."

"Exactly," came Chari's voice from outside the window as his face appeared. "It was the cause for his blindness there."

"You've been eavesdropping again," I mumbled.

"Of course," he said, grinning. "Eavesdropping is the shortest way to the truth. You wouldn't deny this, would you?"

Well, I wouldn't. In fact, denying anything was useless.

55.

I glanced at the clock—5:07—early, much too early in the morning. But my enormous hunger had woken me up. I had no choice; I mustered some strength and stood up under the sound of my own bones screeching, as if my skeleton was finally setting itself back to normal after yesterday's ordeal. I noticed that my phone said I had messages, all from Chari. The first one had come in a couple of hours earlier:

> *I'm in a hurry, Ray, and you're either deaf or you sleep like a log! So, go and take a cold shower and have a double espresso before listening to my second message.*

I was tempted to obey the kid, but in the end my anxiousness won out. Sitting down on the bed, I played the next message, which had been sent only five minutes after the first:

> *Now listen carefully: Isidor Feretti, a computer specialist. He became rich after patenting a new type of mobile processor. A maniac with an expensive passion for hunting exotic animals*

*and a murderer of lonely millionaires whose bank accounts he
later drained in a series of masterful hacking tricks.*

*Yes, Ray, this is about "Lord Darcy," based on informa-
tion I just now extracted from the depths of his personal computer. By the way, his study is filled with stuffed animals, so
I'd better go now. It's disgusting!*

Bye!

"Bye," I replied mechanically before playing the message again.
Strange indeed, I thought. *The murderer was first murdered and then
uncovered as a murderer.* I got back under the covers and thought for a
while, repeating to myself, *Uncovered, the murderer was murdered and
uncovered.* After a few minutes, however, instead of feeling the relief
befitting the situation, I felt that I was on the verge of falling fast asleep
again. Actually, the only thing keeping me awake was the hunger.

I went into the bathroom and stopped in front of the mirror,
which showed me a shockingly familiar image—bruised all over, with
a huge Band-Aid on the nose. I took it off, but immediately regretted
it. The skin came off, too. Tears gushed down my face, rendering the
image in the mirror even more pathetic. I stood there, watching it with
alienation I wasn't supposed to feel. After all, I couldn't renounce my
face only because I smashed it against a wall a couple of times the day
before.

I took the bandages off my arms and stepped under the shower.
The cold water cleared my head. I dressed, sighing like an over-
burdened horse, and went down to the kitchen. I thought that, as
usual, Vanda would be there, but she wasn't.

"It's only five in the morning," I said.

I noted that I had gone back to my habit of talking to myself out
loud, but decided not to pay attention to this, at least for the time
being. I took some sandwiches from the fridge, heated them, and while

preparing the double espresso Chari had recommended, I suddenly felt furious. Last night, the impish kid had tricked me again.

At about midnight, I'd driven him to the gate of his villa from where, despite my wretched state, I walked him to the villa so that his father wouldn't hear us. Then, for quite some time, I waited, hiding behind a tree until he gave me a sign from his room that he had taken all the necessary precautions against a possible visit from the murderer. I had made the effort, I had been worried about him, but he had gone out again after I left. He had gone to Darcy's villa.

"Never mind," I said. "The important thing is that the murderer is now murdered, uncovered."

I finished my coffee without even noticing. I prepared another cup and started eating. I kept thinking about last night, about our conversation with Strauss, and, mostly, about the fact that last night my brain had been working much better than it was now. I wondered if the drug could have such an effect—temporary relaxation and relief, and after waking up, dimness again. Or was the thick fog in my head now caused by something else?

"It is," I answered my own question.

All right, but what? I had absolutely no idea. I finished my early breakfast and decided to return to bed and go back to sleep. First, though, I stopped by the study, sat behind the desk, and wrote Vanda the following note:

> Do not disturb me, even if I never wake up. Darcy is the murderer, and Ludo killed him yesterday, so you don't have to worry anymore.

I stood up and then remembered that last night, after a lot of coaxing, we had convinced Strauss to spend the night here so that he would not be alone in his villa. I added, "Best regards to you and Strauss!" After that, I took it to the kitchen and left it on the table. I headed for the bedroom, but while I was climbing the stairs I realized that the note was not clear enough, so I went back, picked it up, and went into the study. The feeling that I was sobering up after a night of heavy drinking was getting stronger. Maybe during the night, in some dreamlike state, I had drunk something. Or had I taken pills? Maybe both, but I couldn't remember.

I sat behind the desk again and stared at the Butler. Here was someone who could tell me whether I had left the bedroom and if I had, where I had gone.

1. *Opening of the south window at 02:15*
2. *Closing of south window at 05:00*

For a while I gazed at the screen dumbly. I had expected this kind of information, but only regarding the door and not the window. Plus, the times didn't make sense. I was up at 5:00 and had listened to Chari's messages not long after 5:02. I continued to ponder it, and soon came to the conclusion that it was not me who had done this but the Butler, manipulating the window at his "will." Yet, intuitively, I already knew that the truth was completely different, and extremely important to me. I sensed that it was a mystery quite easy to solve, if only my thoughts would become a bit clearer.

"All right, all riiight," I began murmuring encouragingly, adding to the note:

P.S. For more information on the news that Darcy was the murderer, do not wake me up, but call Chari.

My eyes glided over the text *". . . and Ludo killed him yesterday . . . ,"* *". . . Ludo yesterday . . ."*

I stopped breathing for a moment, slumping in the chair. I just realized what I had done. Yesterday. I had left one drugged and wounded man to crawl across the desert, convinced that he was carrying death in him and would die somewhere out there. Where could he be now? Was he still alive?

I took several bottles of mineral water from the fridge, as well as a few packages of dried food, stuffed everything into a bag, and left it by the front door. Then I quietly rushed up the stairs and went into the studio.

How long since my last visit here? Only a few days, but they had stretched out, had swollen like bubbles. How else could they encompass so much death, and not only the physical kind?

I grabbed my binoculars and hurried back to the door, but didn't go out straight away. I remained on the threshold, seized by a profound sense of misgiving, which came to me like a whisper. I had the feeling that it was the last time I would see this studio, in which my hand had painted thirty paintings, none of which I knew about. My eyes had looked at these paintings and I had been blind. The memories of them were now haunting the place, but they did not belong to me. I had other memories, which I now realized were precious, too—a string of early mornings after sleepless nights. I would always come here. I would stand in front of that kitschy screen, hoping that behind it there was a painting in progress or finished, even. I would wait . . . wait to fall into nothingness so that he would come forward—the real Artist.

I slung the binocular strap over my neck, stepped back, and closed the door behind me.

56.

The sun was rising behind my back. Its rays were not warm yet, although the hues they threw over the rocks before me were. The stones I was walking on seemed incandescent, but I could feel only coolness coming from them. I was sweating and shivering at the same time. I was in a hurry, although I knew that after the passing of so many hours, gaining a few minutes would not make much of a difference. Slung over my shoulder, the bag with the provisions rustled with each step, making it hard for me to hear any other sound. But what else could I hear in this place?

The desert was still out of sight. First, I had to go around the chain of rocks, which at this time of day looked to be on fire. My long, black shadow stood out among the rocks, rendering their orange brilliance even more intense. I regretted forgetting my sunglasses back in the jeep. The sun had ascended surprisingly quickly, as if some giant's hand had thrown it up into the sky. The same hand that was now probably throwing me in all directions, while I believed that I alone chose my path through time. "Maybe I did, maybe I did," I repeated out loud, feeling robbed of something. Last night, I'd been convinced by Strauss's hypothesis, but now . . . Now, asking myself whether I believed in anything, I had only one answer: *I don't know.*

When I finally reached the edge of the oasis, the view before my eyes was so different from yesterday's that for a moment I doubted it was real. Gone was the bright, blinding whiteness. Now the rocks on this side looked almost black, and their shadows stretched far out into the distance, making the desert appear in deep metallic gray. I felt even colder and, of course, more anxious. I didn't know why the temperature in the desert dropped so sharply at night, but I knew perfectly well that in such conditions, Ludo, who didn't even have a shirt on, would have had a hard time surviving.

I reached a relatively high outcropping of rock, put down the bag, and climbed up to the highest point I could reach. I stood up and scanned the area with the binoculars. I was looking for the pale figure of a man naked to the waist, faint with exhaustion, but instead my attention was caught by another shape: the black figure of a man sitting down on the sand. Unfortunately, he was sitting with his back to me, so I could see neither his face nor his hands, and his head was drooping so much that I wasn't able to see even the color of his hair.

I climbed down from the rock, grabbed the bag, and hurried in his direction. From time to time, I glanced at the man through the binoculars, and every time he was sitting as motionless as before, as if he were petrified. It seemed to me that I wasn't getting any nearer to him. I could barely walk now. The sweat irritated the scratches and cuts on my face and my arms. I felt as if thousands of ants were crawling over them. I took out one of the bottles of water, soaked a paper napkin, and wiped my aching face. The itching didn't stop, but at least it became bearable. I performed the same procedure with my arms, then took a few sips from the bottle and tucked it back into the bag. I took some more time to rest. I had a long way to go. Seen from here with naked eyes, the man looked like a black dot in the distance.

I used the binoculars again, this time examining the rocks. I estimated that if I had walked along them, I would have passed by the recess where the tribe had performed their ritual and I must have come very close to the sanctuary where, according to Strauss, I had participated in "the greatest mystery." But was it truly like that or had I only participated in my own drug-induced madness?

"I don't know," I replied to myself once again.

I set off toward the man, plagued by more questions. Who was it? Why wasn't he moving? Was he dead? Alive? Drugged? A zombie? Was it Ludo, shrouded from head to toe by that dark cloud of death?

"I don't know, I don't know, I don't know," I shouted. "But I'm sick of all this!"

I tucked two fingers in my mouth and trilled a piercing whistle. Yes! The dot moved. I raised the binoculars to my eyes. The man turned out to be just one of the tribe. I saw his face, now turned to the side. Then I saw him standing up. It was Arlos. He saw me and stepped to the side, revealing the pale shape of a man, naked to the waist, lying on the gray sand, arms crossed over his chest.

It took me a long time to get there. As I got closer I could see how weak Arlos was, but he waited for me without sitting back down. I dropped the bag on the sand, took out one of the water bottles, and handed it to him. He grabbed it with trembling hands. He drank deeply as I stood there freezing and sweating, clenching my teeth so as not to breathe too loudly, still not looking down at the dead man.

"I know what you're thinking," Arlos whispered. "He died yesterday, only an hour after you separated. Even if you had stayed with him, you could have changed nothing. Here, look at them and you'll understand."

"Who?" I asked, also whispering. "Look at who?"

"Him and death. Her death."

I looked down. Ludo's face was deformed, but only from yesterday's fight with the wall. Apart from that, I couldn't even see his death.

He looked like a man asleep, pleasantly dreaming. I leaned over him with the absurd thought that I could wake him up. I gently poked him and felt the lifeless hardness of his body. I dropped my hands and stepped back.

"Come on," I said to Arlos, "we have to take him back to the complex."

"His desire was to be buried here."

"He was alive when you found him?"

"Yes," Arlos said, pointing to the sanctuary entrance, which was only about three hundred meters away. "Yesterday he reached this place and lay down. When I came close to him he asked me to bury him right here. And then he gave in. He gave in to the great rest."

Arlos sat down next to the dead body.

"You've been sitting here the whole night?" I said. "Why didn't you bury him?"

"I am waiting."

"What for?"

"The desert," he said. "The white desert. When it comes back I shall bury him in it. I know that this will make sense. I feel it will mean something to him. Or to me."

I sat down next to the dead body.

57.

Gromov greeted me only with a nod and led me through the foyer. We entered the living room, which was almost identical to the one in my villa. We sat in the armchairs next to the mini refrigerator. He took out two cans of beer and handed me one. I opened it immediately, sipped, and began.

"I'm coming from the desert, but I decided to stop by before going home. Where is Chari?"

"I have no idea. He's disappeared somewhere again."

"Small wonder," I said. "Such a wild child."

Gromov spread his arms.

"We buried Ludo in the desert," I said. "We waited for the sun to rise and shine over it, and we buried him there. He had chosen this place himself. A member of the tribe, Arlos, helped me. He sat with Ludo's body all night out there, watching over it. He respected Ludo's feelings for Natalia, he respected his bravery also, and his selflessness. All in all, Gromov, these people are not savages."

I paused, expecting a response, but Gromov stared at me with a strange, somewhat worried expression on his face.

"So that's how it is," I sighed. "I need a shower and some rest. But first, let's figure out how to put an end to this nightmare."

"I didn't know that Ludo was dead," Gromov said. "I'm sorry."

"Oh! I thought Chari would have told you about what happened yesterday. Did he at least tell you about Darcy?"

"He didn't tell me anything about anyone. I unlocked him this morning, he fed the dog, and he snuck out."

"Well, it doesn't matter." I smiled. "He is safe now because Darcy was the murderer! Yes, Gromov, your son is quite smart. He managed to get into Darcy's computer and find valuable information that nails him as the murderer, beyond doubt. He had the financial motive to drain Natalia's and the Wanderer's bank accounts, and Fouchet had been in his way, impeding his access to the server. The only murder I still don't understand is Felix's."

Gromov's face became a mix of bewilderment, worry, and anger.

"I know it's a lot to process," I told him. "It's hard to believe that Darcy managed to trick us all. I never would have guessed that behind the mask of a maniacal hunter hid a computer genius. It's all over, though. Now we just need to figure out a way to get the servers back online so we can get in touch with the Agency, and the cops. Call Chari. I'm sure he'll have an idea about how to fix the server."

"Wait for me here," Gromov said, getting out of his chair. "I'll get my phone and we'll call him."

He hurried out of the living room. I finished my beer and relaxed in the armchair. I glanced at my watch. It was almost noon. I had forgotten my phone in my bedroom, but now I intended to use Gromov's to finally call Vanda and Strauss. I assumed that Chari was with them. Vanda had probably prepared something tasty, and they were going to have lunch soon. I would tell them to wait for me so we could eat together. I smiled, happy with the idea of the four of us sitting in the dining room, eating, drinking, talking. Everything nice and quiet.

Gromov was taking too long, and it was getting colder in here. I got goose bumps even though the window was open and it was hot outside, very hot.

"What lunch, for God's sake?" I whispered to myself.

What about the personnel? What about Wilma and Hans? The sooner we alerted the outside world about their disappearance, the sooner the search would begin. They might still be alive. Maybe Darcy had not crashed the helicopters and had only landed them somewhere in the desert. I would have to go back again. Go back . . . but why? I couldn't remember. I was no longer able to say whether it was cold here, or hot. My arms and legs felt frozen, as if I were stuffed in a freezer along with Fouchet and Felix. In my head, however, a fire was blazing, writing in flames the question "Why?"

I thought that I was still wondering why I would have to go back to the desert. But I have to, of course, I have to because now it is like an endless white canvas, and my time has come to paint something. There. That's why I shall walk with no direction. I shall walk through the desert, and when my powers have come to an end, I shall lie down on the hot sand under the burning sun, and I shall watch the sky. I shall watch the sky until my eyes run dry, and my blood slowly stops to flow. Yes, this is the only thing I could paint now: my own death.

I closed my eyes to see this final painting more clearly. Indeed, it was a masterpiece. As full of life as I would be full of death in it. Those twenty-five people, though, were they also dead?

"Hey, Gromov, hurry up," I shouted.

"Wait for me here. I'll get my phone and we'll call him."

Was he making fun of me? "No," I answered myself after a moment of concentration. He had not returned, so he had not said anything yet, and I had heard only what he had said to me before. Was this some delayed echo that only now reached my ears? What was this oppressing grayness? Where was it coming from?

Actually, the grayness was coming from everywhere, and with it the faceless shadows. They were walking listlessly, passing me by, passing through me, but I didn't feel them. Although I could see them—short and thin—the shadows of the tribe. Suddenly Darcy's shadow towered over them. His wasn't completely faceless. It had eyes, silver-gray like coins. We looked at each other. We were only two or three meters apart, but there was another distance between us, an inner one, which seemed endless to me.

I started to stand up, my limbs crackling like dry twigs. I stepped toward Darcy, or toward his shadow, toward the Remorite. He stepped toward me, and then disappeared. *He's trying to possess me, to take my body*, I thought in a fit of voiceless hysteria. But when I turned, I saw him pass through the armchair also, continuing on his way, his outlines blurrier and blurrier. He was leaving, and the other shadows were leaving, too, but the grayness lingered. In it, a tiny spot in lighter gray flickered. *It's the window, the open window.* Then suddenly I realized what was happening to me.

I collapsed on the floor and like an insect crawled in the direction of the window. Yes! Insects never fly in through these windows. My heart was beating at an insane rate, my breathing was uneven, and I was overcome by insurmountable panic. I was losing control over my own thoughts, over my feelings and movements. The window was now not even flickering. It seemed to have disappeared like everything else.

Yet, as it turned out, I had been crawling in the right direction. My forehead touched a wall, and as soon as I managed to rise a bit, the wall turned into a hole, which transformed itself into an open window. I clutched at the edge of the sill and finally stood up. My vision was clearer now. The grayness was quickly dissolving into the bright daylight. All I had to do was climb over the sill, fling myself onto the terrace, and, from there, reach the jeep and get out of here. *Now!*

"Now!" I repeated aloud, but stepped back.

I wasn't sure if Vanda and Strauss were in my villa. I also didn't know if Chari was with them. If they were not, if Chari wasn't with them, there was a possibility that I would not find them first, which meant that I would not find them alive. I couldn't take such a risk. I pressed the button to shut the window and collapsed to the floor. Turning my head to the side, so as to have a good view of the door, I waited, while trying to restore myself, at least partly, back to normal. If there was anything normal left in me.

After some time, which felt to me more than an hour, although it couldn't have been more than a minute, the door began to open slowly. Gromov peeked in the living room, and I quickly half-closed my eyes. I relaxed as far as I could, and continued waiting, watching him through narrow slits. He came in, a large, broad-shouldered man in perfect physical and mental condition. There was a gun in his right hand and a rope in his left. He quietly closed the door behind him and walked toward me.

I was making an effort to breathe calmly, but I would not be able to stand this for long, and now I could barely control my twitching eyelids. I hoped that Gromov would immediately try to tie me up, but he stopped a step away from my head. Now I could see only his brown shoes. I saw one of them rising from the ground and freezing in the air. The bastard was preparing to kick me in the face.

I have no idea how I managed not to move or even flinch. Was it due to my stunted instincts or their immediate mobilization? Gromov's hesitation made me realize that he was checking to see if I was playing unconscious. Apparently, he was pleased with the result, because his shoe did not break my jaw and only returned back to the ground.

He moved toward my feet, leaving the narrow range of my vision. Now I could count only on my hearing. The rustling of his clothes was accompanied by a barely audible creaking of his knees. He was squatting next to me. I was glad that the carpet did not reach this part of the floor, and I waited and waited for the short tap of metal on the luxurious mahogany parquetry.

Then I heard it! Gromov left his revolver on the floor. I delayed my reaction for a second or two, and as soon as I felt the touch of the rope on my ankles, I briskly drew back my legs and kicked him. Gromov moaned and fell back. I rose and grabbed the gun. I pointed it at him, and from the terror in his eyes I could tell that he hadn't forgotten to load it.

58.

I didn't allow Gromov to stand up, but I did permit him to get comfortable on the floor. He leaned his back on the wall by the window and crossed his arms as a sign of peaceful resignation. I moved back to an armchair, collapsing into it. I felt horrible but there was no turning back now.

"So Chari lied to me," I said. "You are the murderer."

"Yes, I am."

"Slide your phone to me, would you?"

"Come and get it."

"I will but first I'll blow your brains out."

"Blow yours out, go on, Artist! I bet I revived your desire to say farewell to your life."

"Oh, I'm past that now," I said casually. "Seems that ultrasound does not affect me as severely as you hoped."

"Infrasound," he corrected me. "Ultrasound serves only to chase away insects. Infrasound is what the Butlers use to disinfest the rooms from time to time."

"Only when the tenants are absent," I said. "You, however, decided to eliminate this restriction in the program."

"Yes, though the programs gave me a lot of trouble," he said. "For example, even when they are set on disinfesting mode, they switch on only if a certain window is open. That was a problem."

"I can imagine. We rarely open the windows in this heat, so you couldn't really drive us crazy whenever you wanted to in the daytime. At night, however, you would open them through the Butlers."

"Last night was the only time I used infrasound on you while you were sleeping. Plus, I have been manipulating people during the daytime starting only recently. In fact, it was only you and Natalia, who, by the way, turned out to be particularly susceptible. I was surprised by her last dance."

"You wretch," I said, reaching for the gun.

"What about the kid? How will he feel when he sees his father dead or wounded, writhing and bleeding?"

"You wretch," I repeated, dropping my arm.

"I am a wretch, yes," he said, "and you're a fool."

"I know, I know," I said, realizing I had to bide my time until I got some of my strength back. "Now I know why the window in Felix's study was open. I also know why I fell asleep, in such a weird way, and why I felt so poorly afterward."

"Poorly? You were psychotic, that's the truth," Gromov said, winking at me cheerfully. "But to be honest, if the kid hadn't planted his bug on your bracelet, now everyone here would have been alive and well. Yes, thanks to him I overheard you and the lady talking about your issues. Then it occurred to me that I could get rich by eliminating a couple of millionaires on behalf of the Artist."

"Why didn't you simply drain their accounts? Why did you have to kill them?"

"Because the dead don't want their money back, and these ones don't have any heirs, either."

"What about the others? Where are they now?"

"You should ask God. Or Gunther Strauss," Gromov said through a wicked smile. "I personally don't know where they are."

"So there's a chance that they might still be alive?"

"No, of course not. I blew up the helicopters in the air, just to be sure that none of them would survive. This doesn't stop them from roaming, however, does it? As Remorites!"

"Aren't you worried that if you keep on like this I might really shoot you?"

"I know that you would fire only if I stood up and started walking toward you. As long as I am sitting here, however, you're as harmless as a dove. Yes, Artist, I know you. I know you all too well."

"You're wrong. You cannot know someone only from a few overheard conversations."

"True, but I know you from your diary."

I waited for him to speak again.

"By the way, I forgot to tell you that I also blew up the helicopter with your paintings. After taking your diary out first."

Without taking my eyes off his, I picked up the gun and stood.

"It's hidden in a safe place," he said, now talking faster. "But the cops will definitely find it, and as soon as they read it they'll see what a psycho you are. I have made sure they find other incontrovertible evidence against you. All in all, no one is going to believe it when you claim that I am the killer. Especially if you kill or wound me now."

I went to the liquor cabinet, pulled out a bottle of whiskey, and rolled it toward Gromov. Astonished, he reached out and took it. I sat back in the armchair and aimed at his forehead.

"Drink," I ordered. "You're going to drink until you pass out. Then it will be easy to tie you up."

Something in my expression seemed to convince him that he didn't know me as well as he thought. He opened the bottle and swiftly raised it to his lips.

"Wait," I said. "I have some questions I would rather you answered while still sober."

"Ask!" he said excitedly, placing the bottle on the floor. "Ask me anything. I'll explain all. I have no secrets from you."

"Apart from Fouchet, there was another server administrator, whom you also murdered. Even before eliminating Fouchet, right?"

"Do I look like a victim of suicide to you?"

"You're trying to suggest that you were the other administrator?"

"I'm not suggesting anything. I am the other server administrator."

"You're lying! If you were the server administrator, Chari would have known."

"He didn't know, but he found out last night. He broke into my computer, not Darcy's. Damned kid stole the passwords. Rotten little freak!"

"Shut up," I roared. "You've disowned your own son! You have no idea what an intelligent and deserving child he is."

"Oh, don't make me cry," Gromov said, his eyes filled with hatred. "You made the mistake of attaching yourself to a freak, pure and simple, and now you find the truth painful. The little freak is doomed. He is sick. He will die very soon. His illness has been creeping slowly through his body since he was born, but with the coming of puberty it has become more active. It will take him out any moment now, just like that, while he is running around with his dog."

I wanted to cut him off, but I was at a loss for words.

"He's the reason I am in this complex for lunatics and parasites. When he was little, you couldn't tell he had it at all. Gradually, his freakishness became more and more visible. That's why my wife and I brought him here: to hide him. To hide him from the world, because my father-in-law, Mister Big, could not swallow the fact that his only grandson was damaged goods."

"Quiet, quiet," I mumbled, worried that Chari could be listening to all of this. "Shut up!"

"But I, too, am merely goods. I sold myself! This is what my marriage was: a sale."

"Tell me how come you are both a tenant and an employee here."

"My father-in-law owns this complex, and not only this one. I had many ideas, but I was poor, poor, poor. I was hoping that by becoming his son-in-law he would support some of my ideas. But he only crushed me. He turned me into a slave and sent us here to wait for the death of our defective offspring. And you know what? The rent for this villa for a day is equal to my monthly salary. I am a computer genius, but for the past year I have been doing nothing but maintaining the electronic comfort of this entire trashy place filled with fat ballerinas, gangsters, lords, mad professors, failed artists, newborn farmers, and paranoid newlyweds. I've been working locked in there so that no one finds out. Because my wife could not suffer such a disgrace in the eyes of the trash. Having a husband from the serving class, oh the horror! But she could not stand anything, anyway. After a month or two here, she went back to Daddy. I was left here, waiting for the damned freak to die."

"Enough!"

"He's tougher than he looks."

"Shut your mouth! Or don't. Open it and drink!"

He shook his head, and I aimed at his forehead again.

"You have a choice," I said. "Either sober and dead, or drunk and tied up."

"Damn you, Artist!"

He grabbed the bottle and was just about to take a sip when instead, he threw it at me. He missed. The bottle smashed against the edge of the table.

"Go ahead, shoot. I am now content. The rumors that will swirl around these murders will spread, and my fat father-in-law will go bankrupt!"

Gromov shook in a fit of laughter, which boomed as if not from his chest, but from hell. I listened to it as a monstrous yet encouraging idea formed with torturous slowness.

"The medical article," I said in a hoarse voice. "The day before his death, Felix copied it from the Internet. Yesterday Chari deleted it! He was in shock. Something about it suggested to him that you were the murderer."

"Yes, I got rid of Felix because of that article," Gromov mumbled, frowning. "I forgot to check if he had downloaded it on his computer. The moves of your little friend, however, are beyond me. Why did he delete it? What does he mean to do?"

"What was the article about?" I said. "Is Chari's disease now curable?"

"Yes," Gromov said. "Felix thought telling me the news would make me happy. He wanted to announce it to everyone. I could barely convince him to wait. I made up something about getting a confirmation so as to be sure not to get our hopes up."

"You killed the boy to keep the secret that your son's disease is curable? You monster," I whispered with utter disgust. "Chari put it all together, didn't he?"

"Yes, always poking his nose into everything, damned freak! But if I had let Felix blabber, my stay in the complex would have become suspicious. Everyone would have expected us to leave. But I had just gained some ground after eliminating Fouchet."

I was no longer paying attention to him. My soul felt brighter and clearer.

He will be healed. I'll take care of him.

59.

A car pulled up and someone came in the front door, slamming it behind them.

"Gregg! Where are you, Gregg?" Maggie said.

"We're here, Maggie," I answered, "in the living room."

She looked angry. When she saw Gromov on the floor, her anger changed into puzzlement. When her eyes landed on me, she became terrified and shrieked.

"Calm down," I said. "Calm down, calm down. Everything is fine."

She raised her hands and fell silent. She was like a rabbit staring at the gaping mouth of an anaconda. Then I remembered the gun I was holding. I put it down to reassure her.

"No, Maggie. It's not me. It's him. Gromov is the murderer."

Maggie's unblinking worry did not pass.

"It's true," Gromov said.

"I can't believe it," Maggie said, finally putting down her hands. "Thank God, Rhein . . . I have to sit down. I think I'll faint."

She's playing me, I thought, but it was too late. Maggie swiped the revolver from the table and aimed it at me.

"No," Gromov yelled. "Not here!"

"I know."

I sat there like a potted plant, trying not to look too dumb.

"What took you so long?" Gromov said, standing up and stretching.

"I couldn't find him, Gregg."

"Did you check Rhein's villa?"

"He wasn't there, but Strauss was, along with Vanda," Maggie said, smirking at me. "Can you guess where I locked them, Rhein? Your storeroom. I thought that it would only be natural if you strangled them there."

"Perfect!" Gromov said, looking happy. "We'd better watch out for another trick from the little shithead, though."

"Kid's really getting on my nerves."

"We'll find him, and the Artist will strangle him, too."

Their plan was now all too clear. They would drag me into my villa, tie me up, and disinfest me until my brains started to rot. Meanwhile, they would kill Vanda, Chari, and Strauss on my behalf. After that, they would manage to establish a connection with the city and call the cops for help.

"The cops won't believe you," I said.

"They'll never hear from us," Gromov said devilishly. "Didn't you know? You held a knife to Gaston Fouchet's neck and made him blow up the helicopters. Maggie and I were in one of them. This information has already been logged in the complex records. So we won't have a chance to meet the cops."

They both laughed much longer than warranted and it sickened me to see just how happy they were.

"In love and happy," I said.

"And very rich!" Maggie added, exhilarated.

"No, dear, you're wrong," Gromov said. "We're fantastically rich! We have Darcy's funds now."

"You broke the code? You're the greatest."

I was seething on the inside, yet I managed to maintain my relaxed pose with a sheep-like, resigned expression on my face. After a short while, Gromov came for me, looking as fresh as I was exhausted. He stopped in front of me. I smiled and reached out my hands. I wasn't sure what confused him more—my friendliness or the gesture. I kept smiling, and in the end he smiled, too. He relaxed and became less focused as he leaned in to tie my hands.

I kicked him in the balls and as he fell on me I landed my knee on his nose. Maggie was right next to us and made to hit me in the head with the butt of the gun. I turned to avoid the blow, but fell out of the chair, pulling Gromov down with me. We rolled and he got on top of me. His weight pressed my back into the broken bottle shards and then he punched me squarely on my temple, unleashing a flurry of little stars, chaotic like fireflies.

"Stop," Chari's voice boomed, bringing me back to consciousness.

60.

"Don't worry, Ray. Everything is under control," Chari said, standing in the doorway, his hand raised high, holding a phone. "If I press this button, two messages will be sent. One will land in the Agency's central office, and the other will mobilize a police search-and-rescue crew that will immediately fly here from the city."

Gromov and I both lumbered to our feet, crunching glass. Blood was crawling down my back.

"What are you talking about?" Gromov said.

"I am sorry, Ray," Chari said. "I am to blame. I rushed things with the lie about Darcy. I overestimated myself. I thought I was already in Fouchet's account, but I was tricked."

"What are you talking about?" I said.

"I will be more clear. First, you two step away from each other. Sit at both ends of the sofa," Chari said, eyeing both Maggie and his father. "Ray, sit wherever you want."

Maggie and Gromov looked quite despondent and followed the orders. Chari pulled up a stool, sat on it, and addressed me directly.

"Our connection to the world has been restored, Ray. But I was late, too late. I should have finished everything by the end of last night."

"What?" Gromov said. "What are you talking about?"

Chari paid him no attention.

"That file on Felix's computer opened my eyes, Ray. I realized who the murderer was."

"I know, Chari, I already know. You're going to be okay! We're going to get rid of the damned disease. We're going to pull it out of you like a weed."

Chari lost it, the happiness of the news a painful reminder of how unspeakably horrible his father had been. It was too much emotion for any one person to process, let alone a boy.

"He was only trying to forget about your existence," Maggie said.

"Bitch," I snarled.

"But I knew, from the very beginning I knew that you were his lover," Chari said, emphasizing it as if it were her greatest sin. "He convinced Natalia to offer you a place to stay. But you were his lover before coming here!"

"So what?"

"What I'm trying to say is that I'll let you go. I don't know if you would be able to be happy, carrying the heavy burden of multiple murders, but you can try. I won't stand in your way."

"Ha! You can't stand in our way," Maggie said, shifting her eyes to the revolver in her hand.

Chari, in his turn, shifted his eyes to the phone in his hand. "A moment before you pull the trigger, I'll press this button and the whole truth will be delivered accordingly. I have described everything in detail in the messages. So the rescue crew would be here in no more than two hours, and by that time you two would have reached nowhere. They'll find you easily."

"You're wrong," Gromov said. "They wouldn't have to find us. We will wait for them here, considering the situation."

"It would be utterly stupid to drive like mad through the desert, knowing that your escape is doomed. Stay. But don't think anyone will suspect Ray. The evidence you placed in his garage is now destroyed, as is the Capricorn with his fingerprints. Gaston Fouchet was buried the day before yesterday, so the programming manipulations you did on his behalf yesterday, and especially today, would give you away instantly. His corpse will blow your cover!"

"Chari," I groaned. "Why did you protect your dad and lie to me about Darcy?"

"I know, Ray," he said, blushing. "There was no harm. Or at least that's what I thought when I sent you the lie. In order to register the account properly, I had to migrate to another of Fouchet's accounts, and the real root password resisted my brute-force attacks because it was behind a firewall. The 'anomaly' was also copied into two panels, so I had to hack the anonymous proxy, as well. All those strings just made me dizzy."

Chari continued reeling off all this incomprehensible stuff, but I didn't stop him. I knew this wasn't for me but for his father. He was shining, finally making an impression on the truly pathetic one.

"Stop showing off," Maggie whined.

"Fine. I'll get to the point," Chari said. "Before last night I was going to give you two an oltim . . . an ultimatum: leave immediately and I would never send the messages."

"What's the difference between then and now?" Gromov asked.

"Everyone would have believed that Darcy was the murderer, and the cops would not have suspected you."

"Our disappearance would have immediately drawn all eyes on us."

"It wouldn't have happened like that, because I was going to stage your death," Chari said. "You know that Maggie frequently visits the rocks near the precipice. I was going to tell them that on this particular morning you went with her. Then I was going to play a bit with the program that lifts the sluices. I was going to make it appear as if there had been some glitch and you drowned when the river flooded the precipice. Since it goes underground farther down the river well, it took your bodies deeper into the caves and they are impossible to recover. Am I clear?"

"Absolutely," Gromov said. "But since the Artist now knows that Darcy was not the killer, this well-planned story of yours becomes complete trash. Unless we kill him now, and you say later that he came with us to the precipice."

"Where the Remorites are," Maggie cackled.

"Ray is my friend, you wretches. I would die for him."

"So now what?" Gromov said.

"Now I can offer you only time, enough time," Chari said. "Get out of the complex immediately, and I shall send the messages in three days. Or even four. Until then, I'll maintain contact with the people from the Agency, just as you did. Does that sound good to you?"

"It could have sounded good," Gromov said somewhat bitterly. "But you made a mistake."

"How?" Chari asked, bristling.

"By mentioning the anonymous proxy, that's how. If you had really hacked it, it would have stopped being anonymous to you. You would have known that the role of proxy-server is being carried out by my computer—"

"Wait a moment, Gregg!" Maggie grew excited. "Are you trying to say that he's *bluffing*? That in fact the 'anomaly' is still active? That no messages could be sent from here?"

"Yes, but"—Gromov rubbed his brow hesitantly—"four days would be enough to hide so well that no one would be able to follow our tracks."

"Oh, no," Maggie cried out. "I'm not going to live in hiding like a mouse. There should be no following of tracks. We were in one of the blown-up helicopters and that's it! That's it, do you understand? You have no right to abandon our plan."

"On the contrary, we'll be free. I will have all my rights," Gromov said, suddenly jumping up and heading for Chari. "What are you doing? No, Maggie, no, no!"

I also moved toward Chari, but when the revolver thundered Gromov was there. He stood in front of Chari as a crimson flower opened its petals on his shirt. Maggie just stood there, her mouth gaping. I yanked the gun from her hand, pulling her back into the moment. She looked at me, Chari, and Gromov, who had collapsed. She rushed out of the living room and soon the sound of a revving engine cut the silence.

Chari was kneeling by his father. Gromov's eyes were wide open, staring at his son. A moment before death closed them, he managed to fill them with approval. He also reached out his hand and gently placed it on Chari's hand.

61.

I took a quick shower so I could get back down to Vanda, Strauss, and Chari. When I entered the dining room thirty minutes later Chari had not moved at all. His head was still drooping, his hands were still lying listlessly on the table. Strauss was seated across from him, wearing a worried expression.

"Hey, why are you dressed?" said Vanda. "Come on, take them off, now!"

"How could you want such a thing from me right now, in front of guests? It's indecent."

Chari smiled, something we all noticed.

"Stop it," she snapped playfully. "Decent, indecent! I'm sick of this! I want you naked, and that's it!"

Strauss rolled his eyes.

"The shirt, Ray," Chari said, still grinning. "She wants you to take off your shirt, just your shirt."

"That's all?" I said, summoning disappointment on my face and making his smile grow bigger.

Vanda approached me carrying a large tray, but instead of being full of coffee and sweets it was covered with all sorts of bandages, plasters, gauze, and ointments.

"Off with the shirt," she said.

I took the shirt off and sat down. Knitting her brow, Vanda stepped closer, placed the tray on my knees, and started to examine my back, prodding me with tweezers. Despite her angry mumbling, she was very careful. She dropped shards of glass onto the tray, and I wondered how I had not felt them in the shower.

"It doesn't hurt," I said.

"You really were lucky," she smiled, though her eyes were teary. "The wounds will heal quickly."

"This is all my fault," Chari said with sadness in his voice. "If I had only told you about Maggie and my dad you wouldn't have let her grab the gun."

"Don't blame yourself for not being a gossip," I said.

"It's to your credit that you kept your father's secret to yourself," Strauss said. "People who announce the intimate secrets of others are worthless. But I certainly must accept some blame for not recognizing that Maggie was pretending this whole time. I fell for everything she said about her interest in Remorites."

"I started to think that she had become interested in them after hearing the legend," Chari said.

"Too bad," Vanda said, shaking her head. "It's too bad that she took the jeep and that the gas tank was almost full. That damned woman will get far."

"I doubt that," I said. "The desert is cruel."

We all fell silent and Vanda resumed tending to my wounds.

"You're a thick-skinned man, Ray," Chari said as Vanda finished up and helped me put my shirt back on.

"I'll be as good as new in no time."

Strauss stood up and left the dining room with a forcedly sprightly gait. We could hear the door open and then the bounding excitement of Hector, who ran right to his master. As the two of them caught up, Chari finally started crying. Vanda led him to the sofa and she held him, crying as well.

"So," Strauss said after a long pause. "Now it's time to talk. Chari, do you really believe in the Remorites? Or were you only pretending?"

"I wasn't pretending," Chari said through his tears. "I believe in them."

"Then you can understand the significance of what you've done for your father."

"I've done nothing," Chari sniffed. "I tried to help him, but I couldn't."

"That's not true," Strauss said. "You succeeded because you tried, and gave him the opportunity to start seeing into you, Chari. Through you he finally started seeing into himself. He realized that you were the most important thing in his life and that he loved you the whole time. Imagine how much negative energy he must have neutralized in this sublime moment!"

"Yes, but much of it remained. Will his Remorite be able to overcome it? Will he get a second chance?"

"The only thing I'm sure about is that if your father had continued to live, he wouldn't have gotten a second chance. Not after everything he did. But now, I don't know. It's clear that his Remorite will continue to roam the grayness of the in-between zone for a long time, but will he ever leave it? Maybe this depends on you, too."

"On me?" Chari said, raising his head.

"Ask yourself: If you were in his place what would you want him to do for you?"

"Forget me," Chari said, biting his lip. "This is what I would want from him. To forget all about me."

"Now he needs the same," Strauss said. "This is the only way you can help him: by forgetting him. It is going to be very difficult. Your battle with your own memories is going to be a hard and long one."

"There will come a day, however," I said, "when you will start winning this battle. Then he will be able to help you, so that you both become winners in the end."

"You will get to know him with your heart and soul," Strauss said quietly. "Because now, he also knows that he loves you. There is no power strong enough to break the bond between you. What's choking it, though, are all those heavy memories of the murderer who no longer exists. Now your father is a completely different person. In the gray zone, his only light is you. So be sure to make your light grow brighter. Revel in all you have. Find strength in knowing there is now a cure for your disease. Overcome your memories. Live long and fully. And one day, which for your father will be now again, he will see your shining light and he will start walking in its direction. Perhaps this will be his path to a second chance."

"Maybe," Chari whispered. "Maybe!"

62.

We all helped clean up the dining room, and then Strauss and Chari set off for the lake to feed the swans. I waited for them to leave, checked that the Butler had closed the gate after them, and then let Hector out. Now no one would bother the swans, or me and Vanda.

She prepared coffee, and then sat across from me at the table, brushed a lock of hair from her forehead, and, looking me in the eyes, confessed:

"I'm suffocating, Rhein," she said. "I could barely control myself in front of Chari!"

I was tired. I wanted her to continue controlling herself in front of me, too.

"I did that monster a great favor," she said, pouring us coffee.

"What do you mean, exactly?"

"If I hadn't stuffed Fouchet in the freezer, if I had told you right away, if we had warned the others . . ."

"You're being too harsh on yourself. Just put yourself in your place . . . I mean, you, naturally, are always in your place, but . . . Damn it! Just think about the situation you were in back then."

"A terrible and disgusting situation."

"Exactly! First, you read about my trances and memory loss, and then you find a corpse in the storeroom."

We both laughed— a forced laugh, really.

"You know what makes me furious?" I continued. "The fact that Gromov had fun doing it the whole time. He was eavesdropping on the nonsense Chari was trying to foist on me, mixing it with elements from the legend, and then he played with me, like with the hologram of the Wanderer, in combination with the disinfesting, which I didn't mention to Strauss and Chari, on purpose. They would definitely try it out on themselves."

"Try it on themselves?" Vanda said.

"Infrasound, the electronic narcotic. At certain frequencies its effect is very similar to the effect of the drug the tribe uses. I learned this the hard way today. But it was the infrasound that made me and Natalia see the Remorites. Which once again proves that they do exist when one's consciousness is expanded."

"Stop it," Vanda shouted. "I didn't want to insult Strauss or Chari, but to you I'll put it straight: I forbid you to speak to me about Remorites. Got it?"

Only now did I notice how much Vanda had changed in just a week. Gone was the self-confident, conceited young lady. Gone was the colorful girl-bijou with her ruby lips, alabaster skin, and sparkling emerald eyes. Now her face looked haggard, with a careworn, grayish tinge. There were dark shadows under her eyes, and her lips were pale, almost colorless. She also looked thinner, smaller, and, somewhat touchingly, neat, with her hair pulled back, dressed in her white T-shirt and black cotton trousers.

She was standing before me, looking at me, and waiting.

"Come," I said gently.

She walked around the table, crouched beside me on the sofa, and rested her head on my shoulder.

"You know what?" she mumbled with a sigh. "Maggie didn't leave immediately after she locked us in. She remained on the other side of the storeroom door for a while, describing how painfully we were going to die. I begged her to let us go. I humiliated myself. I was a sorry sight."

"No, Vanda," I said, caressing her hair. "She was a sorry sight, you were only scared."

"I was also desperate. I thought about you and Chari. It drove me mad. Strauss kept his dignity. Maybe what helped him was that he believes in his theory. But all I thought about then was how I don't believe in any other versions of us. I don't believe in second chances," she said, looking deep into my eyes. "What about you, Rhein? Do you really believe?"

"I don't know, and I think that Strauss has his own doubts. But I do think it should remain like this, because otherwise . . . Otherwise, Vanda, we would lose the frightening but also more precious belief that we can have only one unique life. Without this belief, all the versions of ourselves would be cheap and meaningless. No matter how many of them there are."

"You're right," she said, smiling and gripping my hand. "Our chances are always here and now. They are present, floating about us, and we . . . we simply have to be careful not to miss them."

I closed my eyes to feel more fully the touch of her hand in mine, her body next to mine, her presence here and now. Sadly, our time together was coming to an end. Tomorrow the server administrator "Gaston Fouchet" would not file his regular message to the Agency's central office, and the rescue crew would be here no later than noon. And then . . .

"You will leave, Vanda, and will have a new chance. You'll be able to snatch the Martian himself, the genius Marcian Hosepha, from your father."

"Ha! Why should I? I have you."

"Me? You have me, yes. But I am just like those thirty paintings that are now only rags. Singed, carried by the desert winds, rags whose remains of images, ideas, and colors will gradually grow blacker and blacker in the white sands."

"Rhein, you are the Artist, these paintings are yours! They are somewhere in your memory, and sooner or later, you'll pull them out of there. You will see them, feel them again. Paint them once more!"

"What if it doesn't happen like that? What if I never paint anything, ever again?"

"So what?" she said, slowly drawing her hand back from mine. "Life, your one and only unique life, is not just about painting."

I was going to say something, although I didn't know what. Probably some nonsense, but the lips of this wonderful girl touched mine, and then she embraced me and whispered in my ear those three most desired words that made me feel absolutely dumb, and dizzy, and happy.

I love you.

63.

The wind rising from the chasm was cold. The hour in which the sun shone over it had long passed. Gone was the white spirit of the river from my white visions. Now, with the darkening sunset, this empty space looked like nothing more than a dried-up riverbed. Immersed in the twilight, it resembled a grave from whose giant womb the night was to come to life. Again.

"Don't lean over," I said, pulling Chari back by the shoulder.

"I am warning you," Vanda said, panting, "this better be a grand surprise. Or I will never forgive you for dragging me all the way here."

"Look, look," Strauss said, nodding invitingly.

I nudged Chari to move closer to Strauss and stepped forward. I leaned over, but, other than the already-familiar view, I saw nothing.

"Oh my God!" Vanda exclaimed, leaning over the edge. "Oh my God!"

Then I saw them, too. The paintings! They were down there at the bottom—flat, white rectangular shapes, scattered among the gray stones, still wrapped up. I felt dizzy. I drew back from the edge, took a few steps back, and sat down on the sandy ground. I searched for some emotion in my soul, but found none. Complete numbness.

"I thought you were going to be happy," Strauss said.

"He will be. Only later," Chari said. "Now he's afraid."

"Everything is all right, everything is all right," Vanda whispered to me, her hands on my shoulders.

I shook my head. There were no words.

"Don't worry," Strauss said, trying to cheer me up. "I could tell from here they are not damaged."

"The stones down there are smooth," Vanda said.

"The river has rubbed them smooth," Chari said, "over centuries, or maybe even millennia. Now it has saved your paintings!"

"How did you find them?" Vanda asked.

"Maggie called me," Strauss said.

"From the desert," Chari added. "The jeep got stuck in the sand. She deserved to die out there, but we decided to save her, right, Strauss?"

"I promised that we'd send people, as soon as the rescue crew comes. As a sign of gratitude, she told me where the paintings were. Gromov dropped them there from the helicopter."

Chari stepped toward me and reached out his hand. I took it, thinking that I was only returning his friendly gesture, but he pulled me up and then quickly walked away, heading straight for the palm trees at the southern end of the precipice. When he got to them he flung the rope ladder over the edge with a few kicks and started climbing down.

"He's right," Vanda said. "Soon, it will be completely dark down there."

"Yes, we have to hurry," Strauss agreed. "Do you have the rope I told you to bring?"

I thrust my hand in my pants pocket and took out a ball of nylon cord. He patted me on the shoulder and took the lead, urging us to follow him.

Despite being made of rope, the Wanderer's ladder was very easy to use. We were down in no time and without any trouble. Chari was walking to and fro between the rocks. I was sure that he was looking for my diary. I was also sure that the moment we found it, I would destroy it immediately. I hated myself for it.

Vanda and Strauss were already carrying one of the pictures in my direction. I had just been standing by the ladder, doing nothing. Somewhat quietly, they left the painting by my feet and walked away again. I didn't look down at it. I knew that it was wrapped, but I didn't want to see it anyway. Chari had been right. I was afraid. *The end, the end,* I was repeating to myself. *The end is near, my end is near, and only he will remain, the Artist?*

"Ray!" Chari yelled from afar, running toward me. "Go back, go back up! Now!"

He fell and I rushed to him as Hector howled compassionately from above.

"No, no!" Chari said, rising quickly. "Go back *up*! She has lied to us, Ray!"

"Are you OK?" Vanda said.

"She lied to us," Chari said. "She wasn't calling from the desert."

Of course, the range for mobile connections was still limited! How could we not have thought of this earlier? I turned around and ran to the ladder but it was already going up.

"No," Vanda moaned.

"Oh, yes!" Maggie said, peeking over the edge and laughing. "Fools!"

We gathered under the ladder, which was now dangling well above our heads.

"You're the fool," Chari shouted. "We'll go up through the caves, we're going to find you, and this time we'll show no mercy!"

"Wrong again," Maggie yelled back. "You underestimated your father. He had thought of everything! Including programming the helicopter from which all this trash came. It is now very near. All I have to do is climb in. I already have a bank account full of money. So, just imagine the life that's waiting for me. Imagine it before you die!"

She raised her hand to show us the cell phone she was holding.

"But I do owe you for the good idea, kid!"

"Which one?" Chari yelled.

"Farewell!" Maggie screamed, making a point to show us how she was pressing a button on the phone. "You're dead already! Drowned!"

64.

The thunder was still distant but gradually growing louder. Somewhere there, in the darkness underground, the river was leaving the narrow concrete tunnel, and it was coming, rushing toward us, toward its ancient, dried-up path through the rock.

"What's happening?" Vanda said. "What did she do?"

"She has opened the sluice," Chari said, his voice shaking. "While we thought she was in the desert she was preparing everything. That's why she lured us down here."

"And now?" Vanda said.

"We have only five or six minutes left to live," Chari said. "Actually, more, because the sluice-gate won't release the river immediately, only gradually."

Vanda pulled herself together and sat next to him on the rock. She took a motley handkerchief from her pocket, and, with a kind of desperate care, started soaking up the blood on his knee.

Strauss and I stood before them, helpless, as Maggie flung pebbles at us.

"Such a miserable woman," Vanda said, looking up.

"I want you to beg me again!" Maggie shouted.

She was lying on her stomach, peeking over the edge, and waiting for the show. Waiting to watch us drown.

"Come on, Vanda! If you beg properly, I'll spare your lives," she taunted, shaking the ladder like it was bait.

"No," Chari whispered. "Don't beg her."

"Oh, don't worry about that," Vanda said, finishing up on his knee.

"Thanks," he said. "You know, Vanda, in the beginning, I didn't like you. But besides being very beautiful, you're really quite clever."

She embraced him, pressing him against her, as if in this way she could protect him from the looming disaster. Maggie burst out in a weirdly sinister, cawing laughter.

"Sometimes my mother used to laugh like that," Chari cried, staring at the foamy waters that were beginning to spew from the cave. "She used to laugh at me like that."

Suddenly, her disgusting laughter transformed into a scream, which was muffled by barking and beastly snarls. Now we could see that Hector was attacking her! Her head disappeared from sight for a moment, and a moment later, we saw their bodies tangled together at the very edge of the precipice.

"Hector! Back!" Chari screamed in panic, but his voice was so thin that it got lost in the boom of the advancing river.

"Hector, back!" I screamed, not wanting Chari's final memory being the death of his dog. "Hector, back!"

Illuminated by the sunset, the strong yellowish body of the pit bull–mastiff thrust back, leaping backward, and Maggie flew in the opposite direction. She was screaming, falling down along the ladder, her hands frantically reaching for it. She managed to clutch on to the dangling end. But this didn't help her. Close to the ground she crashed down right by us. She hit the stones fast, disappearing under the rushing water with a final scream.

I grabbed the ladder. Vanda and Chari stood petrified, but Strauss brusquely pushed them toward me. They waded closer, knee-deep in the water, slipping on the smooth surface of the stones. The gradual release of the river had come to an end, and soon, very soon, it was going to rush into this place with all its terrifying power.

I reached out, clutched Chari by the shirt, and pushed him to the ladder, but he resisted.

"Vanda needs to go first," he screamed.

Vanda realized that he wasn't going to yield, and started climbing up hurriedly. Strauss and I held the ladder stretched and steady to make her ascent easier. When she reached the top Chari took off after her. I nodded at Strauss, urging him. There was no time; the water was flowing over us. We were swaying under its pull, yet he waited for Chari to reach the top, and only then started climbing.

65.

I am down there, still at the bottom. I am clutching at the ladder. I know that I have to head up immediately, but something is stopping me.

The water is extremely cold, already reaching my waist. I feel it as sharp blades of ice cutting me in half. But there is nothing new about this. My lips curve up in a half smile as I search for the painting Vanda and Strauss had carried here. I want to salvage at least this one. I am looking for it among the foamy wavelets on the dark water. It must be somewhere near. There it is! It has been looking for me, too, pushed by a mystical hand.

It is floating in my direction, wrapped up tight in its waterproof packing. Rocking, swaying to and fro, but still approaching me. I reach out to catch it, and my fingers clutch at the frame, but it slips away. I take a step toward it, still clutching the ladder. My hand reaches out again, but the painting passes me by, floating away. I cannot catch up with it—not without letting go of the ladder. I let go.

The roaring has become deafening. I look back over my shoulder and it seems to me that in front of the opening of the cave there is now a porous, silver-gray wall rising. A moment later, though, this wall arches, transforms into a huge, foaming wave, which rolls in my direction, thundering. I manage to grab the ladder again, and breathe in, just before the wave sweeps over me. Its roar falls into rumbling, booming, grumbling. It pulls at me, and the rope cuts into my palms, but I don't let go. I hold out against the angry might of the water that's been building up and charging with energy in the darkness of the underground.

"Rhein, Rhein!" The voices are coming from the sky.

I look up and see the three of them waving their hands wildly. The reddish halos of the sunset burn around their heads, and their faces are dark above me. I can't tell them apart. I don't remember them. Now they are strangers to me, sinking into forgetfulness like images from a suddenly interrupted dream.

I let go of the ladder. This time for the last time, forever. I fall into the icy embrace of the river, and it carries me down through the chasm. Something bumps my chest—a painting—and I grab it.

I am holding the painting with one hand, and with the other, I am pulling at the wrapping, tearing it. I swallow water, drowning already, here where the river enters the cave, becoming an underground river again. I am pulling, scratching, tearing the wrapping. To see it, to see at least fragments of it, just for a moment—this is all I want. But the current is now extremely powerful, and it spins me, sucks me in, crashing me against the rocky bottom, tossing me back up to the surface. Through my blurry eyes, for an instant, I see something completely different.

At the edge of the precipice, a girl is shielding the eyes of a child with her hand. "Don't look, don't look!"

God, what have I done? I loosen my grip on the ragged painting. What have I done?! The wrong choice. Possibly the worst of them all. *Don't look, Chari! Don't look at me while I am dying. Don't look, Vanda! Although you told me you loved me. Don't look, Strauss. You were like a father to me.*

The mighty river has gone underground again, roaring and booming deeper and deeper into the cave's darkness. While it carries me at breakneck speed along its path, I feel neither its coldness, nor my body colliding with the ancient walls. I am deep into my own blindness, and into the silence that is spreading inside me. It is boundless, inviolable, deathly, yet I am trying to bring it to life with my voiceless prayer.

Please, Lord, give me a chance! Give me a second chance! Give it to me at some moment, Lord, any time, any time that is now.

* * *

The river drifted silently. The Artist was standing in its way and it was passing through him—imperceptible. A ghost of a river, filled with the roaming ghosts of his paintings. He was thinking of them, and only of them. He was smiling. It didn't matter to him that somewhere, in another reality, these paintings were already destroyed. They were still living in his soul, or maybe his soul was living in them.

The Artist was smiling and waiting. He knew what was going to happen. Death was going to happen. He had seen it and even experienced it when the nearest future of that poor man had rushed like agony into his mind. In a moment he was going to let go of the ladder, let it go for the last time, forever, because the Artist in him was going to ask him to do it. His paintings depended on it, on this death, and in it was his chance to reproduce them, a chance more important than the chance the wretched ghost there was about to start praying for.

The ghost of a man who had lost his talent, hanging here now over the mighty element, still clutching at the ladder, overwhelmed by doubts. Should he go up or down? Choose life or death? He couldn't make a choice.

"Come on," the Artist said, smiling. "Let the ladder go, so that I can continue on! Only I should live on, because I carry everything that you have lost."

"Yes, yes, yes." The words of agreement seemed to come as his bruised hands loosened their grip, little by little. "You have to continue, you are the real one."

"Rhein, Rhein!" Unfamiliar voices came from above, worried, pleading. "Rhein, Rhein!"

The Artist heard them, too. He slowly raised his head and tried to recall the faces. Something painful, something hesitant, slipped into his soul. Yes, this man had lost his talent. But he had found love. And friendship. He had even found a father! In his death, he was going to lose them. He was going to lose all. "But it is so much," the Artist thought as he began to realize. "Much more than my paintings."

Now he made another choice. He tightened his hold on the ladder, and continued. He continued up.

EPILOGUE

We travel endlessly down our winding paths through time, and they are always before us: our possible versions—dark shapes woven into dark matter, carrying no life or spirit, or perception. Yet all amazingly different, with different human potential. Designed so as to be able to change us if only we illuminate them with our souls, if only we put our hearts into their silent chests. If only we choose them. And those we pass by? Nothing. They remain the same as they have always been; they remain eternal and immutable in the memory of time.

Yes, they, too, are here; they, too, are now. The versions we do not choose, those that in some strange way, all their own, are still waiting for us, expecting us with the boundless patience of a desert waiting for the rain. And since they are indestructible, and since they are always here, always now . . .

Well, it is impossible for them not to wait until we come. As it is impossible for the human spirit not to turn death into fire. Every time.

ABOUT THE AUTHOR

Born in Sofia, Bulgaria, Nina Nenova is the author of seven novels. *The Capital of Latecomers* is her latest, first published in 2013. Her work was included on the Eurocon/Bulgacon list of Science Fiction Books of the Decade in the late 1990s. For the past ten years, Nenova has worked in seclusion, having contact with the outside world only through her family and literary agent.

ABOUT THE
TRANSLATOR

Photo © 2013 Yanitsa Radeva

Vladimir Poleganov is a freelance translator and writer. His translations and short stories have appeared in various Bulgarian literary magazines and anthologies. His first book, a collection of weird stories, was published by St. Kliment Ohridski University Press in 2013. He is currently working on a PhD in Bulgarian literature.